DON'T PUT THE
BOATS AWAY

DON'T PUT THE BOATS AWAY

A NOVEL

Ames Sheldon

SHE WRITES PRESS

Published 2019
Printed in the United States of America
ISBN: 978-1-63152-602-2 pbk
ISBN: 978-1-63152-603-9 ebk
Library of Congress Control Number: 2019935878

For information, address:
She Writes Press
1569 Solano Ave #546
Berkeley, CA 94707

She Writes Press is a division of SparkPoint Studio, LLC.

For my mother, my sister, and my daughter—
remarkable women scientists.

September 1945

She doesn't know exactly where she's going, but right now that doesn't trouble her. This is the start of the next stage of her life. Harriet Sutton—who's always been called Harry by her family—puts two fingers into her mouth and gives a piercing whistle as soon as she spots a battered black Ford with a small TAXI sign moving toward the West Madison train station.

Brakes squealing, the vehicle stops. She opens the door and tosses her suitcase inside. As she slides in and settles on the cracked leather seat, the cabbie turns around. "You only need wave to catch my attention. I watch for customers." He almost looks like a bum with his unshaven cheeks and chin, but his smile is sweet.

"I'm sorry, sir. I've just come from New York City. I guess I'm used to whistling for a cab."

"No wonder. Where can I take you, miss?"

She gives the address of the boarding house where she has arranged to stay.

The cabbie pulls into the traffic. Watching her in the rearview mirror, he asks, "How was your trip?"

"The train was terribly crowded. Someone told me more than a million people are riding the rails every month."

"It's all those soldiers returning home from the war."

"That's right. They were pretty raucous. I guess it's understandable after what they've been through." Then, inevitably, she thinks about the soldiers who will never return home. Her brother Eddie.

The buildings blur. Quickly quashing her grief, she blinks the tears back. Despite herself, a sigh escapes.

"Miss?"

She looks out the window and spots an arresting white granite dome. "Is that the State Capitol over there?"

"Yep, that's it. You're new to Madison?"

"I'm here to study chemistry at the University of Wisconsin." Her stomach feels tight. While she's excited to start, she's also terrified. "I just hope I can make it."

"You seem like a capable young lady," the cabbie says.

"You're nice to say that." Disarmed by his friendliness, she says, "I can't get over the bombing of Hiroshima and Nagasaki last month. Why did we ever *create* such a powerful weapon and then use it on innocent people?"

Watching her through his rearview mirror, he says, "I've heard that if we hadn't used the A-bomb on Japan, the Japs would have held out until the bitter end, and we would have lost another five million of our soldiers."

"War destroys so much."

The cabbie turns around quickly. "War is hell. I was there in France last time around, in the 'war to end all wars.'"

"My mother was there too," she replies proudly. "Mother drove an ambulance in France."

"Is that so?"

"And for the last two years she's worked as a nurse's aide in an Army hospital on Staten Island."

"We all did our part."

"I'll say!" Harriet had become much stronger working on their Victory Farm.

He signals a turn. "Almost there now."

❧

That afternoon, standing outside Dr. Blackwell's office on the third floor of the Chemistry Building, she knocks briskly on his partially open door.

"Come!"

She steps into the room. Directly ahead, a wall of books and scientific journals face her, and to her right a man wearing a rumpled jacket sits in a club chair.

"Dr. Blackwell?"

As he turns, she sees that his bowtie is askew. "Yes?" He sounds annoyed by the interruption.

"I'm Harriet Sutton. We have an appointment."

"Ah, so we do. Take a seat." He grabs the papers off the chair facing him and places them on top of his messy desk.

She sits, carefully crossing her legs, and then tugs her skirt down over her knees.

He looks at her. "How old are you?"

"I'm twenty-six."

"Why start a master's program at your age?"

She lifts her chin. "I spent the war years running my family's Victory Farm in New Jersey. Our chickens produced 1,500 eggs each day, so my hands were full until now."

"I see." Dr. Blackwell goes on to explain that she should register in the graduate school office, and he spells out precisely which chemistry courses she should sign up for.

"I'd like to take some business courses too."

"Why?" Dr. Blackwell raises one eyebrow, which is as bristly as porcupine quills.

"Because I want to be able to run my father's company when the time comes."

Shaking his head, Dr. Blackwell declares, "That'll never happen."

She sits up straighter. "Why not?"

"You're a woman."

"So what?"

"What kind of company?"

Clenching her right hand into a fist, she says, "It's a chemical company! I'm here to pursue a graduate degree in chemistry so I can become a research chemist." She has never spoken so impatiently to a professor in her life. Her parents would be appalled. She'd better get a grip on her temper.

"Huh."

"Are there any other female graduate students in the chemistry department here at Madison?"

"One or two. I don't know why you women bother with graduate school. After getting your degree, you just marry and leave the field."

Coolly she replies, "That's not my plan." She shifts in her seat. "Are you and Dr. Fowler friends?" Dr. Fowler was her favorite professor at Bennington; he was the one to write her recommendation.

"We were both working on our dissertations here at the same time. I never understood why Fowler would choose to teach at a women's college."

"He's an excellent teacher."

"I always thought he was a little soft."

"I'll stop wasting your time, Dr. Blackwell. Good day." As she exits his office, Harriet realizes she's going to have to find some other advisor. Dr. Blackwell won't do.

She just hopes she'll be able to handle the coursework at this university. Before going to college, she'd needed intensive tutoring, and until she discovered chemistry, she'd thought she was stupid. She loves how much sense science makes. But sometimes she's still afraid that she's dumb. To her SAM looks the same as WAS or SAW, so she learned to read fragments of sentences for context in order to figure out what was being said. She's learned how to manage. On the plus side, the part of her brain that makes reading a challenge is able to visualize molecules in three dimensions, and that's very helpful.

∾

Later that day, Harriet sits at the table in her room at the boarding house that serves as her desk. She writes Professor Fowler to thank him for his help getting her into graduate school, and she tells him about the courses she'll be taking. She doesn't mention Dr. Blackwell.

Her roommate, Klara, a perky freshman who is lounging on her twin bed, interrupts. "Is that your boyfriend?" She points to the small framed photo on Harriet's bureau.

Harriet moves over to sit on the other bed. "Yes. His name is Frank."

Until she met Frank, she'd been afraid she'd never find a boyfriend. She's very grateful that he's attracted to her, even if she's not exactly excited by him. She knows she can be a bit intimidating, but Frank isn't put off. She likes the way he teases her about being so brusque and bossy and sure of herself. She admires his values—he's a pacifist, a Quaker, who works as an administrator at the Essex County Hospital. She respects the way he stood up to her father when he questioned Frank about that the first time the men met. She's glad Frank hasn't pressured her to get married when the main thing on her mind is earning her master's degree. All she wants right now is to see what she can do on her own. "And you, Klara? I bet you have a boyfriend."

"I have lots of boyfriends, but I'm not exclusive with anyone. I just got here—I want to look around."

"That's smart. This is a good time of life to play the field." She almost sounds like someone's aunt.

"I plan to!" Klara rises and goes to stand in front of the mirror.

Harriet watches Klara comb her long blonde hair. Then she notices the lamp on Klara's dresser. Its shade features little round cotton balls hanging from the bottom rim. "I've never seen anything like that lampshade. It's sort of silly."

"I think it's cute."

"I kind of like it myself," Harriet agrees, surprising herself.

Then Klara grabs her bathrobe from behind the door and leaves the room.

Thinking she should probably write a few more letters now before her classes start, Harriet moves back to her table. She ought to write her mother and father and her brother Nat, but the family member who fills her mind is Eddie. She leans her elbows on the surface and puts her face in her hands.

In Eddie's last letter, the one that reached the Sutton home weeks after the telegram from the adjutant general, he said, "I'll be seeing you soon," but he was wrong. Eddie had written, "Our mission is crucially important to the big push ahead, and I know we will help ensure the Nazis' defeat." The family only learned the details months later. A member of the Eighty-Second Airborne Signal Company, Eddie died when his glider crash-landed in France while attempting to deliver a high-powered radio set for communications between the continent and England just before D-Day.

Her mother's spirit is still broken, and her father never mentions Eddie's name, but Harriet knows they both think about him every day. So does she. Harriet hopes that after she gets her degree, she'll be able to step in and assume the traditional role of the oldest son in their father's chemical company—maybe that would help mitigate the loss they all feel. She wants to do that for her father.

Klara returns and climbs into bed. "Good night, Harriet." Klara shuts her eyes.

Eddie must have been the glue that bound the family together. With his death, everything changed. Eddie had been her buddy. They'd competed against each other at tennis, worked on jigsaw puzzles together, joked and kidded each other all the time.

Within moments, Klara's breathing indicates she's asleep.

Her other brother Nat is much younger than she. But she wants to be a good sister to the only sibling she has left, even if they aren't particularly close. A few months ago she tried playing tennis with him, but he isn't athletic. One night he took her to a jazz club in Manhattan where the music was so frenetic it gave her a headache. She promises herself that tomorrow she'll write a letter to Nat, now in his final year at Phillips Academy in Andover.

Shouldn't she write her mother? The problem is that she doesn't have anything to say that her mother would care about. Since Eddie's death Eleanor has continued to work as a nurse's aide at Halloran Hospital, but once she gets home, she retreats to Eddie's empty room. Nothing seems to rouse her mother's interest. Eventually Harriet began to feel she was in danger of becoming infected with her mother's despair. It's a relief not to have to witness her misery every day.

Klara is snoring quietly. Harriet tiptoes over to the stack of books on her dresser and pulls out her copy of *Stuart Little*, the spine of which she's turned to the wall. She finds this recently published volume thoroughly delightful, though she'd be embarrassed to be seen reading a children's book. Harriet loves the tiny mouse and his heroic quest in search of his friend Margalo. She wishes she had a friend like Stuart does. Her best friend at college—Sarah—left after their sophomore year to marry and move to Texas. Harriet has yet to find another kindred spirit.

∾

As she leaves for the lab early one morning a week later, Harriet spots frost on the mums outside the house. Walking quickly up Bascom Hill, she's shocked by how cold the wind feels coming off Lake Mendota. "This is outrageous!" she says out loud.

A young man passing her as he descends the hill replies, "Miss?"

"It wouldn't be this cold at home until November!"

The man's cheeks are bright pink. "Where's home?"

Harriet shakes her head. "Never mind." She doesn't want to be diverted by any man. From now on, she'll keep her eyes down when she's walking around campus.

As she continues up the steep incline, she realizes she'd better buy some long underwear and slacks. She'll stick out among the women on campus in their plaid skirts with sweaters, saddle shoes, and white bobby socks, but at least she'll be warm.

Later that afternoon, she sits in the front parlor of her boarding house reading the *Capital Times* before going to meet Judy, the other woman in her analytical techniques course, for dinner at Memorial Union. According to the newspaper, there's some controversy over the spiral-shaped gallery that Frank Lloyd Wright designed to house Solomon R. Guggenheim's art collection in New York City. A wave of homesickness washes over her. Taking a deep breath, Harriet tells herself she just needs to make a friend or two. Someone with interests like hers, someone who's not as immature as Klara. Maybe Judy will become a friend—she seems thoughtful. There are very few women in chemistry, though one of the teaching assistants in the organic chemistry lab is female; perhaps she'd be another candidate.

What else would help her feel more at home? Looking around the room, she spots a card table pushed up against the corner. She'll ask Mrs. Schmitt whether she could use that table for piecing together the jigsaw puzzle she brought. *And Bach*, she thinks, recalling Sunday mornings when her father played Bach cantatas, concertos, and masses on the phonograph. She should look for a place where she can hear Bach.

∾

A few nights later after Harriet returns from studying in the library, she gets the jigsaw puzzle from her room and brings it back downstairs to the parlor. She pulls a chair up to the card table, opens the box, and starts laying out the pieces right-side up. This is a puzzle she and Eddie had made before he left for basic training. Taking a picture of the barn on their family's farm, they glued it onto a thin piece of wood, and then Eddie showed her how to operate the jigsaw he'd received for his birthday a few years earlier. The pieces she cut aren't nearly as smooth as Eddie's, but they still fit together well enough.

Klara appears at Harriet's elbow. "What are you doing?"

"I'm starting to work on this puzzle. Want to join me?"

"OK." Klara pulls another chair up to the table.

"First I like to pick out the edges."

Klara joins in, pushing the edge pieces to the side. "Then what?"

"We put them together to form the frame for the picture."

"Oh, I get it." Klara starts connecting edge pieces to each other.

Harriet looks at Klara. "This is kind of fun, isn't it?"

"Mmmm." Klara is clearly preoccupied. She fits two pieces together.

"My brother and I used to spend hours working on jigsaw puzzles together. It's such a companionable way to spend time with someone— you can talk or not, it doesn't matter."

The clock on the wall is ticking but otherwise the room is quiet. The hooked rugs on the floor add to the feeling of coziness.

"Harriet?"

She looks up from the table.

"You could look really attractive if you curled your hair. It's thick and such a pretty shade of brown. I could show you how to set it."

Harriet recalls the comment her mother made while seeing her off at the station when she left for Madison. Her mother called her a "handsome" young woman, and her tone suggested that she was giving Harriet a compliment. Harriet knows she isn't pretty, but "handsome"? What does that even mean when you're talking about a female?

She doesn't want to hurt Klara's feelings, but there's no point in learning how to curl her hair. "Not tonight," she says. "Maybe some other time."

"Sure."

Harriet says, "You're kind, Klara." She smiles warmly at her room-mate. Klara seems almost like a younger sister.

They return their attention to the puzzle pieces on the table before them.

After a few moments, Klara says, "Didn't your mother ever show you how to set your hair?"

"No, she wasn't that kind of mother. But then, I never asked her about that sort of thing."

❦

On December 4, Harriet waits for Judy in front of the University Club, where the initiation ceremony and banquet for Sigma Delta Epsilon, the club for graduate women scientists, is being held. She knows she's a little late, but apparently Judy is too. They agreed to enter the intim-idating red brick building together.

A stout young woman with very short red hair, wearing a navy blue suit, rounds the corner.

"I'm so sorry!" Judy cries. "I broke the heel on my shoe, so I had to go back for my other pair."

Harriet starts up the steps toward the triple archway, saying, "Don't worry. You're here now." She grabs the knob and flings open the heavy wooden door. Inside, exquisitely rendered oil paintings of local land-scapes framed in gold are mounted along the walls, and an enormous Persian carpet covers the floor.

"This is fancy!" Judy says.

"Very nice," Harriet agrees.

They proceed to a reception room where forty women stand talking in groups. Everyone is wearing a dress or a suit and heels. Most of the women hold a cocktail in one hand. Harriet's glad she dressed up in the gray flannel suit her mother had bought for her at Lord & Taylor.

Judy says, "I wonder what the decibel level is in here?"

"Oh, you and your penchant for measurements," Harriet jokes, lightly tapping Judy's arm. She scans the room, looking for the bar. "Can I get you a drink? Scotch and soda?"

"Thanks, Harriet, that would be terrific." Judy steps toward the nearest group of women.

As Harriet approaches the bartender in the far corner, she sees that many of the women here are much older than she is. Some of the eldest women look quite forbidding with their severe haircuts and tailored suits, though there are a few women with softly curled hair in silk dresses as well.

After cocktails, everyone heads into the dining room, where they have an unobstructed view of Lake Mendota. Harriet and Judy sit next to each other at a round table for eight covered with a white cloth, glasses, silverware, cups and saucers, and plates of iceberg lettuce with slivers of carrots. A small round votive candle graces the center of the table.

Harriet leans toward Judy. "Isn't this nice? We can almost forget about the war."

"Lots of the guys are still coming home and being demobilized," Judy counters. "The war's not over yet for some people."

"It's not over for my mother," Harriet replies, thinking of Eddie.

Judy doesn't say anything.

After taking a deep breath, Harriet reaches for the basket of rolls. "Thank goodness the United Nations' charter has been ratified by twenty nations now, including the Union of Soviet Socialist Republics and the Republic of China. I hope the UN can ensure that atomic weapons will never be used again. We've got to be able to guarantee there won't be any more wars."

Judy swallows a forkful of salad before she replies. "I'm with you. I'm not sure they can ban atomic weapons, but here's hoping they'll figure out some way to keep the world safe from mass destruction."

A tall woman wearing a tweed suit walks over to the podium. Her short hair is graying at her temples, and wrinkles appear around her mouth and eyes as she smiles at the audience. "Can you all hear me? I am the president of the University of Wisconsin chapter of Sigma Delta Epsilon, and I'd like to welcome all our new initiates and the rest of you established members of Sigma Delta Epsilon. My name is Marjorie Pennington—Dr. Pennington. As most of you know, members of Sigma Delta Epsilon are distinguished for demonstrating originality, independence, and initiative in scientific research work."

Harriet leans forward.

"To be a scientist requires a high order of intelligence, with strength in mathematics and spatial ability. It requires persistence and an intense channeling of one's energy so that one derives significant satisfaction from the activities of the work itself."

She identifies with what Dr. Pennington is saying; she loves to work hard on things that interest her.

Dr. Pennington continues, "A preference for working alone is another characteristic of the best scientists."

Really? Harriet prefers to be in charge of a group of people working together. Is this going to be a problem for her?

"And to be a *woman* scientist requires an even higher order of dedication and hard work. We must prove ourselves because many of our male colleagues doubt that we are truly dedicated to our profession. It's up to us to prove them wrong."

The audience breaks into applause.

She whispers to Judy, "Isn't she inspiring?"

Judy nods.

Once Dr. Pennington concludes her remarks, Harriet says, "Thank God there are women like this at Madison! The hell with Dr. Blackwell."

"Will you go on for a PhD after we get our master's degrees, Harriet?"

"No. I want to work for my father. He's president of Sutton Chemical Company in New Jersey."

"Really?"

"My brother Nat isn't likely to want to work for the company, and Father will need someone to hand it off to. Nat hopes to be a musician. Besides, I want to please Father and earn his respect. When I ran the farm for him, we got along better than we did when I was struggling in high school. He called me his 'right hand man,' and I kind of liked that, though he did require me to report in to him every day. He's so critical and demanding. He's not easy to please." She's not going to tell Judy that the man she calls Father is not the man who sired her—which is why she has to work extra hard to win his approval and, if she's lucky, maybe even his affection.

Judy says, "I see."

ᠺᠥ

On Saturday, Harriet invites Klara to go skating on Lake Mendota with her. The ice is very hard and smooth because, though it's been cold, it hasn't snowed much yet. Harriet races back and forth, hungry for fresh air to fill her lungs after hours of breathing pungent odors in the organic chemistry lab. Klara skates figure eights and twirls. Afterward they head home to their boarding house. Once they've added a log to the fire, have drawn the brown corduroy drapes closed, and hold cups of cocoa in their hands, they sit down at the table in the parlor with a new jigsaw puzzle Harriet bought earlier that week.

When all the pieces are face up and the edges have been separated out, Harriet looks at Klara. "Your cheeks sure are red."

"I know. They always get that way when I go outside in the winter." Klara picks up the box the puzzle came in and scrutinizes the picture.

"You're not supposed to look at the box for clues, Klara." Her mother was very strict about this rule.

"Then how do you know what the puzzle is supposed to look like?"

"Use the shapes and colors to guide you."

Ralph, their fellow boarder, looks into the room. A former GI, his grown-out buzz cut stands straight up. "How are you girls doing?"

Glancing at his midsection, Harriet admires how flat his stomach is. Frank isn't nearly so svelte. She lifts her eyes. "We're fine."

"This is hard!" Klara picks up a corner piece.

"I'm off to the library," Ralph says. "Tell Mrs. Schmitt not to wait dinner."

Once he exits, Harriet asks, "How are your classes going, Klara? Are you getting some good grades?"

"I don't want to talk about it."

"OK, sorry I asked." Harriet would like to be able to tell someone about her own grades. She's been studying extremely hard, spending most of her waking hours in class, or at her lab bench, or in the library, and she's happy about how well she's doing.

They work awhile in silence. Klara says, "I got some of the new Breck shampoo this week. I really like how it makes my hair feel."

"Hmmm."

"You're welcome to try some."

"Thanks." After a few minutes, she says, "Would you be interested in going to hear Bach's *Christmas Oratorio* with me tomorrow at the Congregational Church? It's directed by one of the faculty members in the music school."

"No, I go to Calvary Lutheran Church."

"It's a special afternoon concert, so you could attend your own church first."

"Thanks anyway, Harriet." Klara stands up. "I give up! It'll take forever to finish this puzzle."

"There's no rush. It's relaxing."

"Well, I need to get ready for my date."

"A date? Well, have a good time."

∾

The next day as Harriet listens to the *Christmas Oratorio*, her heart rises to the rafters. She feels as though she might ascend toward heaven herself. Tears fill her eyes. This is even better in a sanctuary than listening to music on the phonograph at home. When the man sitting in the pew in front of her turns to the woman at his side and tenderly kisses her cheek, Harriet feels stabbed suddenly with envy. She yearns for tenderness. Unfortunately, that's not Frank's strong suit.

Everywhere on campus now she observes men and women holding hands.

When Klara returns from dates flushed, Harriet can't help noticing the lipstick smeared across her mouth. She tells herself she's just got to wait—her time for being madly in love will come. After she gets her degree. Weeks ago she decided that instead of going back East for Christmas, she would stay in Madison and work through the break so she could make sure to ace all her courses. Every night she rereads the two letters Frank has sent her. He warned her he wasn't much of a correspondent. By now she's memorized his letters, and they're starting to seem a little boring.

In the last few days before Christmas, Harriet finds herself walking through town every evening, admiring the shop windows filled with wooden toys, the holiday decorations, and all the lights. This is the first Christmas since the war ended, and she senses the exuberance and relief of the people around her as they bustle about, preparing for a holiday they will celebrate more fervently than they have in years. Mrs. Schmitt must have been hoarding her supply of sugar for months, because now she bakes every day. Plates of Christmas cookies and stollen filled with dried fruit and nuts appear for dessert, and an elaborate gingerbread house adorns the dining room table.

Once Klara and Judy return to their homes for Christmas, Harriet starts to regret her decision to stay in Madison during the holiday break from classes. What was she thinking?

December 1945

On December 24, when Harriet sits down at the table with Mrs. Schmitt, her son Hans, and his pregnant wife, Marie, for a dinner of carp and potato salad, she realizes she's made a horrible mistake. This is such a strange meal with people she barely knows. She feels overwhelmed with loneliness. She's always been home for Christmas, even during the war when she was at Bennington and travel was difficult. She misses her parents and Nat so much! Why isn't she sitting at the holiday table with them? She longs to see Frank too. Sighing, she decides she'll telephone them all tomorrow, now that nonessential calls are permitted.

As a disabled veteran, Hans is another source of discomfort. Harriet knows it's terrible that he lost his leg in Salerno, and she's sorry for him, but she's afraid to ask about his war experience, and she certainly doesn't want to think about Eddie's. She hurries up to her room as soon as they finish eating the main course.

On Christmas Day, not wanting to intrude on the Schmitts' time together as a family, she spends the morning at the lab, and then at noon she joins them for their holiday dinner of goose stuffed with apple and sausage, red cabbage, and potato dumplings. She has never eaten any of these dishes before, and they're delicious, but as soon as the meal is over, she escapes to her room. She pulls out all the letters she received over the previous four months: there's one from her father, three from her mother, four from Nat, and the ones from Frank. Nat's letters make her laugh, but now that she's reading her mother's more carefully, she starts to cry.

The telephone rings at the end of the hall, and after a few moments, Mrs. Schmitt calls up that the phone's for her.

She runs down the hall and lifts the black Bakelite receiver from its heavy square base. "Hello?"

"Harry?" Her father's voice booms across the line.

"Merry Christmas, Father. I've been thinking about all of you. How are you?"

"Fine, fine. Your mother wants to speak with you." Harriet isn't surprised that her father passed her off right away; George doesn't like talking on the telephone. Maybe he's been conditioned—as they all were—to the three-minute rule imposed by the government during the war.

After a pause, Eleanor shouts, "Dearie!"

"I can hear you, Mother."

"What are you doing?"

"I was actually sitting in my room reading your letters. To be honest, I'm feeling a bit blue."

"We miss you terribly, Harry. I wish you were here!"

"So do I, Mummy."

"Did you receive the Christmas package I sent last week?"

"Not yet. Did you get the presents I mailed?"

"We did. The handblown glass ornaments you sent are beautiful!"

"I'm glad you like them. A friend of mine dragged me along to the German Christmas market they hold here in Madison, and those globes caught my eye."

"They're simply super," Eleanor replies, slurring the s's a bit.

She doesn't want to talk with her mother any longer if she's loaded. "May I speak to Nat?"

"Certainly."

Another voice comes on the line. "Harry?"

"Is that you, Nat?" He sounds like Eddie.

"Of course it is."

"How *are* you? I've been thinking about you a lot."

"I'm all right."

"Your voice sounds lower."

"I guess it is."

"What's happening there?"

"We're all sitting around, stuffed with turkey, listening to the opera. The Met is performing *Lucia di Lammermoor* today, and they're recording the performance live, so we can hear it right now while it's going on in New York."

"That sounds like fun."

"Thanks for all the letters, Harry. I really wish you were here. Christmas is awful without you. Mother put up Eddie's Christmas stocking again this year, and it just hung there empty."

She groans.

"The other night Father said if he'd encouraged Eddie to enlist in officers' training school, maybe the outcome would have been different."

"Oh no. I'm sorry I'm not there with you. Is Mother drinking a lot?"

"Yes."

"I hate it when she gets like that."

Quietly Nat says, "Me too."

"Thanks for your letters, Nat. It sounds like senior year's going pretty well."

"So far. I started jamming with some guys the other week—that's a lot of fun."

"Playing your saxophone?"

"Yep."

"Great," she says, nodding to herself. "Well, we should wrap it up. Keep those letters coming, Nat. Take care of yourself."

"I miss you, Harry."

"Me too, Nat. Say goodbye to Mother and Father for me."

As she returns down the hall to her room, she realizes that she actually feels a bit better now, though she's worried about her mother. Should she write Eleanor a letter expressing her concern? Conflict with her parents makes Harriet feel sick to her stomach. And Frank— she'll call him tomorrow. Picking up a recent issue of the *Journal of the American Chemical Society*, she turns to the article she's been assigned to read, but then she sets the journal down on top of the pile of journals on the floor. She can't face reading this on Christmas Day. Going over to her dresser, she grabs the Christmas present she bought for herself—it's a copy of the Swedish book *Pippi Longstocking*, which has just been translated. She settles onto her bed with a sigh of pleasure and opens her new book to the first page.

∼

Sunday night

Dear Harry,

Thank you for the navy blue sweater you gave me for Christmas. I like the white diagonal stripes—they make me think of lightning bolts. I'll wear it all the time this winter. The wind when I cross campus is really fierce.

I'm back at Andover now for the long haul till spring break. I know I'm going to have to work my ass off to get decent grades from Dr. Marling. He's the toughest teacher we have here. He used to teach at Harvard, and his expectations couldn't be higher. Half the senior class routinely flunks his course in American history. Dr. Marling assigns us so much work it seems he doesn't realize we have classes and homework for English and physics and Latin and religion too.

I wouldn't be able to survive my senior year if it weren't for

Mr. Pratt. Father has been very clear that I can only study sax-
ophone with him so long as I keep my grades up. At a minimum
I've got to earn second honors. Mr. Pratt plays in the Boston
Symphony Orchestra, and he's kind of funny looking. You
should see him, Harry. He looks like a little old squirrel stand-
ing on its hind legs, because he's a tiny man with grizzled gray
hair and round, rimless glasses, and he always wears the same
brown suit and tie when I come to his studio for my lesson. He's
super—classically trained but he likes jazz and Charlie Parker
as much as I do. He told me that after I graduate from Andover,
I should consider enrolling at the Schillinger House of Music,
which was started in Boston's Back Bay by Lawrence Berk, a
pianist with an engineering degree from MIT. It sounds like a
great school.

Somehow when I'm with Mr. Pratt, I don't miss Eddie as
much as I do at school or at home. But I sure am lonely without
him. What about you? Does being so far away in a new place
help you not miss him as much? At Andover I am reminded of
Eddie everywhere I turn.

I wish I could see you, Harriet. Christmas was very odd
this year.

Love,
Nat

ॐ

During the winter Harriet focuses on her work so intently that she no
longer notices couples holding hands. When she looks at her photo
of Frank, she discovers she doesn't miss him all that much—isn't that
strange? Days and weeks fly by.

In March, along with Judy, Harriet attends a Sigma Delta Epsilon
talk by Dr. Elizabeth McCann on the studies to increase production

of penicillin. She learns that scientists in England and the United States are struggling to produce these powerful antibiotics in quantity. During the war penicillin was found to be remarkably effective in treating soldiers' bacterial infections, pneumonia, osteomyelitis, gonorrhea, and other diseases, but because of the limited quantities, its use was restricted to the military. Now scientists in labs at the universities of Wisconsin and Minnesota are working to develop a promising green mold that was found on a cantaloupe in Peoria by a very observant housewife.

While Judy and Harriet walk back toward their respective boarding houses, Harriet says, "I can't believe research this important is going on at our very own school. What an opportunity!"

"You want to get in on this, Harriet?" Judy sounds skeptical.

"Of course I do! The chance to work on something that could help save people's lives?"

Judy says, "Penicillin research must be PhD-level work."

"Not necessarily. I'm going to ask Dr. McCann."

∾

May 20, 1946

Dear Frank,

I have an incredible opportunity to do some very important research on penicillin with Dr. Elizabeth McCann here at Madison over the summer, so I will not be coming home until Christmas. I am sorry. I hope you will understand that I need to do this. Not only will the research be the basis for my master's thesis, but hopefully I'll be able to help in the quest to ascertain which strains of penicillin can be reproduced in the greatest quantities, which ultimately will result in saving lives. I'm terribly lucky that Dr. McCann wants to have me on her team. I'll be working with her and other graduate students who

are further along in their training than I am, so I'm bound to
learn an enormous amount. I might even get my name on the
paper when we publish our results.

This means another six months before we'll see each other,
but maybe we can write letters and talk on the telephone more
frequently than we have been. I feel increasingly out of touch
with you and your life, and I don't like that.

Please don't be disappointed. I want to hear all about what
you're up to and how your mother and sister are doing as well.
Please write.

Missing you,
Harriet

She thinks about signing off with "Fondly, Harriet," but that seems
awfully stiff. She can't say "Love" because Frank hasn't used that word,
and she's not sure she loves him either. She does miss him when she
thinks about him for more than a moment, so the way she ended her
letter is the truth.

Over the summer, Frank calls her a couple of times, and she telephones him once a month during the fall semester. She writes a few
letters to her parents and Nat during that time, but her attention is
really riveted on her research with Dr. McCann. She doesn't even
notice as summer changes to autumn until the snow starts to fly.

December 1946

Heading home on the train back East to New Jersey for Christmas, Harriet starts thinking about her family and Frank. She's been so immersed in her research that she hasn't written many letters to them lately, and she didn't hear from them as frequently as she did last year. She's getting really excited to see everyone now.

Her parents' farm manager, Hamilton, meets her at the train station in Plainwood. As they approach the house, it looks larger and more imposing than she recalls. She can tell it's been repainted recently in a paler shade of yellow than before.

Once he pulls to a stop, Harriet jumps out as her mother hurries down the path.

"Mummy!"

"Harry! I've missed you so much." Eleanor grabs Harriet's upper arms and leans her torso toward Harriet's in their usual version of a hug. Pulling back, she eyes her daughter. "What happened to your hair?"

"I'm growing it out. How are you, Mother? You look good." Eleanor seems more energetic than she did when Harriet left home last year.

"I'm so glad to see you," Eleanor says, taking Harriet's arm in hers. "Now, what's this about wanting to be called Harriet?"

"Harry was my name when I was a kid. I've grown up."

"It might take me a while to get used to calling you that."

Together they walk quickly up to the front door. It isn't snowing yet, but the air smells like snow is on its way.

Inside, Eleanor says, "Dinner is ready. We'll eat as soon as you wash up." She heads down the hall while Harriet ducks into the powder room.

When Harriet enters the dining room, George stands and pats her shoulder.

Nat hugs her fiercely. Then they all take their usual places around the gleaming mahogany table. Except for Eddie—his spot is vacant. Harriet shuts her eyes. Eddie should be here. Her heart hurts; she feels as though she's losing her brother all over again.

When she opens her eyes, she sees that the table is set with the fancy china, crystal, and silver tonight, along with ironed linen napkins at each place. A vase of miniature peach-colored carnations stands in the middle of the expanse, mirroring the hue of the blossoms on the wallpaper; the green of their leaves is the same shade as the room's cabinets, woodwork, and doors.

Harriet says, "Everything looks lovely, Mother."

Rosalee, wearing a spotless white chiffon apron over her white uniform, bustles in with a platter. "I cooked your favorite meal, Miss Harriet, fried chicken with mashed potatoes and green beans." She hands the plate of chicken to George.

"Thank you very much, Rosalee," says Harriet. "You're looking well. How is your family?"

"We all just fine, thank you. Ham Junior be growing like a weed. And see, we've got another one on the way." She pats her bulging stomach.

"Hamilton told me. That's wonderful, Rosalee."

As Rosalee exits, Harriet notices that the glasses on the table are filled only with water. This is surprising—typically her parents have bourbon with dinner. Has her mother stopped drinking? She looks around the dining room table at her father, mother, and brother.

George appears much older than he did when she last saw him; his hair is thinner, and his jowls have started to sag below his jawline. Eleanor, wearing pearls and a becoming green sweater Harriet has never seen before, looks well, and her hair is still quite red despite threads of gray. Nat, on the other hand, is so pale that Harriet wonders whether he's ill.

Rosalee returns with the other dishes, which she gives to Eleanor and Harriet. Once Rosalee retires to the kitchen, Harriet turns her attention to her father. Feeling the old pull to please him, she starts asking questions about the farm. His replies are so brief that she moves on to asking how things are going at Sutton Chemical.

Thin-lipped, George says, "Fine." It's clear that he doesn't want to talk about anything. Harriet finally notices that the atmosphere around the table is tense.

Eleanor tells Harriet, "You'll be glad to know that Abba will be joining us for Christmas."

"Ew, I never thought to write her."

"Did your grandmother send you any letters?" Eleanor asks.

"No."

"Then I wouldn't worry about it. You may invite Frank to join us for Christmas Eve or Christmas Day—one or the other."

"When we spoke a few weeks ago, he said he'll be celebrating with his mother and sister, but I don't know the timing on that. I'll call him later and see when he's available." One of the things she admires about Frank is the way he cares for his ailing mother and young sister.

"We'd be happy to have him join us."

"Thank you, Mother." Harriet wipes her mouth with her napkin. "I was sorry to hear that Halloran Hospital no longer required your services after the doctors and nurses got back from the war—I know you enjoyed your work there as a nurse's aide."

"Plainwood Hospital doesn't want my assistance nursing patients on their wards either. But two days a week I assemble CARE packages—now it's for regular citizens in Europe who are hungry. Not nearly as satisfying as caring for wounded soldiers, but at least I'm doing something to help."

"Good for you, Mother."

"I got bored only doing things that anyone can handle, so I signed up for a class at Douglass."

"You're kidding!"

"Not at all. They have a college re-entry program for mature women."

"What class are you taking?"

"A course on Shakespeare. Since I enjoy his plays, I figured this would be a good way to ease back into college."

"That's great, Mother," says Harriet.

"Don't know why you bother," George puts in. "It's not as though you need a degree so you can get a job."

"I'm doing it for the intellectual stimulation, George."

Harriet is about to ask Nat a question, but his head is bent over his plate in such a way that it's clear he doesn't want to engage in conversation.

After several minutes of silence, George rouses himself to ask, "How was your trip, uh, Harriet?"

"It was fine, Father. I actually got a berth in a sleeping car this time."

Again the conversation dies. Although Harriet loves Rosalee's fried chicken, she doesn't ask for seconds because she isn't getting as much exercise these days as she did when she was working on the farm.

Finally the family rises and moves toward the parlor.

On the way, Harriet pulls her brother aside. "Are you all right, Nat? Your face is as white as a sheet of paper."

"I've been expelled from Yale. They told me not to come back. We just found out."

"Oh no, I'm so sorry." She puts her hand on his arm. "That's terrible."

He steps away from her. "Father is furious. I don't know what he's going to do."

George calls, "Harriet?"

Nat turns and scurries up the stairs toward his room.

Harriet enters the parlor, two walls of which are lined with books.

"Do you want a glass of bourbon with your mother and me?"

"Sure. Thanks, Father. Lots of ice, please."

Once they all have their drinks, Harriet sits on the cushy couch with her mother, facing her father, who takes his red leather chair.

"Now, Harriet," George says, "I want to hear all about Madison." He crosses his long legs and leans forward.

Delighted to be asked about her work, she replies, "I'm learning *so much*. Chemistry is absolutely fascinating, especially in the lab. I'm doing research on penicillin."

"Yes, tell me more," George replies. "You haven't written in a long time."

"I've been so busy, really *consumed* by my research. It's such important work. Penicillin saved the lives of thousands of wounded soldiers during the war—soldiers who would have died from their wounds without this antibiotic. But it's finicky. Penicillin has an unusual chemical structure that no one could replicate for a long time. The Brits tried at Oxford, and then in 1941 they brought some samples over to the US for our scientists to see what we could do. You'll like this, Father. The very first patient cured by penicillin, Mrs. Ogden Miller, is the wife of the athletic director at Yale University. She developed streptococcal septicemia after a miscarriage in 1942 and would have died if she hadn't been treated with penicillin." When George doesn't respond, Harriet continues, "Anyway, clinical trials were conducted during '43, and on D-Day every medic landing in Normandy carried penicillin in his pack."

Eleanor says, "Doesn't penicillin come from some kind of mold?"

"That's right, Mother. The first strains came from a fluid given off by the green mold that grows on bread, the same mold that's used to produce Roquefort cheese. The stuff we're working on now comes from moldy cantaloupes. The problem is figuring out how to produce large quantities of penicillin quickly and cheaply so it's available to anyone who needs it."

"What kind of luck are you having?" Eleanor asks.

"Dr. Demerec of the Carnegie Institute took the strain of penicillin from cantaloupe mold that was isolated at a lab in Peoria and treated it with X-rays. Then he sent it to us at Wisconsin and to scientists at the University of Minnesota for testing. We're working to confirm that this strain provides ten times more yield than the best of the other strains. X 1612 may prove to be the most effective strain yet for the mass production of penicillin."

"You might as well go work for a drug company when you're through with this," George remarks. "There are plenty of them around here."

Harriet feels as though he slapped her. "I have no interest in working for a drug company, Father. I was hoping to work for you."

"That's news to me." George drains his bourbon and sets the glass down before he speaks. "I don't see how your research relates to any of the products we make at Sutton Chemical."

Harriet's voice rises. "I've taken courses in accounting, financial reports, and budgeting, along with my chemistry classes. They should be useful."

"Perhaps."

Harriet hoped her father would be proud of her work in chemistry. Hurt and confused—devastated, actually—she turns to her mother.

Eleanor says, "Let's not discuss this anymore tonight. Everyone's tired." Quickly swallowing the rest of her drink, she stands. "It's late. Time for bed."

Harriet rises from the couch. After years of critical comments from George, she wonders whether she'll ever be good enough as far as he's concerned.

George stays in his seat. "Don't mind me, Harriet. I'm in a foul temper. It's been a very bad day, and I have a difficult decision to make."

Together Harriet and Eleanor climb the stairs to the second floor. When they get to the landing, Eleanor says, "I'm sorry George didn't show more interest in what you had to say, dearie."

"Research excites me, Mother. I'm finally doing something that really matters."

"I'm so glad. And I must say it almost makes me weep to think that you want to save people's lives. You've definitely got Henri's blood running through your veins."

"Really? You've told me so little about my real father."

When Harriet first figured out for herself that George wasn't her biological parent, she was angry at her mother for hiding the truth from her. Eleanor always pretended that George was Harriet's father until the shocking revelations about Eleanor's service in the Great War and her marriage to a Frenchman came out three years ago, the night they learned that Eddie had enlisted. That night her mother was so upset that she lost control and started telling them all about how horrible war actually is—and she knew, from her own experience. Since then Harriet has come to understand more about why her mother held on to all her secrets.

"I told you Henri was a surgeon in the Great War. He died at the front. "

"I know that much."

"He was a very good doctor, a serious scientist who kept himself informed about the latest medical information, but he was also a most compassionate man. Your wanting to save people's lives reminds me of him. You're following in his footsteps."

Harriet throws her arms around Eleanor. "Thank you, Mother. That makes me feel better."

After a moment, Eleanor pulls back. "What about Frank? Do you think he'll propose while you're home?"

"I hope not! I'm not ready to think about that yet."

"He seems to be a very patient man."

"I really appreciate how direct and matter-of-fact Frank is. Do you remember the first time he came here to have dinner with us?"

"I'll never forget that evening," Eleanor says. That was the night they received the telegram about Eddie.

"When he said he figured you'd all want to take a good look at the guy who was going out with me, I thought Father would choke."

"Remember, George said 'good for you to call a spade a spade.' He liked Frank's forthrightness."

"I do too." Harriet embraces her mother again. "Oh, Mummy, I'm so glad to see you acting more like yourself."

Eleanor murmurs, "I'm trying."

"I've got to call Frank now. I can't wait any longer."

∾

All during Christmas break, whenever Harriet invites Nat to take a walk with her, he refuses. When she asks him a question, he answers in an angry monosyllable, so eventually she gives up trying. He keeps to himself, playing the piano at all hours. Nat seems to have placed himself in isolation while he awaits his father's decision about what's next for him.

Although Nat is unavailable, Eleanor is more candid with Harriet than she's been in a long time. During one late night tête à tête, Harriet is shocked to learn that her mother blames herself in part for Eddie's death. Eleanor claims that if she hadn't kept her role in the Great War a secret all those years, if she'd talked about the horrors she'd seen, maybe Eddie wouldn't have been so quick to enlist. Harriet assures her mother that's completely irrational, hugs her, and they say good night.

While Harriet's home for two weeks, she and Frank go to a lot of movies. They first met at the movies in the winter of 1944. They were sitting one row apart, and they both laughed at the same things. Afterward, Frank sought her out and asked for her telephone number.

As they watch *The Big Sleep* with Humphrey Bogart and Lauren Bacall, they hold hands. Afterward, Frank drives to their favorite parking spot. Since they both live at home with their families, his car is the only place they can find real privacy.

"Just like a woman," he teases, slowing to a stop. "You *would* prefer a story with a romantic angle to *The Best Years of Our Lives*." He turns off the ignition.

She says, "In the midst of all those murders, that was the part of the movie that made the most sense to me." She found the chemistry between Bogart and Bacall absolutely mesmerizing.

"Shhh," he says. "Stop talking so I can kiss you."

After they neck for a few minutes, she yawns uncontrollably. "Sorry. I guess I'm still catching up on my sleep. What time is it, anyway?"

He glances at the new glow-in-the-dark wristwatch she gave him for Christmas. "Eleven thirty."

"I should go home."

~

On the last night before Harriet has to leave town, Frank takes her to a popular supper club. He looks spiffy in his new navy suit, and she can tell he's just had his blond hair cut. She's wearing a new dress as well, a green satin frock with a fitted waist and full skirt her mother bought for her. She's looking forward to a fun evening of dancing, but then she notices him fingering his pocket as though there's something precious in there. Now she feels nervous. She's very fond of Frank. He was there at the front door with them when they received the telegram about Eddie's death, and it was wonderful the way he offered his help, and then when no one answered, he had the sensitivity to walk out the door. She's terribly grateful to him for caring about her. Picking at her food, she chatters about anything she can think of.

Finally he asks her to dance. Before she went to Madison, she'd gotten him to take a couple of dance lessons with her. Now he's pretty good at swing dancing, and they're having fun twirling around each other, starting to sweat. When the bandleader sings the slow song "Five Minutes More," she pulls Frank closer so their bodies are touching all the way from their shoulders down to their groins. As she presses into him, her heart starts to pound faster. She doesn't really like the way Frank thrusts his fat tongue into her mouth when they kiss, but she loves the feel of him against her stomach. Abruptly, Frank pulls back, inserting several inches of space between their torsos.

"What's wrong?"

"I don't want to embarrass you," he says.

"But that feels so good!"

Later, after they park in their usual spot, Frank kisses her so hard that she tastes a little blood.

"Can't you be gentler?" Is he kissing like this because she's not responding enough?

"I'm sorry, I know you've asked me before. I just get so pumped up when we're together." He leans over to brush his moustache tenderly against her lips.

"That's better."

"I want to discuss our future, Harriet. I love you, and it seems to me—"

She interrupts. "I'm not ready to make a commitment, Frank. I need to know where I'll be working once I get my degree. I hope you can wait a few more months."

Once she's back home in bed, she faces the fact that she feels frustrated by the physical side of her relationship with Frank. He's rough when he kisses and caresses her—but maybe that's the way all men are. She knows he's inexperienced with women, and of course, she's inexperienced too.

She knows it's unfair of her to refuse to discuss marriage with her boyfriend, but marriage is such a serious commitment, even if everyone around her seems to be diving in. Her mother told her that three different cousins would be tying the knot next summer. She wants to love and be loved. But she wonders now whether she could possibly be more attracted to the idea of Frank than the reality.

∽

The next morning, George informs Harriet that he'd like to speak with her after breakfast. When she knocks at the mahogany door, her father is sitting at his desk. He stands and gestures to the two armchairs facing the fireplace. Aside from the windows looking out on the back-yard and the doors, all the walls are filled with bookshelves crammed full of volumes. A fire crackles in the grate. They sit facing each other.

George says, "What are your thoughts about your future, Harriet?"

"As I told you the other night, I want to work for Sutton Chemical after I graduate in May." She's never said this so directly to her father before. When she first went to Madison, she wasn't sure she'd turn out to be good enough at chemistry for him to hire her. Since then she's felt more confident about her abilities.

"Given the kind of research you're involved in, you'll probably get any number of offers from drug companies."

"My advisor asked whether I'd consider going on for a PhD. She says I'd be a strong candidate for their doctoral program, but I can't see pursuing a career in higher education. I'm more interested in solving practical problems with chemistry."

Lighting a cigarette, George inhales deeply. "We'll talk after you finish your master's degree. You never know what sort of opportunities may present themselves to you in the next few months."

Why won't he give her a straight answer? Harriet takes a deep breath. "Will you consider taking me on, Father? You don't owe me a job—but would you think about it?"

He taps his cigarette on the edge of the ashtray on the small table at his elbow. "We'll discuss your options when the time comes."

January 2, 1947

Harriet and Nat are traveling west together on the Viking Train to Madison, and then it'll continue on to St. Paul without her. She's anxious to get back to school, whereas Nat appears horrified by the prospect of going to work in a mill owned by their father's cousin in Northfield, Minnesota.

On the leg from Chicago to Madison, Nat jokes frenetically, and she realizes that he's becoming more and more nervous the closer they get to her destination, where she'll leave him on his own.

She says, "Let's go get breakfast now." Maybe eating something will help calm him down.

As they pass by a lady wearing thick rayon hose, Nat whispers, "If she stands up, she'll find her stockings still have knees."

She laughs out loud. What an image! "Where did you get an idea like that, Nat?"

Looking gratified, he says, "It's a line from a song I wrote a couple of years ago. You remember those baggy, tattered, rayon hose from the war years."

"I certainly do. I didn't know you'd written a song."

"I've written a few songs about life at Andover."

"Lyrics and music?"

"That's right."

"What can you do with them?"

"I don't know."

Once they sit at a table in the dining car and the waiter serves their coffee, Nat says, "I can't believe Father wouldn't let me go to music school once my career at Yale was over."

"What did you expect?"

"I worked really hard at Andover—I made the first honor roll senior year. I thought I'd proved to Father that I was mature enough to know what I wanted to do next. He was supposed to let me choose my own school after graduating from Andover. But no, Father would have none of that. He said I had to go to Yale."

"Yale *is* his alma mater."

"I don't care." Nat clenches his fist. "He should respect my opinion. I'm eighteen years old. Guys my age were trusted to drive tanks and shoot the enemy, while I'm still being told what to do."

She tries to be gentle when she says, "Well, you did flunk out of Yale."

"Father knows how important music is to me. All the piano and saxophone lessons, the Gilbert and Sullivan performances, the concerts, the jazz clubs, all of it was meant to prepare me for music school. I have to go to music school so I can become a professional musician."

"Yes, but—"

"Don't you understand? I've got to be true to myself!" He sounds like he's on the verge of tears. "I *love* making music more than anything in the world, and I'm really good at it!"

"I know, Nat."

"My piano teacher at Andover and my saxophone teacher from the Boston Symphony Orchestra *both* said I should go to music school. Dr. Honiger told Father that again at graduation. After Yale booted me, I was sure Father would finally let me go to the Schillinger House of Music."

"Father's not going to reward you for failing."

"He's punishing me. He's sentenced me to work as a manual laborer in some kind of mill. Now all I can hope is that if I do a really good job in the mill for a while, he'll relent and send me to Schillinger next fall."

She says, "Pressuring Father will never work, Nat. I'm sure he thinks he's looking out for your best interests. He takes his job as your father very seriously."

"Too seriously!"

She looks out the window. After a few moments she turns back to Nat. "Maybe it's time I tell you something. It's a huge secret."

"What are you talking about?"

"George is not my real father."

"What?"

"My actual father was Mother's first husband, Henri."

"No way!" Putting his elbows on the table, he leans toward her.

"It's true. He was a surgeon in France during the Great War."

"I can't believe it!" He pauses. "Well, maybe I can. That would explain why you don't look like the rest of us."

"That's not a very nice thing to say." She looks down.

"I'm sorry, Harry, it just slipped out. I wasn't trying to make you feel bad."

She lifts her chin. "I'm still your sister—your half sister."

"Of course you are."

"Sometimes I feel like I don't really belong in our family, especially around Abba."

"When did you find out about your real father?"

"Right after Eddie left for basic training."

"You sure kept it to yourself for a long time. Why didn't you tell me before?"

"I haven't discussed this with anyone except Mother. It's really her secret." She looks out the window at the passing scenery for a moment. Then she admits, "Maybe I'm embarrassed too. I don't exactly fit into the family. Not like Eddie and you."

"Of course you're part of the family!"

"Learning that secret helped me understand why Father has always been so hard on me. I have to work harder than anyone else to win his approval."

"Father's hard on me too. I don't know if I'll ever be able to earn his respect."

"At least you know your father, Nat. You've looked into his eyes, and maybe you've even seen something of yourself in him. Mother doesn't have a single photograph of Henri."

"I had no idea."

"After Mother admitted the truth to me, I wanted to know everything about Henri. Eventually, though, I realized that George has always done his best to be a father to me."

"Father was awfully proud of the job you did on the farm."

"He seems to have some reservations about what I'm doing now."

Nat says, "Do you suppose Father knows about Henri?"

"I assume so, but I don't really know. We've never discussed it." She takes a sip of coffee. "Tell me, what happened at Yale, anyway?"

"I hated being there. I wasn't able to take any music classes first semester, and the other students were so suave and snobby. They made me feel like a slob."

"You must have had classmates from Andover at Yale."

"None of my Andover friends went to Yale—they went to Harvard and Cornell. Of course Eddie would have been there if he'd survived the war. That would have made being there much better." He grimaces. "Anyway, I escaped from campus whenever I could get back to the city."

The waiter deposits plates of bacon and eggs sunny-side-up in front of them.

Spearing a piece of bacon, she asks, "How often did you go to New York?"

"A couple of times a week. I went back to my favorite clubs, and sometimes I'd see what was going on at Minton's."

"You went up to Harlem by yourself!"

"Minton's has some really good hot music. You remember the time when we went to the Downbeat and heard Dizzy Gillespie's band?" He smiles now.

"They played so fast I thought my head would explode."

"It's energetic! And all those flatted fifths—I love hearing them. Dizzy and a bunch of the guys meet up for jam sessions at Minton's after their regular gigs. They really get groovin'. I'm just sorry Charlie Parker wasn't in town. He's my idol."

"That's why you started playing alto sax."

"Of course. But I still play piano."

"If you were flunking, I'm not surprised Yale dismissed you. These days every college and university in the country is overwhelmed by all the GIs returning to school. Last year the student population at Madison *doubled*. They had to bring in trailers and Quonset huts and temporary barracks to house everyone. Classes run from seven-thirty in the morning until ten-thirty at night."

"I thought sisters and brothers are supposed to stick up for each other."

She touches his hand. "I'm just trying to help you understand how you got into this mess."

"I know how I got into this mess! Now I have to live with the consequences."

"It seems to me that Father has set you free."

Bitterly, he replies, "He sent me into exile."

"You know, you don't *have* to go to Northfield."

"What else would I do? Where would I go? I have to follow Father's plans for me."

"Why?"

"I told you—so I can go to music school!"

He turns to stare out the window while a dark-skinned waiter wearing a white coat removes their plates and silverware. "All I can see are fields of snow. Everything's this monotonous white."

Trying to get him to find some other perspective, she says, "Not only white, Nat. The leaves on the trees are bronze, and see the tips of the sumac—they're a deep rusty red."

"It all looks black and white to me. The landscape is totally bleak. Doesn't it depress you?"

"Actually I like having a view that goes all the way to the horizon. The sky is so big and open here. It makes me feel like I can do anything. You can too."

"What must I do to make Father believe in me?"

Dropping her eyes, she says softly, "I wonder the same thing for myself." Then she looks up. "Nat, I bet after some time at the mill, if you wanted to go back to college, Father would support you."

"I'm never going to ask him for anything again."

Now she's growing impatient with him. "Never say never, Nat. You don't know what the future will bring."

"I know I sound like a spoiled brat. I'm sorry for whining, Harry."

"More coffee, ma'am?"

She looks up. "No thanks." She looks back to Nat. "You can't see what's coming—that's hard."

"I don't know anyone in Northfield."

"You're bright, Nat. You'll land on your feet. I know you will."

When the train pulls into the Madison station, she gathers her belongings. Putting her arms around Nat, she gives him a warm hug. "You'll be fine, Nat," she says, patting his back. "Why don't you visit me in Madison sometime? We aren't that far apart. Come for Easter."

"That would give me something to look forward to." Pulling away, he promises, "I'll write you."

After squeezing his hand, she picks up her bags and departs.

January 2, 1947

As the train leaves the station in Madison, Nat looks out the window, hoping for a glimpse of his sister, but she's out of sight. He settles back in his seat. Then he reaches into his pocket and pulls out the last letter Eddie wrote to him. He looks again at the final paragraph. "Do not be led by your sense of duty. Your life is yours to live as you see fit." That's what Nat thought he was doing. All last year he worked his ass off at Andover. He earned good grades; he even did well in Dr. Marling's impossible American history course.

He played soccer and kept the team amused as they struggled in their games against Exeter and Deerfield. He belonged to the rifle club too—an easy choice since he'd had lots of practice shooting rats around the chicken coops at home. He studied piano with his beloved teacher Dr. Honiger and sax with Mr. Pratt. He did his part.

Pulling the woolen scarf off his neck, he twists it with both hands, imagining it's his father's neck he's wringing. He hates his father. As the train takes him farther and farther away from everything he cares about, he turns the scarf until it's as tight as a rope.

At the same time he longs to please his father.

And he's young—he knows he's young. There's not a lot he can do to change his father's mind. Years ago he refused to go to Andover, but he didn't get anywhere with that. His father insisted that all the men in their family attend Andover.

Eventually Nat came to appreciate Phillips Academy. Andover raised the bar on his aspirations, and he managed to prove himself there academically and musically—if not socially. He gained some self-confidence, enough so that he came to believe he should be able to chart his own course going forward. Having Eddie there with him during his first two years at Andover forged a special bond between them, and with the school.

Lifting his scarf from his lap, he untwists it and drapes it around his neck.

Now what?

～

After the Rock Island Rocket from St. Paul pulls into the train station in Northfield, Nat descends the steps and looks around. Walking along the street, suitcase in one hand and saxophone case in the other, he sees that he has landed in an awfully small town on an unimpressive river. The sky is blue and so sunny it looks as if it should be warm, but it isn't. With each step he takes, the snow squeaks under his feet— actually, the snow is so dry that it shrieks. When he reaches the Cannon Mill looming over the falls, he hurries inside. A woman with a lopsided smile who's sitting behind a desk tells him to take a seat. While he waits, he removes his leather gloves and flexes his fingers, trying to get the circulation going in his numb digits. Soon a short wiry man appears, looking as if he's been sprinkled from head to foot with tan talcum powder. Nat stands.

Wiping his hands on his trousers, the man says, "I'm Mr. Hagman, head miller here. You must be Nathaniel Sutton."

"Yes sir." Nat shakes hands with Mr. Hagman. "I go by Nat."

"All right, Nat. You won't start work today—we're already in the middle of the second shift. You might as well go get settled."

"Where will I stay?"

"After Mr. Campbell called to let us know you'd be coming, the wife looked around for a room, but nothing's available because of all the men back from the war. The colleges, Carleton and St. Olaf, are overflowing too."

Nat starts to feel nervous.

"So Mrs. Hagman and I decided we'll take you in. We have an extra room now that our kids moved up to the Cities for work. We'll charge $5 a week for room and board."

"That's very good of you, sir."

"Not a bit. We'll enjoy having a young one around the house again."

"Thank you."

"Mr. Campbell said you're a relative of his—did I get that right?"

"I think he's a cousin of my father's. That's how I came to be here instead of somewhere else."

"You're welcome here."

"What kind of mill is this?" Nat feels really stupid that he can't tell. Then, considering the dust on Mr. Hagman, he asks, "Is it a flour mill?"

"No. They started milling flour on this site in the 1860s, but after the Campbell Cereal Company bought the mill twenty years ago, it was adapted for milling cereal grains."

"I didn't know Minnesota existed in the 1860s," Nat says.

"Northfield was founded in 1855 and Minnesota has been a state since 1858," Mr. Hagman replies. "My family's been here since the beginning."

"Is that so?" Nat responds politely.

"Yep. Well, you'd best take your gear along to the house. It's just a few blocks up the hill."

∾

Mrs. Hagman calls Nat down for supper at five-thirty. Mr. Hagman is already seated at the table, which is covered with a blue-and-green plaid oilcloth and set with white dishes decorated with blue flowers and vines. Mrs. Hagman, her thin blonde hair falling out of the bun on the back of her head, carries a platter of something covered with tomato sauce, surrounded by noodles. He hears a man on the radio in the front room reporting the day's prices for wheat, corn, and other commodities.

"I hope you like meatloaf, Nat," she says as she places it on the table in front of her husband.

"I like meatloaf very much," he replies truthfully, pulling out the chair Mr. Hagman indicates he should occupy.

Mrs. Hagman returns to the kitchen, so Nat hovers, thinking he shouldn't sit until she does. She returns with a bowl filled with sliced peaches in green Jell-O, which she sets down near Nat. The Jell-O is the same color as the tiny circles all over her apron. Taking her chair, she says, "Please sit down."

Mr. Hagman serves the meatloaf and noodles and hands the plates on to his wife.

"Jell-O salad?" she asks.

Nat says, "Yes please," though he has never eaten Jell-O before. He picks up his fork.

Mrs. Hagman clears her throat. "We like to say grace before our meals," she explains mildly.

Nat returns his fork to its place, folds his hands, and bows his head.

Mr. Hagman says, "Bless this food to our use and us to thy loving service. Amen."

After Mrs. Hagman takes a bite, she says, "I hope you have some warm clothing, Nat. Earlier this week it was thirty below—broke the record for the last day of December—and the temperature's still below zero."

"I've never experienced anything like the cold you've got here. How can it look so warm and sunny when the air feels like we're in Antarctica?"

She laughs. "It's a bit nippy. But you're in luck. There's a sale on this week. You could buy a blanket-lined work jacket."

Mr. Hagman says, "Good idea. Nat, do you know what Northfield is famous for?"

"No, I don't, sir."

"In 1876 the notorious outlaw Jesse James came to town with his gang, and they robbed the Northfield National Bank."

"Whoa."

"They shot and killed Joseph Lee Heywood, the bank employee who wouldn't open the vault for them, and some of the robbers were killed or wounded during the shoot-out."

"How many were killed?" Nat asks.

"Three died during the robbery, and others died from their wounds over the next few days. Jesse James and his brother Frank escaped, but that was the end of the James-Younger gang," Mr. Hagman says.

Nat says, "The employee who was killed—Heywood? He was a hero."

"He sure was. Northfield has been pretty quiet since then."

"Thank goodness!" Mrs. Hagman adds.

Nat wonders whether to use his fork or his spoon on the Jell-O salad. He looks at each of his hosts, hoping for guidance.

Mrs. Hagman says, "You can bring your laundry to me when it needs washing. I'm happy to do it."

"Are you sure, Mrs. Hagman?"

"You betcha."

Mr. Hagman stabs a piece of Jell-O and fruit with his fork. "What kind of church do you belong to, Nat?"

"I'm not really religious, sir. No one in my family goes to church."

"Really?" Mrs. Hagman's brow creases and lines cross her forehead. "Where do you turn for comfort?"

"Comfort?"

"Everyone needs comfort from time to time."

"That's true," Nat agrees. He wonders where he could turn for comfort.

"You're welcome to come along to church with us anytime you like. We belong to St. John's Lutheran. It's the biggest church in town."

"Thank you, Mrs. Hagman." Nat tries the Jell-O salad. It's surprisingly tasty. "Good meal."

Mrs. Hagman says, "I was thinking about making château rabbit on toast for supper tomorrow night—do you like that, Nat?"

"I've never had château rabbit." Nat tries to swallow the yawn that's threatening to emerge. Standing, he puts his cutlery on his plate. "May I take my dishes to the kitchen?"

"Of course," Mrs. Hagman replies. "But that's enough clearing. You look like you could drop in your tracks. Let me know if you need anything. There are extra towels in the bathroom and a clean glass on the sink for you."

"Mother, that's enough. Let the boy go to bed."

"I think I will head up. Thank you for dinner, Mrs. Hagman, and thanks for your hospitality. Good night."

∾

Once he is lying under the covers, Nat thinks about the Hagmans: they seem to be very nice people, but he figures he doesn't have much in common with them. He could certainly use some comfort, though.

Two weeks ago his paternal grandmother did her best to help him. A few days before Christmas, Abba took Nat to hear the Metropolitan Opera's matinee performance of *La Bohème*. The opera was sublime, but getting to spend time alone with Abba was the highlight.

During the first intermission, as they stood near the bar, Abba raised her glass of champagne and murmured, "Ah, the pleasures of civilization!"

Nat suddenly saw his grandmother with fresh eyes. Abigail was dressed in an elegant silver gown, and she wore a large diamond ring, a diamond bracelet, and a diamond pin. Nat realized he'd never seen his grandmother in anything but fancy clothing. During the war while his family worked the farm, Nat assumed that Abba hadn't participated because she was too old. Now he understood that she was too refined to take part in that kind of labor. Nat didn't mind if his grandmother thought she was above life on the farm—she cared about music as much as he did.

He took a sip from his champagne flute. She was watching the crowd. "Abba, did you ever play an instrument?"

She turned her attention back to him. "I studied the piano for many years, but once I was married, I stopped taking lessons."

"I've never heard you play."

"I haven't touched the piano in ages."

"Then why do you have such a beautiful Steinway in your apartment?"

"I have musical friends—and a grandson who plays very well." She smiled at him.

"Your piano sounds so bright and alive."

"It should. I have it tuned regularly." She brought her glass to her lips.

"Abba, what am I going to do? Father won't let me go to music school. I *love* music! The summer we heard about Eddie, playing the saxophone was the only thing that kept me sane."

Swallowing, she said, "I know you're passionate about music, Nathaniel. I'll speak to your father, but I must warn you, I may not be able to change his mind."

"Really?" Nat was surprised.

"George hasn't listened to me in years."

"So I'm not the only one."

"I'm afraid not, dear."

January 3, 1947

A little before seven the next morning as Nat prepares to leave, Mrs. Hagman hands him a pair of earmuffs. "For the cold?" he asks.

"It's for the noise. The machines are really loud when they get going. You'll want to wear the muffs while you work."

As Nat and Mr. Hagman approach the huge four-story structure built of sturdy timbers on a limestone foundation, Mr. Hagman says, "I'll show you around first."

They start on the fourth floor. "This mill operates in the traditional way, from top to bottom, using gravity to move the wheat and malt from one point down to the next. The product moves through big tubes that go through the floor. First we sterilize the grain, and then the rollers start breaking up the wheat kernels, which go through the purifier and then back through finer rollers until you get down to farina."

Surrounded by individual machines that are at least five feet tall by three feet wide, Nat is daunted by their size and number. He can't see into the machines, which are made of pale yellow-grained wood, so he has trouble visualizing what they do. "Farina?"

"Farina is fine meal. Since we're making breakfast cereals here, we stop grinding the wheat once it reaches the consistency of farina instead of taking the wheat all the way down to flour."

On the next floor they encounter the sifters, large machines as well, suspended from the ceiling by flexible hickory rods; the sifters are shaking from side to side. Shouting over the racket made by the machinery, Mr. Hagman says, "When we grind the malted barley, it goes through the sifter, and then it's ground some more and sifted again—it keeps making that loop. We sell the dust off as animal feed."

Nat sneezes several times.

"You have to be careful, Nat. This is a dangerous place. You must move cautiously around all the turning wheels and pulleys and spinning belts. Make sure your shirtsleeves and fingers don't get caught."

On the ground floor, Nat watches the cam-driven packaging machine insert a pour spout into a box, glue the bottom, then drop the cereal in and close and seal the box before it moves along the belt. Mr. Hagman says, "In the next room the boxes are wrapped with paper, packed into cases, and then rolled out for loading onto the freight cars outside."

"Wow. It's amazing that the whole process, from raw wheat to boxes of cereal, is completed right here in this one building."

"It's efficient." Turning to him, Mr. Hagman says, "Your part in this is very important. It's up to you to sweep the floors and make sure to remove all the dust."

"That's it? I'm going to be sweeping?"

"That's right—all day, every day. You must make sure we don't have a disaster. Flour dust is fifty times more explosive than gunpowder. This mill, with its wooden walls and machinery, would burn faster than you can imagine. All the men working here rely on you to keep us safe."

"I understand. This is a serious job."

The work is more monotonous than anything he has ever done. After four hours, he's amazed to see how much dust he accumulated sweeping the floors. He keeps sneezing every few minutes, and he's afraid he's going to have an asthma attack; he tries to breathe shallowly so he doesn't take all the dust into his lungs.

He finds it hard not to feel humiliated by the mind-numbing labor he's been assigned. He can't even talk to anyone because the rollers, grinders, and sifters make so much noise. By the end of his first day his arms are shaking. He worked on the family's Victory Farm, but somehow sweeping turns out to be much more tiring, perhaps because it's so repetitive. He feels as if he already knows every slat in the wooden floors by heart.

Over supper that night, he asks Mrs. Hagman if she has a large handkerchief he can borrow to wear over his mouth while he's working.

"If you're bothered by the dust, we'd better get you several kerchiefs so you have a fresh one every day. I'll go to the store tomorrow."

"That would be awfully kind of you, Mrs. Hagman. I can reimburse you right away."

"Oh, for gosh sake. I'll just tack the charge onto your bill for room and board."

Before bed, Nat sits in the living room awhile with the Hagmans, listening to the dance music that plays on the radio and exploring the local newspaper. From the front page of the *Northfield News*, he learns that rail traffic on the Milwaukee and Rock Island lines through town was stopped all day when a freight train derailed at the south entrance to the yards. That's news? The paper's eight pages also contain articles announcing lectures at Carleton and St. Olaf colleges. He wonders why there are two colleges in one small town. He sees announcements of weddings, christenings, and engagements, births at the hospital, obituaries, church notices, legal notices, advertisements for sales, reports on the high and low temperatures over the previous week, summaries of the movies showing at the Grand and the West Theaters, and classified ads. The contrast between the *Northfield News* and the *New York Times* reminds Nat all over again just how far from home he is.

He's very grateful to have a room of his own. After closing the door behind him, he sits on the bed. Other than the howling of the wind, the house is quiet; there's nothing to distract him from his thoughts.

It's beginning to dawn on him that when he flunked out, he ended up hurting himself more than his father. His father said this experience in the mill would be good for him. Really? What is this job as a sweeper going to do to him over time? If his lungs or his hands or his ears are injured, impacting his ability to play the sax or the piano, he will never forgive himself.

He has never felt so alone.

ॐ

The next day the temperature is twenty below, and a bitter wind blows while Nat and Mr. Hagman walk to work. Nat hunches his shoulders and clenches his whole body against the cold that cuts through his clothing. The air is so frigid he feels as if he can't inhale. Then he notices that Mr. Hagman has tied his scarf around his face in such a way that only his eyes are exposed. Nat pulls his own scarf out from around his neck and rewraps it to cover his nose and mouth. Breathing through the wool helps a lot.

At the mill Nat keeps his head down and sweeps, hour after hour. Midmorning, when he is working next to one of the dust collectors, he discovers that wheat dust is drifting down from the machine onto the floor as fast as he can remove it.

"This is futile!"

A guy passing by shouts, "There's always new dust. That's what they told me when I was a sweeper."

Nat looks up. "You had this job?"

"Yeah, everyone starts sweeping. It's the lowest paid job. You work your way up from there. I'm a loader now, and the money's a lot better, but I have to work outdoors."

"In this weather?"

"Doesn't matter what the weather is—blizzards or lightning storms, we still have to keep loading the boxes into the railcars."

"I guess I should be grateful that I work indoors."

Nat wears a red neckerchief from Mrs. Hagman over his mouth and nose, but he still sneezes constantly. He figures he must be allergic to the grain dust—even his eyes itch. By noon Nat's neckerchief is sodden, and he doesn't have another with which to dry his upper lip, so it quickly chafes and becomes raw. By the end of his second day of work, he's miserable. In the bathroom mirror at the Hagmans', he sees that his juicy red nose and watering eyes make him look pathetic.

Sunday morning, when Mrs. Hagman reiterates her invitation to attend church, Nat says, "Thank you anyway. It's much too cold to go outdoors if you don't have to." He's too tired and discouraged to have to smile at strangers.

While the Hagmans are at St. John's, he reads the newspaper more closely. There's a lecture next week at Carleton that he'd like to hear, but it'll be held Friday morning when he's at work. Then he spots an ad from Eide Radio & Appliance: "New records 35 cents. We have purchased the Leigh Studio's complete record stock." Feeling a spurt of excitement, he wonders whether he could buy a record player for his room here. He has some money: his father gave him $50 for expenses, and his mother sneaked an additional $50 into his suitcase along with a note. Before long he'll receive his first paycheck too. Of course he'd have to promise not to play his music too loudly. Then he realizes that right now he can make all the noise he wants; the house is empty, the windows and doors shut tight.

Dashing up to his room, he pulls out his saxophone for the first time since he landed in Minnesota. As he plays "Comfort Ye, My People" from Handel's *Messiah*, his heart feels less heavy. Once he sets the saxophone down, he thinks about writing a letter to Peter, his best friend from Andover, who's at Cornell University now, and he should write Harry after he checks with Mr. Hagman about the work schedule for Easter weekend.

၉

The Hagmans agree that Nat can have a record player as long as he doesn't play it after nine in the evening. When he goes to Eide's, he finds a limited selection of records, but he buys a record player, a Billie Holiday album, and two recordings of Brahms's early symphonies. He doesn't bother to acquire a radio because he's already learned that he can't get jazz on any of the stations here. He used to love listening to Duke Ellington on the radio at home.

Before long he grows bored with feeling stuck, and his curiosity reasserts itself. One night, even though the thermometer reads minus ten, he goes to the public library for a glimpse of the world beyond Northfield. He learns that even the Boy Scouts are experiencing the housing shortage, to which an Air Scout Squadron in Armonk, New York, has responded by buying a secondhand naval transport plane, taking off its wings, and equipping it for use as their clubhouse. This story amuses him, makes him smile. In *Life* magazine he reads, "The Russians tried to steal Europe and failed." What does that mean? He doesn't know much about Russia.

An ad for *The Secret Heart* with Claudette Colbert and Walter Pidgeon catches his eye. Apparently the film concerns two women who love the same man. Nat's experience with women is practically nonexistent. For a couple of months at Andover, he had a gorgeous girlfriend named Emma. But she never answered his letter about Eddie getting killed, and in the fall she didn't return to Abbot Academy, the girls' school down the street from Andover. He thinks having two women in love with him would be great.

On Friday night he makes his way to the Grand Theater. The film opens with Larry Adams playing a passionate rendition of Franz Liszt's Piano Concerto No. 1. Both women are in love with Larry, but after Larry's suicide and revelations about the financial disaster he caused investors, the movie gets creepy. Larry should never have become a banker—he would have been a great concert pianist, but his father forced him into a practical career instead. Unnerved by the eerie resonance with his own life, Nat leaves the theater before the end of the movie.

Every Sunday Nat pulls out his saxophone as soon as the Hagmans depart for church. He's set up the record player on top of the desk in his room, and one day he is so engrossed in playing along with Billie Holiday's rendition of "In My Solitude" that he doesn't hear them return. When Mrs. Hagman raps on his door, he puts down his instrument and stops the record. "Come in."

"Was that you playing?"

"Yes, ma'am."

"Holy buckets, you're good!"

"Thank you." Her praise warms him, though he knows he still has a long way to go.

"No wonder you don't come to church with us. This is your chance to practice with no one around."

Nat nods.

"I have an idea. On Wednesday nights when I go rehearse with the choir at St. John's, maybe you'd like to come along? I'm sure we could find an empty Sunday school room you could practice in."

"That would be great, Mrs. Hagman. I didn't realize you sang in the church choir."

"I don't. I play the organ."

"Really? I love organ music. I'd like to hear you play, Mrs. Hagman."

"I could be worse."

"I played a little organ in high school, but mostly it was piano."

"Is that so?"

"I'd like very much to come along with you Wednesday night. Thank you."

༃

January 31

Dear Nat,

I'm glad to hear you can come to Madison for Easter week-end. That'll be a treat. It sounds like you're settling into life in Northfield. Have you had a chance to go skating yet? I love to get outdoors here when I can grab the time.

Dr. McCann thinks I should consider going on for a PhD in chemistry. It would require more years in the lab, and then what? I can't imagine teaching at a college or university. I prefer to do chemistry, not talk about it. What do you think, Nat? You know me well. What would you advise?

Love,

Harry

Nat is amazed—Harry has never asked his advice before. He writes her back immediately to say she should *do* chemistry if that's what feels right to her.

༃

Next Sunday after lunch Nat spots a notice in the *Northfield News* about an organ recital at Carleton that afternoon. While he points it out to Mrs. Hagman, he remembers thinking he didn't have anything in common with the Hagmans. He sure was wrong.

"Would you like to go with me to hear Mr. Woodworth?" Nat loved listening to Dr. Honiger play Bach in the chapel at Andover.

"Thanks, Nat, but I need a nap."

Walking toward the college campus, Nat is surprised to see all these clapboard houses with light trim, which make him think of

Massachusetts. It's easy to find Skinner Memorial Chapel, for it's a massive stone structure with a square bell tower dominating a large lawn; there's nothing close by except for trees, and now he is reminded of Andover. Suddenly he realizes how much he likes being on a college campus. And this place has coeds, which makes it even better than Andover. As a pretty girl in a red wool cap covering long blonde hair approaches him, Nat stops.

"Hey," he says. "Hi."

She smiles but passes by without saying anything. How is he ever going to meet a girl like her?

When he sits in the audience before the recital begins, Nat looks at the stained glass windows with elemental floral images and crosses, and up at the wooden beams just under the roof of the sanctuary. Then he drops his eyes to the crowd of older people, who must be members of the faculty and their spouses, and older students—GIs—and a few people closer to his own age. He fits in here. Once the music surrounds him, Nat starts to feel more like himself. He thinks about Andover and Eddie, performing Gilbert and Sullivan operettas with him, defying the rules by playing poker there with his brother and pals, and also the sobering occasion when he comforted Eddie after that brutal hazing by the ACB club. Then it dawns on him that he has the time now to go back to work on those songs he started writing about life at Andover. That would be fun—and it could be a way to connect with memories of Eddie.

∾

At the mill the next day, Nat watches a guy called Dick come up to a machine, and as the pulleys are going, Dick takes one belt off and throws another on in its place while all the wheels keep turning. The machine never stutters or slows. Nat is terribly impressed.

56 Ames Sheldon

The roar of the machine is deafening, so he grabs Dick's sleeve. With exaggerated face and hand gestures, he mouths, "Wow!"

Dick grins and nods at Nat.

During the afternoon break, Nat finds Dick sitting in the cafeteria, smoking a cigarette. Then Nat notices the hand holding the fag has only three fingers. Nat sits down next to Dick. Opening the lunch box Mrs. Hagman gives him every morning, he says, "That was remarkable, Dick! Aren't you afraid of getting pulled into the machine?"

"Pretty slick, huh?" Dick replies proudly. "I've kept those machines going for more years than I can count. I know their workings better than the workings of my wife—'course the machines are more predictable."

Nat laughs as he opens the thermos and pours himself a cup of Mrs. Hagman's weak coffee. "I wouldn't have thought you could change a belt like that without incurring major damage."

"I got banged up in the beginning till I learned my way around. I have to say, you wield a mean broom. The mill has never been so clean. You go all the way into the corners."

Ridiculously pleased, Nat blushes. "Thanks, Dick." Unwrapping a piece of apple pie, he asks, "Want some?"

"No thanks. You're not from around here, are you? You've got an accent."

"I grew up in New Jersey."

"Ah! That explains it. What's a young fella like yourself doing in a place like this?"

"I guess my father thought it would be good for me to get out on my own. It's time I start earning my way." As he hears himself, he notices that he feels a bit of pride about this. At last it occurs to him that when he earns his own money, he can do whatever he wants. He's independent of his father. He can be his own man.

Dick says, "That's not bad."

"I've been wondering about something. The machines are all

operating at different rates, and they're out of sync with each other. It's kind of jarring. Wouldn't it be better if they worked together, in some sort of harmony?"

"Oh no, if they moved all together, they'd vibrate the mill to the ground—the building would break apart. The machines are purposely adjusted so they don't do that."

"No wonder it sounds so clunky."

"You get used to it."

❧

Nat's arms are growing stronger from his work in the mill, and he becomes confident enough to jump onto the open man lift when he needs to move from one floor to another. During lunch he often sits and talks with Dick, but most of his conversations are with himself. He enjoys his own company.

He writes another stanza for the song "Must I Go to PA?"

> *Foll'wing Dad's a tough act,*
> *All I'd do is detract*
> *From his great saga*
> *That's told to this day:*
> *While at PA*
> *Grades are all A;*
> *He caught the pass*
> *Beat the big Red and Gray.*

He knows Eddie would agree with those lines. Is that why his brother played football at Andover, hoping to beat Exeter like their father had? As he composes the lyrics, Nat finds that he feels closer to Eddie than ever.

In the town library, he studies a variety of newspapers and

magazines. A battered issue of *Life* dated January 13 has an article about the Communists in France, who make up the largest party there; apparently, they follow Moscow's directives. Having the Communists come to power in France would be "the surrender of the French Republic, the greatest bulwark of liberty on the European continent, to a totalitarian and foreign influence. For England and the US it would mean that the Soviet sphere had reached the shores of the Atlantic." This image gives him the shivers.

Nat decides to write his father, asking him to send articles from the *New York Times* about Communism and whatever Russia's up to so he can better understand what's going on. He's starting to realize how much he doesn't know. At an evening lecture about immigration by a Carleton professor of sociology and anthropology, he learns that 500,000 Italians are asking for admission to the US, but the quota for Italians is 5,800 persons. What can they do about all those people?

A few weeks later Nat receives an envelope of clippings from the *New York Times* with a note from his father simply stating, "As requested." A letter from Peter arrives too; Peter likes Cornell very much, and he's decided to major in the history of art. Nat wonders, *What is the point of a degree in art history?* He thought Peter wanted to be a cartoonist.

ॐ

Late one afternoon, Nat is sweeping the top floor of the mill, where the largest grinders start the work of breaking up the kernels of wheat. As he moves the broom rhythmically, he thinks up sax riffs to go along with the *swish swish swish* of the broom; those swishes almost sound like brushes stroking the top of a snare drum. He'll have to try those riffs out tonight in the room Mrs. Hagman arranged for him to use at the church.

He hears a change in the sound of the machinery, as though one of the grinders has suddenly stopped. That's strange. He removes his earmuffs. Stomach tightening, he moves quickly into the next room.

Dick stands in front of the huge steel wheels, a five-inch-wide belt on the floor beside him, his right hand jammed in the tiny gap between a wheel that's two feet wide and another that's eight inches in diameter.

Dick's face is white. Between clenched teeth, he cries, "Turn it off!"

Nat scurries around the machine, looking for a switch, but he can't find one. He shouts, "Mr. Hagman, Mr. Hagman!" but realizes no one can hear him over the clamor of the other machines, so he races for the open man lift. Flying down to the first floor, whispering, "Oh God, oh God, oh God," he finds Mr. Hagman and quickly leads him back to the fourth floor, breathlessly describing the situation.

Once upstairs, Mr. Hagman makes the grinder reverse direction and release Dick's hand. When it's free, Dick cups the middle finger of his right hand in his left.

Nat is surprised to see that there isn't any blood, but Dick's finger has been flattened. Mr. Hagman tells Nat to accompany Dick down the street to the doctor's office.

After examining and x-raying Dick's hand, Dr. Jones says, "All three phalanges, the bones in your finger, have been thoroughly crushed, so much so that I don't believe they can heal. I recommend we amputate that finger."

Dick replies, "At least I'll still have two fingers on my hand— enough to hold a cigarette."

Fortunately, Nat is asked to leave the room while the doctor performs the operation. As he starts to calm down, he thinks how much he admires Dick for his bravery and his jaunty attitude. Dick is a real man.

Later that night Nat can't sleep. He keeps seeing Dick's smashed finger. His own hand twitches at the thought of losing one of his digits.

❧

Early in March, Nat spots a notice about an upcoming performance of *H.M.S. Pinafore* at Carleton College. Nat and Eddie performed that operetta for their family during the summer of 1943, along with a cast of neighbors and friends, and it was more fun than anything—even more than the production at Andover they'd been involved in earlier that year. His second year at Andover, after Eddie joined the Army, Nat got to play the piano accompaniment to *Pirates of Penzance*, and that had been thrilling.

"Mrs. Hagman? How would you and Mr. Hagman like to attend a performance of *H.M.S. Pinafore* at Carleton College with me this weekend?"

"I'm not familiar with that," Mrs. Hagman says.

"It's a very silly operetta with beautiful songs by Gilbert and Sullivan."

Mr. Hagman says, "Count me out. I don't go for that kind of thing."

"We've never been up to the college," Mrs. Hagman replies.

Surprised, he says, "Never? The performance is open to the public. There's no reason not to go."

"All right, then. I'll give it a try."

On their way over to Carleton, Mrs. Hagman holds her coat closed around herself so tightly that Nat wonders whether she's embarrassed. Maybe she's intimidated by a college campus, but he feels very much at home here. He's glad to be able to expose Mrs. Hagman to something new about her own town.

During the performance, he is tickled anew by the nonsense. When Mrs. Hagman asks about confusing parts of the story, Nat explains that you have to suspend your disbelief and simply go along with it. Mrs. Hagman is very impressed by the student playing Josephine, who has an excellent voice, but Nat's disappointed by the guy in Rafe Rackstraw's role—he isn't nearly as good a tenor as Eddie was.

On the way home, Mrs. Hagman says, "Thank you, Nat. That was enjoyable. You know, I never heard you laugh before."

"Really?"

"You're such a serious young man. You don't even smile very often."

"Well, I have felt a bit like a fish out of water. I'm not used to small towns or working in a mill, but I'm starting to get the hang of things."

"You're certainly a hard worker."

೦ಌ

The next Saturday after work, Nat takes an afternoon train up to Minneapolis, hoping to find a record store where he can buy some new jazz recordings now that vinyl is no longer reserved for military use. As the train from St. Paul to Minneapolis crosses over the Mississippi River, Nat recalls the pleasure he had reading *Tom Sawyer* and *Huckleberry Finn*. Leaving the Great Northern Depot, he walks halfway across the Hennepin Avenue Bridge so he can view the great waterway. Although snow and ice cover the banks, the middle of the Mississippi is wide open and flowing freely.

He turns back toward the city and passes a group of men standing together at the end of the bridge in rough clothes, smoking. Hennepin Avenue strikes him as slightly seedy, so he moves over to Nicollet Avenue. Most of the buildings are two and three stories high, constructed of brick or stone. He passes by the J. C. Penney and Powers stores, aiming for The Dayton Company, which he spots up ahead. This is a name he recognizes from ads in the *Minneapolis Star*. The Dayton store is a strange-looking conglomeration of structures—one three stories tall, another five, and another eight. He figures it must have been added to over the years. Inside, he finds the record section downstairs near the books, and a sales clerk informs him that the best place to buy records by Ella Fitzgerald, Count Basie, and other jazz artists is actually Gabberts at 3035 Nicollet Avenue.

"How far away is that?" Nat asks.

"More than twenty blocks. You'll want to hop a trolley to take you down Nicollet and get off at Lake Street."

Back outside, he spots the Foshay Tower, a skyscraper with thirty-two floors that rises high above the surrounding buildings, which aren't very high by Nat's standards. He walks over to Marquette Avenue and enters the foyer. The Art Deco interior is beautiful with its marble floors, gold-plated doorknobs, and silver-and-gold-plated ceiling—this is more like what he's used to. The Foshay Tower may not have as many stories as the Chrysler Building in Manhattan, but it reminds him of home.

A young woman wearing a navy coat and high heels walks by.

"Miss?"

She stops and smiles at him. Her lipstick is bright red. "Yes."

"Do you happen to know when this building was constructed?"

"Sorry, I don't know the date. It's been here as long as I can remember."

Glad to find that he's not invisible to all women, Nat grabs a streetcar down to Lake Street. In Gabberts, he snatches up the only copy of the new Charlie Parker Septet album and heads for the front.

A tall skinny man with a protruding Adam's apple, the cashier, says, "I see you got the last one. Charlie Parker's albums fly out the door as fast as we can get them in."

"I'm really glad you had this. Parker's my favorite saxophonist."

"He's a great one."

After paying the man, Nat asks, "Is there any place to hear live jazz in this town?"

"The Flame Room in the Radisson Hotel is probably your best bet."

"Where's the Radisson?"

"Downtown between Nicollet and Hennepin Avenue, next to The Dayton Company. You can't miss it."

On the train back to Northfield, he pores over the liner notes accompanying the album. Back at the Hagmans' he listens to the whole record, and then he plays "Yardbird Suite" over and over again. If only he had some other musicians to jam with.

∽

The following Saturday, in order to look as old as possible, Nat dresses up in the only jacket, tie, and pair of trousers he brought to Minnesota, and he makes sure to tuck the bottoms of his long underwear into his dark socks so the white doesn't show. This time he takes a later train up to the Cities, figuring that the music at the Flame Room won't start before eight,

The clerk at Gabberts was right—Nat has no trouble finding the Radisson Hotel. He buys a package of cigarettes. Entering the Flame Room, he sees a table for two near the back and sits there. It's been months since he's smoked a cigarette, so his first inhalation makes him cough repeatedly, and then he feels dizzy. Maybe having asthma means he shouldn't smoke. Once he recovers his breath, he looks around. Most of the tables are occupied by people dining, the men wearing suits, the women in dresses and high heels. The room is dim despite the small lamps on each table, though spotlights are trained on the bandstand, where a drum set, piano, string bass, music stands, and microphones wait.

Nat wonders what he should drink. He's not twenty-one yet, but he had no trouble ordering alcohol in the clubs in New York. When the waiter comes by, he stops the man. Adopting his father's manner when he gives an order at his club, Nat tries to sound assured. "Please bring me a rum and Coke, sir."

The waiter nods.

Soon the musicians emerge, chatting with each other as they take their places. Nat is shocked to see that all of them are white. Back home his favorite jazz musicians have dark skin. He wonders how good these white guys can possibly sound. At least the band has an appropriate mix of instruments, with trumpet, trombone, and saxophone to go with the piano, bass, and drums.

He takes a slug of his drink. The band starts off playing "I'm Just a Lucky So-and-So," a tune by Duke Ellington that Nat recognizes. He relaxes. Leaning back in his chair, he closes his eyes. This is more like it. This is the life he wants.

April 1947

A devout Lutheran, Mr. Hagman closes the mill at noon on Good Friday so his employees can attend church. Instead of heading over to St. John's, though, Nat hurries to the station to board the train to St. Paul, where he changes to the Milwaukee Road train to Madison.

As he heads south, he recalls the despair that crushed him the last time he rode this train. He no longer feels quite so desperate about his plight, but his sister didn't seem very sympathetic. After Eddie died, he and Harry should have clung to each other, but they didn't. He doesn't know why. Maybe it was because Harry is so much older than he—nine years is a lot. Maybe it was because that first summer after they got the news, Harry leaned on him really hard to get the farm work done since Eddie wasn't there to help with his muscle and can-do attitude. Nat tried to fill the gap, but he isn't as strong as Eddie was. That summer Harry got even bossier than usual, and she lost her sense of humor entirely.

He pulls out a piece of paper and thinks about another stanza of "Must I Go to PA?" *Must I live in a dorm? What rhymes with dorm? Conform. What are the ways in which we were expected to conform? Our haircuts? Our clothing?* He was always afraid his ties were wrong, though he felt sure Eddie's were perfect. Eventually he writes:

Must I live in a dorm,
Feel that I must conform?
Though I'm a perfect
Brooks Brothers' size,
I'll be despised
By all the guys,
If by some gaffe
I wear really bad ties.

When he climbs down from the train in the West Madison station, he grins to see Harry waiting for him on the covered platform.

"Nat!" she cries, throwing her arms around him.

He stands stiffly, still holding his suitcase, though he leans his shoulders toward her.

"You really don't like hugs, do you?" she says, still holding tight.

Pulling back, he replies, "I'm not used to them."

"I'm so glad you're here!" She looks wonderful: pink cheeked and as familiar as his own face.

"I'm glad too." He puts his suitcase down and gives her a peck on the cheek.

"Gracious!" she says. "That was unexpected."

He picks up his suitcase.

"Have you eaten?"

"I bought a sandwich on the train."

"All right, then. We can head home."

"Home? Where's home?" he asks. The relevance of this question for himself strikes him momentarily.

"I live in a boarding house nearby."

Outside the station, Harry motions for a cab.

"Where will I be?"

"You'll stay with me in my room. Klara and my two other room-mates have gone home for the holiday, and I managed to convince Mrs.

Schmitt to let you take one of the empty beds. We're really crammed in tight this year, but I think we can manage."

Once they enter Harry's room, Nat feels her eyes on him.

"You're taller, Nat. You must have grown two inches since Christmas."

Nat says, "No wonder my pants keep getting shorter! I thought they'd shrunk."

"Why didn't you buy some new ones that fit?" She sounds snippy.

"I suppose I look like a scarecrow. At least I didn't wear my dirty work jacket. You should be glad about that."

"I *am* glad about that. We'll go shopping tomorrow." She points to the corner.

"Your suitcase should fit over there."

He squeezes between two of the four narrow cots crowded into the middle of the room on his way to the spot she indicated. After putting his bag down, he says, "I've never slept in a lady's boudoir before. This is kind of exciting."

She laughs. "I hadn't thought of it in those terms, but I see what you mean."

He wanders over to a lamp standing in the corner and gingerly touches its lacy shade, and then he moves to a chest of drawers, the top of which is covered with bottles of nail polish and remover, tubes of lipstick, baby powder, cotton balls, earrings, and bracelets jumbled together. "Who uses all this stuff, anyway?"

"That's Klara's. She's not very well organized, but she's a nice girl. Young."

"Would I like her?"

"She's not bright enough for you, Nat. Besides, she's engaged."

Pleased to be reminded that at least he has intelligence going for him, he leans in to scrutinize himself in the mirror over Klara's bureau. He purses his mouth.

"Are my lips too big?"

"They're fine."

He turns away from the glass.

Sitting down on her bed, Harry says, "I'm sorry I didn't write you as often as I meant to this winter, but I've thought about you lots of times. I've just been so busy working."

It seems to him that she's practically bragging, or maybe it's just that he envies her being preoccupied with work she enjoys so much. "That's okay."

She yawns. "Tomorrow I want you to tell me all about life in Northfield."

"There's not much to say." He opens his suitcase and hands Harriet five Hershey's chocolate bars. "I know you love chocolate, so I brought you a present. Hershey's Sweet Milk Chocolate—it's 'more sustaining than meat,' as the advertisement claims."

"Thank you, Nat, that's very thoughtful." She gets up to put the candy bars in the top drawer of her dresser. Turning back to him, she teases, "I might even share some with you."

He smiles. "You'd better."

In the bathroom together, while Nat brushes his teeth, he sings, "I polished up that handle so carefullee, That now I am the Ruler of the Queen's Navee!"

She chuckles.

"Do you remember that song from *H.M.S. Pinafore*? Eddie and I used to sing it while we brushed our teeth."

"You guys would laugh so hard you'd make a huge mess on the mirror."

Back in the bedroom, she says, "Let me know if you need another blanket or an extra pillow."

Once he slides under the covers, he thinks how happy he is to be here with his sister. Then he shuts his eyes and sleeps more soundly than he has in months.

∽

The next morning over breakfast, as Mrs. Schmitt moves in and out of the dining room with orange juice, coffee, and platters of eggs and sausage and toast, Nat chatters away, telling Harry about sweeping the mill and living with the Hagmans, practicing his sax at St. John's Lutheran, going to free concerts at St. Olaf and Carleton. He tries to make his current life sound like it has all sorts of charm. It's certainly different from anything he's known before.

When Mrs. Schmitt leaves them on their own, Nat comments, "She makes me think of Mother."

"Mrs. Schmitt looks nothing like Mother. She's old and stout."

"Her hair is the same."

"Well, they both roll their hair up around their ears and across the back of their head. It takes long metal hairpins to keep that 'do' in place, and I can't imagine how that could be comfortable."

"I guess." Nat pours himself another cup of coffee.

"It's good to hear you sounding more like yourself. When I left you on the train in January, you really had the blues. I've worried about you."

"I feel better now."

"What are you thinking about your future, Nat? Have you made any plans?"

"Not really. What about you, Harry? How's the work on your master's going?"

"I just handed in the first draft of my thesis this week. I hope that my advisors won't have any major criticisms. After breakfast I'll show you my lab."

"I'd like to see where you work. That'll help me picture you when I go back to Northfield."

∾

The day is overcast, the clouds are gray, and the wind off the lake is piercing as they walk past the Quonset huts and the Historical Library.

Nat wears his new raincoat with the flannel lining, but he's sorry now that he didn't bring his warmer blanket-lined work jacket after all, even though it's grubby. While they trudge up Bascom Hill, Harry points out the Music Hall and the Science Hall, the Radio Hall and the Law Building, the Education and Engineering Building, and finally Bascom Hall.

At the top, breathing hard, he leans over.

"Are you all right?" she asks, putting her hand on his back.

After a few moments, he stands up straight. "I'm afraid my asthma's getting worse from all the dust I inhale while I'm sweeping."

"You should see a doctor."

He shakes his head no. "What's with the statue of Abe Lincoln?"

"I think he's here to inspire us to be honest and study hard. People rub his foot for good luck before exams."

"That's why the front of his boot is so shiny."

"After graduation, students climb up and sit on his lap."

"I bet you can see a long way from there." He turns to look at Bascom, North, and South Halls. "I can't believe the size of these buildings—they're massive."

"Usually the campus is really crowded. We have more than twelve thousand students at UW now."

Harry takes Nat over to the Carillon Tower to show him her favorite view of Lake Mendota. Dutifully he admires the scene, but now he's shaking with cold, despite the sweater beneath his raincoat.

"Don't you get lost? This campus is huge."

"I only spend time in a few buildings."

As they turn down Charter Street, he says, "Are we almost there?"

"Two more blocks."

Once they enter the Chemistry Building, he feels his shoulders relax. She points out the lecture hall with the periodic table of the elements hung from the ceiling, large blackboards behind the instructor's lab table, and seats for four hundred students. They look into smaller classrooms and laboratories before they arrive at Harry's lab. There, chemicals in labeled glass bottles with glass stoppers fill several shelves against the wall, and clear glass beakers and Erlenmeyer flasks are ranged on other shelves. Nat runs his hand along the gray soapstone counter, which is as smooth and cool as it looks. A Bunsen burner sits nearby, along with a metal clamp for holding test tubes above the flame.

He wrinkles his nose. "I smell gas."

"We don't get much circulation in this room." She walks over to open the window.

Grabbing a stool, he sits. "Tell me what you do here."

She stands next to him "We're testing different kinds of mold to see which produces the most penicillin. Penicillin cures lots of infections and diseases that used to be fatal, so this is really crucial work."

"I can tell you love what you're doing, Harry." He's proud of her—envious too.

"I love doing something that can help people live longer and healthier lives. I just hope we find the key to being able to mass produce the stuff."

"I bet you will. You can do anything you set your mind to."

She smiles. "Thanks for the vote of confidence, Nat, but it's an enormous challenge that many leading scientists have been wrestling with for a very long time."

"I mean it, Harry. I've always been in awe of the things you can do. Remember the time we changed that flat tire on the way to see *Oklahoma*? You were wearing stockings and a dress, but you jumped right out and had that tire switched out in seconds."

"It wasn't quite that fast."

"Was too." He swivels in his seat, gesturing toward the test tubes. "Tell me more about penicillin."

Sitting on an adjacent stool, she says, "Penicillin was first discovered by accident by a Scottish scientist named Alexander Fleming in 1928. He wasn't able to attract any interest in his discovery of the antibacterial properties of penicillin mold, which must have been frustrating as hell for him. Finally, a few years ago scientists in the UK and in this country started experimenting with different molds, trying to find a method for producing the drug in quantity. At first they just used what they had—milk bottles and other small flasks to contain the culture. Someone estimated it would require a row of bottles stretching from New York City to San Francisco to generate the penicillin needed during the war."

He snorts. "That's quite an image."

"Now scientists are fermenting penicillin in deep tanks in a process that's something like brewing beer."

"Speaking of beer," Nat says, "isn't that something Wisconsin is known for? Maybe we could get some with lunch."

"You aren't hungry already, are you?"

"I guess I'm still growing."

"We'll go to the Rat for lunch—they have beer there. Just let me check a few of my beakers."

As he wanders around the lab, careful not to touch anything, he asks himself whether he misses Yale. No, but he does miss being in school. Heading out to the corridor, he stands in front of the flyers posted on bulletin boards. A young woman in a white lab coat comes out of a door across the hall.

"May I help you?" she asks.

"I'm just waiting for my sister, Harry—Harriet—Sutton." Nat's eyes skip down to her breasts and then back up to her face.

She says, "All right, then."

As she walks toward the stairs, he admires her shapely legs, and then he recalls telling Eddie once that he is a "leg man." But that's not something he can say to his sister.

∾

In the Union, Nat and Harry descend to the lowest level and move through the main archway into Der Rathskeller. He heads right to the fireplace, steps onto the hearth, and holds his hands out toward the heat. Turning back to Harry, he says, "Boy, it's nice in here!"

He looks up at the mural above the fireplace, which depicts a bespectacled professor in a gown with very wide sleeves, an open book, a skull, a bone, and tools on the desk before him, standing in front of an audience of seated young men wearing suits.

Pointing up, he says, "Is that guy meant to be a physician?"

"Of course."

"I'm just trying to make conversation, Harry."

"Sorry."

He spots the German slogans painted inside banners on the walls. "We could almost be in Germany."

She says, "This is a real German rathskeller. Wouldn't you know, women weren't allowed in here on a regular basis until the war started." She leads him over to the lunch bar, where she orders beer, grilled cheese sandwiches, and pickles for two.

They find an empty table and sit down with their food. She picks up her glass of beer. "Once Prohibition ended, Congress declared that 3.2 beer wasn't intoxicating, which meant it could be sold in all sorts of places. Soon the university's officials figured out they'd better make beer available to students here in the Rat if they wanted to keep them on campus." She takes a sip.

"Lucky for us," he replies, lifting his own glass as he looks around the room.

"I noticed you looking at every girl we passed coming down Bascom Hill," she teases.

"I don't see pretty girls in the mill."

"Do you think you'd be happier at a coeducational university rather than a men's school?"

"Maybe. Are those frescoes on the walls?"

"Not exactly." She bites into her sandwich.

Returning his glass to the scarred wooden table, he starts flexing the fingers of his right hand.

She says, "Someone told me the artist used oil paint on the plaster after it dried, so it's not quite the same technique—"

He interrupts, "I'm still reeling from the news that my father isn't *your* real father."

"I consider George my real father—I've never known any other. He and Mother raised me."

"Tell me more about Henri." Watching Harry intently, he picks up his pickle.

"I don't know much. He was a Frenchman, a surgeon Mother met on the front during the Great War when she was driving that ambulance for the Red Cross."

Nat replies, "I knew she'd been in the war, but I had no idea she'd married Henri until that horrible night we found out Eddie had enlisted. Mother was so upset about Eddie going to war that she drank too much, and then her secrets about being in France and having a husband before Father came blasting out."

Harry says, "I know. I couldn't believe it when she threw her glass at Father!"

"Why did Mother keep all those secrets?"

Returning her sandwich to the plate, Harry replies, "Father didn't want her talking about *anything* that happened when she was in France. I think he was ashamed that he hadn't been over there fighting himself."

"That's probably true," Nat says. "Once when I asked Father about his contribution to the Second World War, he got all huffy about running a company that was essential to the war effort. Then I asked what he did in the Great War since he was at Yale when the US got into it. He told me he had to stay home to run Sutton Chemical but he always had regrets."

Harry takes another sip of her beer. "Mother and Henri fell madly in love, and they got married. Not long afterward, Henri was killed right in front of her. She tried to save him, but he was too badly wounded. She came back to the States right after he died."

"How long were they married?"

"I don't really know. A few months?"

"His death must have been horrible for Mother."

"How about coming home pregnant, with no husband to help establish a home and pay the bills? That had to have been terrifying."

"Then she found Father," Nat says, absently rubbing the hearts and initials carved into the table.

"She already knew George. He was a childhood friend of her college roommate."

"What roommate?"

"Janice Finch. She married a man from Tennessee. I don't think Mother has seen much of her since college." Harry finishes the last bite of her sandwich.

"Does my father know that Henri's your real father? Does Abba know?"

Harry replies, "Father must know, and I assume Abba does too—she's always treated me like a second-class citizen."

"Really?" Nat feels embarrassed that he never noticed.

"Abba's good to you."

Hoping to make Harry feel a little better about the way Abba treated her, he explains, "Well, we do have a common interest in music."

"You know what's heartbreaking? Mother blames George for Eddie's death because he encouraged Eddie to enlist, although she blames herself as well. She thinks that if she hadn't kept those secrets, if she'd described the horrors of the war she experienced, maybe Eddie wouldn't have thrown himself into the line of fire."

"Are you sure?"

"Mother told me."

"Why would she tell you that but not me?" He believes he's closer to their Mother than Harry and Eddie. At least he used to be.

"We were talking one time when she was really low. I told her it was not her fault, though I'm not sure I got through to her."

"Why wouldn't she tell me?" He shuts his eyes for a moment.

"Once the truth about Henri came out and you were away at school, Mother and I talked about all sorts of things we'd never discussed before."

Wanting to reestablish his own credentials in their family, he says, "Eddie had his own reasons for enlisting in the Army. He felt it would help him when he went into politics."

"I miss Eddie," she says, putting her arms around herself. "When I need a break, I work on one of the jigsaw puzzles we made together and think about him."

"I think about him too. The summer of '44 I tried to make up for his not being there on the farm, but I couldn't."

"I know." She sighs deeply. Then she shakes her head and stands. "Let's go get you some new trousers. Do you have any money?"

"Of course. I'm earning my own dough now."

၅

Later that afternoon, Harry and Nat lounge in Mrs. Schmitt's front parlor, which is separated from the dining room by a plaid curtain that hangs between the two rooms, containing the heat in each space. Doilies cover the arms and backs of every stuffed chair. Pewter beer mugs stand in rows on a shelf attached to the wall.

She says, "Want to work on a jigsaw puzzle with me? I've got one with a picture of our barn."

"I don't think so."

"Are you sure? It's really fun."

"I don't have the patience, Harry." He feels annoyed that she doesn't believe what he says. "Sorry, I'm not Eddie."

She folds her arms over her stomach.

He stretches his legs out in front of him on the rag rug patterned with stiff–looking flowers. "What do you hear from home?"

"Father writes that he's been hiring new staff to work at the company because orders are way up, and Mother is organizing a special dinner to raise funds for the Red Cross. Frank says they're swamped with all the babies being born at his hospital. I guess that's not surprising when you think about all the soldiers returning home from the war over the past eighteen months. Frank has never seen anything like it."

"Hmm," says Nat. He doesn't think Frank is good enough for Harry.

"I'm thinking about sending Father a formal letter of application to work at Sutton Chemical."

"Why would you do that?"

"To let him know that I'm serious about wanting to work for the company."

"I could never work for Father."

"Do you hate him, Nat?"

"Not the way I did a few months ago."

"What do you think you want to do with your life now?"

"I don't know—stop asking me stuff like that!"

She inhales audibly, then sighs. "What would you like to do this evening?"

"Is there someplace we can hear jazz?"

"Let's look in the newspaper."

All they can find are advertisements for dance bands led by musicians they've never heard of.

"Nuts," says Nat. "I was hoping we could hear a good band tonight. At least I've found a place where they play jazz in Minneapolis."

"You know those times you went to hear music on Fifty-Second Street in New York with your friend Mark? I've always wanted to ask you: is Mark a homosexual? Not that I have anything against

homosexuals. I was just wondering. When he was at the house tutoring you, he never seemed the least bit interested in talking to me."

Although Nat has mixed feelings about his former tutor, he feels
protective of Mark. Besides, her questions are starting to irk him.
"That's none of your business!"

Speaking softly, Harry asks, "Are *you* attracted to men, Nat?"

"No!" Now he's really offended.

"Are you sure?"

"I first knew I'm attracted to women that time during the war when
you had me feel how smooth your leg was after you pulled on your
last pair of silk stockings. I had to run out of the room. I could hardly
contain Mr. Snake."

"Who?"

"My . . ." He gestures toward his crotch.

"You have a name for it?" She smiles tentatively.

"*Him.*"

She gives him a playful push. "You certainly had eyes for every girl
on campus this morning."

Nat likes it when Harry teases him. "I guess Mark is a homosexual,
but we've never actually talked about that. I know my old roommate
from Andover is homosexual—he's also my best friend."

"Isn't it tricky being good friends with a man who might want more
from you? How do you handle that?"

"The same way you would handle an unwelcome advance from any
guy."

She guffaws. "Right. How did you get to be so smart?"

"I'm not smart. Ask Father."

She doesn't respond to that. "Let's go see a movie. That way I'll have
something to write Frank about."

"You met Frank at the movies, didn't you?"

"That's right—at the Palisades Movie Theater. We laughed at the
same things. I don't suppose our paths would ever have crossed

otherwise." She picks up the *Capital Times* and turns to the back pages. "*The Lady in the Lake* is showing tonight. It's based on a Raymond Chandler novel. Robert Montgomery and Audrey Totter are the stars."

"That should be entertaining. Do you have any chocolate left?"

"Of course. I only eat one or two pieces a day—I want it to last."

"May I have one?"

∾

Sunday morning Nat and Harry skim the newspaper while they sit in the dining room over coffee and toast. He spots a headline declaring that a nationwide strike by the telephone workers will start tomorrow. This won't bother him personally, but how are people supposed to report fires if the phones don't work?

She says, "According to this, representatives of France, Britain, and the United States are proposing to give all the Saar's coal to France if the French agree to economic unity in Germany with the United States and Britain. What's 'the Saar's' coal?"

"I think Saarland is in western Germany. This is probably a move to form a more united front against Russia. They've been awfully tough to deal with since the war ended. Father sent me some articles from the *New York Times* that were pretty scary."

"You've been corresponding with him?"

"Not exactly. He just forwards clippings to me."

"That's something." She stands. "Would you mind if I put a record on?"

"Please do."

When the opening chords of Bach's *St. Matthew Passion* fill the room, she sits in the chair next to him. After a few minutes, as tears begin to stream down his face, he looks over and sees that Harry's face is wet too. He reaches for her hand. She squeezes back.

After the piece concludes, he says, "I'm so glad you played that, Harry. I love Bach!"

"So do I!" They grin at each other. Then she checks her watch. "We should get going now. Our lunch reservations are for noon."

Up in Harry's room, they remove their shirts and trousers. Once they're standing in their underwear, backs to each other, he picks up a towel and flicks it at her bum a few times.

"What?" Grabbing her dress and holding it against her front, she turns around.

"Eddie used to do that to me. We'd play with towels or else we'd shove each other around, but it doesn't seem right to shove you."

"I'm not Eddie. This must be something guys like to do."

He'd hoped she would want to play.

She turns away again and drops a flowered dress over her head. After buttoning it up the back, she says, "I chose the best German restaurant I could find for dinner today—German seems appropriate for Easter in Wisconsin. The Hasenpfeffer is supposed to be very good at Heidelberg Hofbrau on the Square." Then she picks up his towel and flicks it in his direction.

"Here, let me show you. You need to snap the towel quickly. It's all in the wrist." He demonstrates.

She says, "Let me try again." She does so.

"That's better."

A little later, as they walk down State Street toward the restaurant, she asks, "How do you feel about being in Northfield now?"

"I'm not as furious as I was. Working with my hands hasn't been a bad thing for me, though I don't want it to continue much longer. I have lots of time to think while I sweep the mill day in and day out, which is kind of nice. And I definitely like earning my own money."

"I'm glad to hear that, Nat."

"How about you, Harry?"

"I can't tell whether Father's pleased by what I'm doing or not.

Maybe it doesn't matter so much what he thinks as long as I'm convinced I'm doing the right thing."

"Makes sense to me."

Walking into Heidelberg Hofbrau on the Square, Nat can hardly see where he's going. The lights are low, reflecting only slightly off dark oak walls. Deep burgundy fabric covers the tables, and the closed curtains are the same color.

He says, "This is swell."

"My friend Judy told me about this place. It looks like it'll be good."

A waitress wearing a burgundy dirndl leads them to a small table in the corner. The menu is in German; a translation appears beneath each item.

She orders the Hasenpfeffer and he the Veal Geschnizeltes with spaetzle. The waitress departs.

He says, "She's got nice big bosoms."

"Nat!"

"Sorry. I can't help it." He thinks any guy would agree with him. Well, maybe not Peter.

Leaning forward, she says, "Mother and Father are coming out for my graduation in May. Why don't you join us? If we're all here together when the focus isn't on you, it might be easier for you and Father to put your differences aside."

"I'll think about it."

After lunch they're so full of rich food they decide they need to take a long walk. They change out of their dressy clothes and head out along the lakeshore path to Picnic Point, where they sit on a bench.

"What's next, Nat? You seem to be saying that you don't want to work at the mill much longer. What *do* you want to do?" Her legs are crossed, and she's shaking her foot back and forth.

"I don't know. I have to make money. I'd like to get a job working in Minneapolis, but I don't know anyone who would hire me. Maybe I can teach music somewhere."

She lifts her chin. "I really don't think music school is the answer for you right now, Nat. You should finish college before you do anything else."

Despite the fact that he has already figured this out for himself, he explodes. "Don't tell me what to do! You're always telling me what to do." He knows he's being unfair.

Her foot moves faster and faster. "Who else is going to discuss this with you? You've got to take charge of your own life."

"Why are you so impatient with me?"

"I don't want to have to worry about you."

"Then don't!" He stands abruptly. "I came here looking for comfort, not the third degree." He starts walking back.

"Nat, stop! I'm just trying to help."

He keeps walking.

"How can I help?" She hurries after him. "Wait! I have an idea. I'll talk to the head of the music department here at Madison. He must know people in the music business in Minneapolis."

June 1947

Harriet has been home from Madison for ten days. Saturday morning at the breakfast table, her father asks her to come to his study right after they finish eating.

Her stomach clenches. Is he finally going to talk to her about working for him at Sutton Chemical? It's what she's wanted ever since she realized Eddie wouldn't be able to follow in George's footsteps.

Once they're seated, George says, "Your mother tells me you've had a job offer from the Rockefeller Institute for Medical Research."

"I had an interview there earlier this week," she replies. "I was very impressed by all the PhDs and MDs I met. They're doing great research on antibacterials and they're developing all sorts of vaccines."

"Why didn't you tell me you were going there?"

"I didn't want you to feel like I was pressuring you, Father."

"How much would they pay you?"

"The starting salary is $300 a month."

"I'll pay $400 per month if you come work for me."

"Really?" She jumps to her feet.

"At your graduation, I was impressed by what Dr. McCann had to say about your research, and I must say I'm glad you graduated with honors."

"Father, this is fabulous!"

He rises to face her. "I would like you to join me in the company my father created. I'll have you learn every facet of the business."

"This is what I've wanted for years! It's why I went to Madison in the first place. Yes! I accept your offer."

"What did you say to the Rockefeller Institute?"

"I told them I'd think about it—I *would* take their offer if I couldn't work for you."

"I see. How soon do you want to start?"

"Right away."

"Let's say a week from Monday. I need to talk with the guy you'll be reporting to, and there's paperwork we'll need to get going."

"Thank you, Father."

Why isn't she happier? If only her father had made the offer as soon as she got home from Madison. The Rockefeller Institute must have roused his competitive spirit.

∾

"Nervous?" George glances over at Harriet as he drives his new Lincoln in to Sutton Chemical.

"I'm excited!"

He smiles at her.

Practically vibrating with anticipation, she can't wait to show her father he was right to hire her.

As they drive through the main gate to the facility, she exclaims, "It's so big! I had no idea. Why didn't you ever bring me here before? Eddie and Nat got to see the place years ago."

"I didn't think a girl would be interested."

She resists pointing out that he was obviously wrong about that.

After he shows her around the plant, he escorts her down a long hallway to the executive suite.

He stops in front of an open door. A small sign on the wall reads,

DR. VERNON BRYNE, EXECUTIVE VICE PRESIDENT. "This is the man you'll be reporting to."

Dr. Bryne quickly stands up, though he stays behind his desk. He opens his mouth, exposing buckteeth in what must be his idea of a greeting.

George steps into Dr. Bryne's room. She follows.

"Vernon, this is my daughter, Harriet. She just completed her master's degree in chemistry with honors from the University of Wisconsin. I know she'll be a good addition to your staff.

"Harriet, your boss, Dr. Vernon Bryne."

Dr. Bryne dips his head at her. "Miss Sutton," he says in a frigid tone of voice. He moves around his desk toward them, but he does not stick his hand out to her. "I'll show you to the lab."

"Harriet," says George, "come find me in my office at five-thirty. It's at the end of this hall."

As Dr. Bryne leads Harriet down several corridors, he doesn't say anything. Once they arrive at the research lab, he opens the door for her. "You'll have the station on the bench that's nearest the window. The boss's daughter gets the best spot in the room."

Harriet walks over to the area he indicated. The bench is a long two-sided soapstone counter with gas, water, and steam plumbed in the center; on each side three high stools stand in the spaces between drawers that extend from the counter to the floor. Much of the bench is crowded with Bunsen burners, glass beakers and flasks, test tubes in a rack, tongs, and spatulas, but the spot Dr. Bryne indicated has nothing on it. She's surprised to see that they haven't prepared for her. Does that mean she isn't really welcome here? "Dr. Bryne, where might I find glassware and tools to work with? And a lab coat?"

"Dr. Gallagher is in charge here. He'll explain everything to you. He's in a meeting now with all the scientists, but they should be back before long. You can sit at your place until they return." Dr. Bryne turns and exits.

She's supposed to twiddle her thumbs? That's not very efficient. Harriet can tell Dr. Bryne doesn't like her one bit. She doesn't like him either. Does he doubt her abilities as a chemist because of her sex? Or is it because she's "the boss's daughter"? No wonder her father told Dr. Bryne she got her master's with honors. She knows she's lucky to have this job, but she worked hard to earn it. Did she take the job away from someone Dr. Bryne wanted to hire? She knows there are lots of men back from the war looking for employment.

Wandering around the room, she looks over the shelves of chemicals on the wall, the fume hood, the stained sink, the refrigerator, the incubator, and, in the corners, the microscopes on the desks. What will the five other chemists at the bench think of her? She'll need to prove herself right away.

Fortunately, Dr. Gallagher turns out to be much friendlier than Dr. Bryne. Explaining that he was under the impression she wouldn't start until next week, Dr. Gallagher apologizes for the fact that her station hasn't already been set up.

He shows Harriet where all the equipment is kept, and then he assigns her the task of assessing the water resistance of a piece of canvas that's been treated with a new chemical coating developed in their lab. This is actually a job for a technician, not a chemist, but she isn't affronted; she's eager to begin.

∽

Each day during their drive home from work, George fills her in on the history of the company.

On Friday George tells her, "Getting access to the materials we need, which has been difficult ever since Pearl Harbor, continues to be our biggest challenge."

"I can imagine," she replies. "Even the supply of new nylon stockings is still limited."

George pushes in the cigarette lighter. "We've made the transition quite nicely from producing industrial finishes for war—for shells and bombs and gas masks and aircraft wiring systems—to peacetime uses like finishes for new cars rolling off the assembly lines. Sutton coatings that were used to waterproof fabrics and oilcloth for our fighting forces are now applied to awnings for buildings and homes and boats."

He pulls the lighter out, touches it to the cigarette in the corner of his mouth, and inhales. "Printing ink is our biggest seller of all, thanks to the new formulation invented by one of our chemists. Printing presses require a series of rollers to spread out the ink, but that ink used to dry on the rollers before the paper reached the type."

"Hmm."

"Sutton ink doesn't dry at room temperature, but it dries almost instantly once you apply heat. It's used for printing glossy magazines like the *New Yorker*, *Collier's*, and the *Saturday Evening Post*."

"I didn't know that."

He taps the ash off his cigarette. "The ink doesn't cost much to produce, and we price it as high as the market will bear. That robust profit margin has been great for our bottom line."

"If it's such a good product, Father, why don't you bring down the price so more printers can afford to use it?"

"We need to make up for the development costs and to underwrite the cost of doing research on other new products."

"That makes sense. How do you decide the price for Sutton products? Do you charge the same as other companies with similar products?"

"Proper pricing is both an art and a science. You need to know who your customers are, how much your competitors charge, and the relationship between quality and price. If you believe your product has extra value and you want it to be known for quality, you price it higher to reflect that quality."

"Who are our competitors?"

Exhaling smoke, he says, "Dow Chemical and E. I. Dupont, of course. Also Union Carbide, National Starch, and Pennsalt Chemical."

"I see."

"I'd like you to investigate what we can do in the area of fungicidal coatings to preserve foods after being harvested so they survive shipping and storage without rotting. Your experience with penicillin should come in handy here." He grinds his cigarette out in the ashtray.

"What! You want me to develop a fungicide to inhibit mold? That's the exact opposite of everything I did at Madison!" Immediately she feels an immense sense of resistance to this idea. It's as though her father wants her to turn herself inside out.

"You know something about molds now, Harriet."

Scrambling for something to say, she asks, "Has Sutton Chemical ever done any work with fungicides?"

"Not yet. I want you to give it a try. Read up on the literature and then start experimenting. I think there's a lot of money to be made in this area."

❧

That night Harriet tells Frank she'd like to see a movie. From what she's read about *The Farmer's Daughter*, she hopes that watching the feisty Loretta Young character will help inspire her to figure out how to meet her father's challenge. After they watch the movie, Frank drives his new Mercury to their private place on a deserted road overlooking a swamp. The songs of frogs fill the air—otherwise it's quiet. Frank stretches his right arm along the back of the seat and angles his long legs toward her. She turns toward him.

Thirty-three years old, he has a few crow's feet at the corners of his brown eyes now, and his pale blond hair doesn't look quite as thick as it used to, but he's just as good looking as he was when they started dating. She feels safe with him.

She pinned up her hair last night the way she learned from Klara so it would be wavy today, and Harriet feels quite pretty for a change. She's even wearing lipstick and a light cotton dress.

"You sure look nice tonight, honey," he says.

"Thank you, Frank." She doesn't know what else to say. She's still so unsettled by her reaction to the assignment her father gave her that her mind is roiling, but she's not going to talk with Frank about that now. He probably wouldn't understand. She just wants him to put his arms around her and pull her to his chest and hold her.

"Hug me, Frank."

He slides across the bench seat and embraces her. After a moment, he crushes her lips against his.

She leans back. "Gentle, please!" How many times does she have to say this? She's asked him over and over to handle her gently, but he can't seem to do so. He's a big strong man, and maybe it's passion that makes him so heavy handed.

"I'm trying to get you to kiss me back."

"That's not the way to do it."

Removing his arms from her shoulders, he asks, "Is something wrong?"

"No. I don't know." She looks down at her lap, discouraged by their inability to communicate with each other. "I should go home. It's been a long week."

"Of course. We can talk tomorrow." He turns the key in the ignition.

Over the weekend she thinks about why she's struggling with the idea of working on a fungicide. Eventually she realizes it has to do with intention. She loved working on the mold that produces penicillin because it was about saving lives. Now her father wants her to work on *killing* molds for the purpose of making money. But of course generating income is what business is all about. Her resistance was naïve. In fact, she can see that her father is smart to make use of her knowledge for the company's benefit. And if she succeeds in discovering an effective fungicide, she will have helped ensure that people don't get sick from eating fresh produce. That's a worthy goal.

❧

June 23
Dear Harry,

I have a job! Thanks for your idea. The referral from Dr. Callahan at Madison led me to the St. Joseph's School of Music in St. Paul, where I will start teaching this fall. Mother sent me some money—don't tell Father about the dough!—so I quit the mill and moved up to the Cities. I've enrolled in the summer school program at the University of Minnesota and found a room to share with some guys near campus. Everything is coming together. Now I just need to find a jazz combo to play with.

I've been thinking about what you said, Harry, and you were right. Father really did set me free. I can do whatever I want with my life. I can even go to music school once I figure out how to pay for it. I am the master of my own fate.

Thank you for all your help along the way, Harry. It means a lot to me.

Love,
Nat

❧

One steamy morning in July, George tells Harriet to wear her new suit. "We're going to meet with my banker today."

"You want me to accompany you?" She's surprised.

"Absolutely! This will give you a look at another aspect of our business."

She and her father go into the plant for a couple of hours, which she spends reading about fungicides. At ten when she heads for George's office, a hat on her head and her purse on her arm, she encounters Dr. Bryne in the hall.

"Where do you think you're going, Miss Sutton?"

"My father asked me to accompany him to a meeting in the city, Dr. Bryne."

His face turns red. "I see. I guess I have nothing to say about that." He changes direction and walks away.

On the train into Manhattan, she asks George, "Does everyone report to Dr. Bryne, Father?"

"Yes, but I'm contemplating some changes in his position. He has too many people under him now that we've hired all these new men."

"What will Dr. Bryne think?"

"Doesn't matter. We need to be able to grow. One of my most important responsibilities is to select, train, and motivate the right people, who are placed in positions they're capable of handling."

"I see."

George is finally treating her like a capable adult. She'd better not disappoint him.

The meeting with his banker takes place in a corner office on the top floor of Manufacturers Bank at Fifty-Five Broad Street in Manhattan. They enter a large room with huge windows on one wall, prints of sailboats on another, and bronze statues of ducks and pheasants on a credenza against the third wall. A trim gray-haired man in a crisp seersucker suit strides toward them, hand extended. "Georgie, good to see you."

Wearing a white shirt, club tie, and navy blue suit, George is taller and he looks even more impressive to her than the banker. Her father shakes the banker's hand, then says, "Ben, my daughter, Harriet. Harriet, this is Ben Goodrich—we were at Yale together."

"How do you do, Mr. Goodrich." *And how,* she wonders, *do you keep your suit so impeccable in this heat?* Her beige linen suit is already a mass of wrinkles. She just hopes her Tampax doesn't leak onto the back of her skirt.

Mr. Goodrich leads them to stuffed chairs facing each other around a table, where they all sit. "Coffee?" he asks, gesturing toward the carafe.

"No thanks," says George.

She shakes her head no.

A fan on the credenza turns slowly, moving air across their faces as Mr. Goodrich and George exchange news about classmates from Yale and then comments about what the Soviets are up to in Germany. When George asks Mr. Goodrich how business is going, Mr. Goodrich talks for several minutes, using technical terms she's never heard before. She's delighted to discover how charming her father can be, and he must be asking good questions, because Mr. Goodrich answers at length.

Finally George says, "I don't want to waste your time, Benny. I've come here today to see about a loan. Now that we've moved out of war production, we're experimenting with new uses for our products, and we're doing a lot of hiring in the research and development areas. Our new hires are impressive. These men have learned to follow orders, and they're motivated to work hard after fulfilling their military obligations. In this last fiscal year, sales topped $6 million. Now we need to expand our factory in Bayonne so we can accommodate all this growth."

"What was your net income last year?"

"After expenses, $250,000, which we're plowing back into the company."

Mr. Goodrich nods.

"Five years from now, if things go according to plan, I expect we'll take the company public." George turns to her. "Wouldn't it be great to see Sutton Chemical on the New York Stock Exchange, Harriet?"

She smiles. She doesn't presume to interject anything into this conversation.

Mr. Goodrich says, "Let me know when you go on the market—I'll certainly want to invest in Sutton. How much do you need, George?"

"One million dollars, payable over five years."

One million? The number shocks her.

"No problem. We'll charge two percent."

"Understood."

"I'll have the papers drawn up and get them to you tomorrow. How soon do you need the cash?"

"A week from today."

"Right."

Both men stand and shake hands. Startled by the speed with which they conducted their business, she jumps to her feet as well.

Back on the train, George says, "Ben's a good man, and he's done very well for himself. He married a wealthy woman, and he's made a lot of money at the bank. I bet he brings home $100,000 a year, on top of his investments and real estate."

"That *is* a lot of money," she agrees, comparing that to her annual salary of $4,800. George certainly likes to talk about money—this is something she never really noticed until she started working for her father, but now that she thinks about it, she realizes it's always been true.

∾

Doing research on fungicides turns out to be quite fascinating. In the course of her reading, Harriet learns all sorts of things. Wax coatings were applied to preserve citrus fruits as early as the twelfth century.

By the 1930s growers in the United States were spraying a thin film of hot-melt paraffin wax on their fruits to preserve them, which allowed the fruit to respire. Like anything living, fruit that's been harvested continues to breathe throughout its life. During respiration, carbohydrates are broken down to produce energy to operate cellular processes, keeping the cells alive. Respiration is also essential to the ripening process. She'll have to think about other possible waxes she might use to provide a carrier for the fungicide.

∾

Late one afternoon as Harriet exits the building with George, she remembers that she forgot to put the Agatha Christie whodunit she was reading over lunch into her purse. She hurries toward the lab, but when she hears her name, she stops outside the open door.

She recognizes her colleague Mark's voice. ". . . Miss Sutton's spot. Why is Dr. Bryne suddenly spending so much time in the lab now, asking questions, nosing around the bench—especially Miss Sutton's spot? What's he looking for?"

Dr. Gallagher replies, "Bryne made a huge mistake last month when he ordered three times the amount of ore we'll need for production of titanium dioxide in the coming year. Mr. Sutton was furious. The price of the ore is likely to come down as mining operations and shipping become normalized, so Bryne cost the company a lot of money. He's probably trying to make up for that error by paying more attention to everything we do in here."

"Why focus on Miss Sutton?"

"She's the newest hire. He wants to make sure of her work."

Harriet is skeptical about Dr. Bryne's motivation. She suspects he'd be delighted to see her fail.

Deciding she can read something else tonight, she tiptoes away.

∽

The next night when Frank calls, he asks Harriet to go for a drive with him. He sounds so serious that she assumes he's going to propose. As she dresses for their date, she feels anxious. She's not ready to say yes. What's wrong with her? He's a good, honest, honorable man, and he seems genuinely to care for her. What's holding her back? Does she feel she should be more established in her career first? Or maybe she's simply afraid of commitment.

When she greets him at the door, she sees he isn't smiling.

As he walks around the back of the car, she repositions the rear-view mirror to inspect her face, searching for whatever he must have found disappointing about her appearance tonight.

After he gets in and starts the car, she asks, "Is everything all right, Frank?"

"Sure," he says, glancing at her before he heads down the driveway.

The way he's acting makes her nervous. "Where are we going?"

"Our usual spot—it's a good place to talk."

She stares out the window at the passing scenery, trying to appear unconcerned. Why hasn't he called her honey?

Once they reach their destination, Frank turns off the car. He takes both her hands in his.

"I've been thinking about us," he says.

"Yes?"

"Now that you're working for the family business, it seems to me like we're going down two very separate paths. I work for a hospital, after all."

"I know you do."

"I don't understand why you turned down the opportunity to continue doing research on penicillin at the Rockefeller Institute. You could make a big difference there."

"I loved research at Madison, and it was tempting to consider working at the institute, but Father asked me to join him at the company—and that's what I wanted."

"I never thought you were interested in business."

"I liked the accounting and finance classes I took at Madison. They made sense to me."

"It looks like you've decided to pursue a direction that's rooted in your past instead of choosing a future with me."

"What are you talking about?"

"You chose your father and his world over me and my world."

"Oh, come on. That's a weird thing to say."

"Tell me what we have in common now—besides movies." When he smiles, she realizes that he simply wants to be convinced they should stay together.

She replies, "We both care about people and their health and well-being."

"That's true." He reaches for her hand.

She keeps her hands in her lap as she considers the visceral revulsion she sometimes feels in response to his kisses.

Then she lifts her chin. "We *should* call it quits, Frank."

He turns away.

"We're awfully different."

He fires up the engine of the car.

Trying to be nice, she says, "I really appreciated your patience with me all the time I was away in Madison."

Bitterly, he replies, "A lot of good that did."

"Your family will be relieved. Your mother doesn't like me at all. She's so formal and cool to me."

"Let's not get nasty."

She feels such a confusing mix of fear and anger and relief now that she cannot speak.

When he pulls to a stop in front of her house, she jumps out, kicking the car door shut.

She runs into the house and slams the door.

"Harriet, is that you?" Eleanor calls from down the hall.

Her mother is sitting in a wingback chair in the parlor, a highball on the table next to her. Harriet perches on the edge of the couch.

"What happened?"

"I just broke up with Frank. Is that a mistake? You know he has no sense of humor. And he has such a boring job!"

"Frank is a good man, but it wasn't the right match, Harriet."

"He *is* a good man. There are lots of things about him that I admire. But I really didn't like the way he kisses." She shakes her head. "I guess that's pretty petty."

"Did you tell him that?"

"I tried." She jumps up. "I'm going to get a drink."

"Good idea."

When Harriet returns with a bourbon and water, she sits back on the couch. "Mummy, how did you feel when you were in love with Henri?"

Eleanor closes her eyes for a few moments. Softly she says, "I couldn't get enough of him. I loved running my hands all over him. I wanted to crawl inside him."

"Really? I've never felt anything like that."

"I loved the way Henri smelled. I could inhale him forever." Smiling to herself, Eleanor raises her glass and drinks deeply.

"Frank smells like antiseptic—the smell of the hospital must stick to his clothes. In June for his birthday I gave him a bottle of Bergamot aftershave, but it didn't make much difference." She sighs. "Maybe I didn't love him after all—at least not the marrying kind of love."

"You seemed to be good friends."

"I didn't feel passion with Frank."

"Then it's just as well you called it off."

"Yes." At the same time, fear claws at her throat. "What if I never find someone to really love me?"

"You will, dearie. You know the old saw, 'There are plenty of fish in the sea.'"

"Not as many as there used to be, thanks to the war."

Eleanor grimaces. Then she reaches out to pat Harriet's hand.

∾

During Nat's Sunday night phone call home, Harriet gets on to talk with her brother. He tells her about the jazz combo he's started sitting in with, and she reports that she broke up with Frank.

"I'm not surprised it didn't work out," Nat says. "He wasn't smart enough for you, Harry."

"I wonder whether I'm too ambitious for him. Maybe he just wants a wife who'll sit home and cook and knit and take care of the babies."

"He did tease you about being too bossy the first night I met him."

"Well, I *can* be bossy at times."

"I'll say! When you were running the farm, there was no discussion. You just told us what to do—all the time."

"I know—I admit it."

"Frank didn't know how to scratch your itch."

Startled, Harriet says, "Whoa! That's right." She chuckles. "What do you know about scratching that kind of itch?"

"I'm very familiar with my own."

She's tickled by his insight. Nat really *is* her brother. "You're the best, Nat. When will we see you?"

"Maybe Christmas."

∾

Later that summer Eleanor insists that Harriet accompany her and George to a cocktail party the Wrights are throwing at a country club in Far Hills. Her mother tells her, "You need to get out and meet some new people, dearie."

As soon as Harriet enters the large reception room, she notices a trim man with dark brown hair who seems to be mesmerizing a crowd of young women around her own age. She edges closer to see what's going on. He's wearing a plaid navy-blue-and-green jacket, navy slacks, and a jaunty green bow tie, and he's terribly handsome, teasing and flirting with everyone. Although he looks intriguing, he's much too debonair for her. She steps back to join her parents, who are talking with their hostess.

Mrs. Wright says, "You must be Harriet. Welcome. Have you met my son Ron?" She nods at the tall man who'd just caught Harriet's eye.

"No, I haven't, Mrs. Wright."

"As you can see, he's very popular with the girls. Ever since he got back from the Pacific, they've been throwing themselves at him."

"I can see that."

"Let me introduce you." She grabs Harriet's hand and pulls her over to the group surrounding Ron.

Ron's eyes are dark blue, and his thin nose is as straight as a knife. He inclines his head toward her, saying, "And what's your name?"

She can scarcely breathe. "It's Harriet, Harriet Sutton." She's glad that she's wearing her new burgundy dress with the tightly fitted waist and skirt.

Mrs. Wright adds, "Harriet's the daughter of our new friends from Plainwood. I'm told she plays a mean game of tennis—you should challenge her to a match sometime, Ron."

Harriet is so attracted to Ron that it scares her. "Actually, I'm pretty busy."

"Doing what, Miss Harriet?" The formal locution sounds charming on his tongue.

"I'm a chemist. I work at my father's chemical company."

"Really? That's unusual. I don't know any chemists, much less lady chemists." He grins at her.

"Lady?" she replies. "I don't think of ladies as women who work— but perhaps that's unfair."

"No, I know what you mean," he says.

"You do?"

He nods.

"Just call me a chemist."

"As you like." His eyes twinkle. "I can't believe you work all weekend. You must have a little time for tennis once in a while."

She can't help herself from smiling in response. "Feel free to call me if you're serious about tennis."

He telephones her the next day.

∽

One evening in October, Harriet knocks briskly on the door of her father's study.

"Come in!"

She opens the door and enters quickly. The room smells smoky from the fire and the cigarette in his hand, but it's her father's smell, so she finds it comfortably familiar. Rachmaninoff's Concerto No. 2 in C Minor is playing full blast on the new Philco 1213 Chippendale radio-phonograph.

"Doesn't this sound great!" George gets up from his favorite leather chair and moves to turn down the volume. As he does so, she spots tears on his cheeks. The sight touches her. Her father can seem so forbidding at times; she's glad he has his soft spots too.

"I've got some exciting news for you."

"Tell me." He resumes his seat in front of the fireplace.

She takes the adjacent chair. "This is nice," she says as she looks around the room and then at the flames darting among the logs.

"What's on your mind?"

"I've learned that the dithiocarbamates were more effective, less phytotoxic, and easier to prepare than the inorganic compounds previously used as fungicides."

"That sounds like a start."

"Since the 1930s paraffin waxes have been used to coat citrus fruits, but I'm thinking carnauba wax and oil in a water emulsion will make a better carrier for a fungicide like dithiocarbamate—"

"I'm pleased you're moving along with your research, Harriet. Let me know when you're sure you've got the right stuff for us to sell."

She's so proud of her progress that she expected he'd want to hear all about it. Pushing her disappointment down, she crosses her legs and starts shaking her foot.

He goes on. "Now that you're here, I'd like to get your take on the restructuring plan I've been sketching out. We need separate divisions for research, sales, and manufacturing. Dr. Bryne can head research, and I'll make Mr. Oswald vice president for sales and Mr. Sheehy vice president for manufacturing."

"Would that be a demotion for Dr. Bryne?"

"He'd still be a vice president."

"I guess that makes sense, though I really wouldn't know—I'm not a manager, after all. I'm a chemist," she replies.

"Fair enough." He gets up and goes over to his desk to get his glass of bourbon. "I'll have a talk with Art Donohue—he owns a business about the same size as ours." He returns to his chair. "Would Dr. Bryne make a good research director?"

She looks up at the banjo clock on the wall as she considers her response. She doesn't know what Dr. Bryne's job is exactly. He doesn't seem to do any science or lab work. She turns her eyes back to George. "I don't know, Father. I don't trust Dr. Bryne, but maybe that's because he doesn't like me. You should ask Dr. Gallagher."

"You must have some impression of Dr. Bryne."

"Well, he seems to be terribly critical of mistakes, but maybe that's how it has to be in business. Dr. Bryne likes to tell people exactly how to do their jobs."

"That's not good," says George. "Destructive criticism kills initiative. I'll speak with Bryne about this."

"Don't mention my name!"

"I won't. Being willing to make mistakes is a crucial component of experimentation." He lifts his glass. After swallowing, he says, "Dr. Gallagher speaks highly of your work, Harriet. How are you getting on otherwise?"

"Are you asking whether I miss Frank?"

"I have some respect for the guy, but you can do a lot better."

"I don't miss Frank." She's a little surprised to hear herself admit this. "Besides, my new tennis partner, Ron Wright, keeps me busy."

"Glad to hear it."

February 1948

One night at an elegant supper club in Far Hills four months later, Ron leans over the table so far that he appears to be bowing. "Are you thinking what I'm thinking?"

Harriet bends her torso toward him. Ron's straight dark hair, which is a little long, brushes her forehead as lightly as a feather. She shivers. Their noses come close to touching.

She's thinking she must be in love with Ron because she even likes the smell of his sweat, which she notices after they play tennis on the indoor courts at his club each weekend. She's attracted by the scent of his aftershave as well.

She says, "I'm not sure what you're thinking."

"We've been having a lot of fun together, haven't we?"

"I'll say!" She and Ron, who returned from the South Pacific apparently untouched by the war, have gone out to parties and dinners and concerts and plays several nights a week. Like many others these days, Ron seems to be intent on making up for everything he missed during those years he spent defending freedom, and Harriet's happy to accompany him. She's never felt like this, but then she's never been actively wooed before. Being with Ron feels so easy, so natural, so right. He's even the perfect height for her to snuggle her head against his neck when they embrace.

Ron reaches for her hands. "I think we should get married, Harriet.

I love you. I love your intelligence and your drive and your ability to beat me at tennis—at least some of the time. Besides, you have great legs!" As he grins, adorable dimples dent his cheeks. "I want to marry you, darling. What do you say?"

"How would you feel about my continuing to work?" She holds her breath. There's only one acceptable answer to this question.

"That's what I would expect."

"Then . . ." She gulps. This is what she wanted, isn't it? She's thrilled to have snagged such an eligible bachelor. On the other hand, the thought of losing her independence is frightening. Ron seems to respect her and her aspirations—and isn't it time for her to grow up, to become a complete adult woman? But would marriage mean she'd start down the slippery slope that ends in her being stuck all by herself in a house with a baby? That's the thought that truly terrifies her.

"Yes," she finally says, squeezing his hands tight. "I will marry you."

"Wonderful!" Pulling her closer, he kisses her tenderly.

She's so excited that she can hear her heart beating in her ears. After she pulls back from the kiss, she teases, "But, Ronnie, you have to admit, I win more than half of our matches."

"You're right, Harriet. I've got to work on my serve."

"We should talk to Father."

Ron lifts his martini. "I've taken care of that." He takes a sip.

She's startled by the news, but she's pleased by how confidently he has taken charge. "What did Father say?"

"I have his blessing. I told him I expect Smith Barney will make me a vice president this year."

"I didn't know that."

"Well, it hasn't happened yet. Anyway, your father didn't see any obstacles."

"When did you talk to him?"

"I invited him to lunch last week."

She's tickled that Ron and her father conspired behind her back toward something she desires. "Father never said a word."

"Of course not." Putting his martini down, he reaches into the pocket of his navy blue Brooks Brothers suit. He pulls out a black velvet box and flips it open, revealing a large emerald-cut diamond set in white gold.

"Oh, Ronnie, it's gorgeous!"

"Put it on."

She tries to slide the ring onto her finger, but it won't go over the knuckle. This makes her feel slightly anxious. "I'm sorry."

"Don't apologize, darling. We'll see the jeweler tomorrow. They'll make it fit." He takes the ring back and returns it to his pocket. "Let's dance."

"Yes!"

Grabbing her hand, he leads her to the dance floor. The Glenn Miller Orchestra is playing "I Know Why (And So Do You)." Her pink satin dress, which flares out from its snug waist, sways with their movements. She's never felt so happy. When he twirls her around and around again, she grows dizzy—she's not used to drinking more than one martini.

❧

Harriet's research continues. She reacts ethylene diamine and carbon disulfide in a glass beaker, and then she salts it with sodium hydroxide. Next, she adds carnauba wax, oil, and water. After spraying the mixture on two apples and two oranges that she has carefully cleaned, she sets them out to dry at the back of her section of the bench. After that she goes to her desk to record all the details in her lab book. It's late Friday afternoon when she finishes.

Early Monday morning, she hurries to her workspace. The apples and oranges are no longer there. Assuming they rolled off the bench, she gets down on her hands and knees to see where they've gone.

Mark, the colleague who works opposite her, asks, "Miss Sutton? *What* are you doing?"

She looks up at him. "I'm looking for the apples and oranges I treated on Friday. They must have fallen off the bench." She moves around her colleagues' empty stools.

"Here, let me help you." Mark crawls around the other side. After a couple of minutes he stands back up, his face as red as his hair. "Any luck?"

She straightens, brushing down her skirt. "No. Thanks for your help. And please, I've asked you before, call me Harriet. 'Miss Sutton' is much too formal. You call the others by their first names."

"All right, Harriet. But I must say, I can't understand how your experiment would simply disappear."

She looks in the refrigerator to see if someone placed her apples and oranges inside, but they aren't there either. Very puzzling. She walks across to Dr. Gallagher's office. A man with unruly white hair and round wire-rimmed glasses, he's sitting at his desk reading some papers. He looks a little like Albert Einstein. She knocks on the frame of his open door.

He glances up and smiles. "Miss Sutton."

"Dr. Gallagher, could the people who clean the lab over the weekend have done something with my experiment? I can't find the fruit I left on the bench Friday."

"They have explicit instructions not to move anything on the bench. Their job is to clean the sink and floors. I can speak to their supervisor."

"Never mind. I'll start again. This time I'll put my experiment in the incubator."

∿

Harriet and her mother make plans for the wedding, a simple outdoor ceremony that will be held at their home on the farm. The date has been set for late August after Nat's summer school classes at the

University of Minnesota end, before the regular academic year starts. As they sit together at Eleanor's desk in the parlor one evening, the women study their lists while Beethoven's *Pastorale* Symphony plays on the radio. They're both drinking Manhattans.

After taking a swallow, Eleanor says, "It's so nice to think about something positive for a change!"

Her mother looks old. Her red hair has faded to a sort of strawberry blonde, and though she's smiling now, the strong lines around her mouth suggest a frequent frown. Harriet puts her hand on her mother's arm. "I'm grateful for your help, Mother."

"I'm happy to do what I can. With your job, you don't have time for all the phone calls and appointments we need to make with the stationer, the florist, the caterer, and so on."

"I couldn't do this without you." She's happy that her mother is taking responsibility for all the tedious details.

Eleanor says, "I believe four bridesmaids and four groomsmen would be about right."

"That's more than I want. I'm serious about keeping this wedding as simple as possible. I'm thinking about cousin Susan and Ron's sister, Dottie, for bridesmaids."

"Who's your maid of honor?"

"I haven't asked anyone yet. I'd like it to be my friend Sarah from college, but she's married and living in Oklahoma now, and I know she's been trying to get pregnant. I'm not sure what to do about her."

"If not Sarah, how about Susan?"

"Good idea. It'd be nice to have my cousin in that role." Harriet takes a sip from her drink, then gets up and goes over to the ice bucket. She adds a couple of cubes to her glass.

"We should start drawing up the invitation list so we have an idea of the numbers. Your father will have friends and colleagues and customers he'll want to invite, and I'm sure the Wrights have people they'll wish to include."

Harriet sits again. "I'm not ready to think about the invitation list yet."

"Tomorrow, then? I've got to start on my calls."

"All right—tomorrow." After taking a big sip of her Manhattan for courage, she says, "Mother, I know now what you were talking about when you told me how much you loved the way Henri smelled. It's that way for me with Ron. He smells so yummy, and the way he touches me feels so good I could almost jump out of my skin."

"I'm glad you're strongly attracted to each other."

"Mummy, do feelings like these last a lifetime?"

"Your father and I weren't together long enough for our desire to diminish, but I don't believe that hunger you're talking about goes on forever. Once you have children, they soak up a lot of your energy."

"Then I guess we'd better enjoy every minute while we've got these feelings."

"Marriage can be challenging. It hasn't always been easy with George. You just have to stick with it during the tough times."

"Of course."

Looking down, Eleanor says, "I'm going to miss you terribly when you don't live here with us any longer."

"I'll miss you too, Mother, but I won't be far away." Harriet notices tears standing in her mother's eyes. "Now, tell me how your economics class is going. Do you like it?"

"I thought this class would enable me to have intelligent discussions with George about the business, but the truth is, it bores me to tears. The concepts are so theoretical, and none of it pertains to anything I really care about."

"How about something to do with biology?"

Her mother shakes her head. "I'm not going to embark on a career in medicine. I don't know what I want to pursue. I've been casting about for something that will really grab me."

Harriet can't imagine not knowing what she wants to do.

Her mother goes on. "I might try a course in psychology."

∾

Harriet is dealing with a variety of variables as she experiments with her fungicide solution—the combination and concentrations of the chemicals, the quantities of wax and oil and water are all factors to test. Ever since her first batch of fruit disappeared, she has kept her apples and oranges in the incubator next to her desk—that way she can control the temperature, the humidity, and the amount of fresh air to circulate through the incubator so the CO_2 and other gases don't have a negative impact on her experiment. From time to time she uses the microscope to look for mold that could be growing on her fruit. Every day she makes meticulous notes.

One morning three weeks later, her apples and oranges are no longer sitting in the incubator. She can scarcely believe it. Who would do this to her? She looks around to her fellow chemists and then over at the technicians at their bench. They're all intent on their own work.

Telling herself to calm down, she goes to Dr. Gallagher's office.

"Would it be possible to put a lock on the incubator I'm using for my fungicide experiments?"

He replies, "I'm sure that could be done, but why would you want to lock it?"

"I just don't want anyone but me to be able to open the door and compromise the environment I need to control."

"I'll put in an order with maintenance. It might take a couple of days."

"Thank you, Dr. Gallagher."

∾

The next morning she makes up a fresh batch of fungicide, sprays a new set of apples and oranges, and places them in the incubator. Then she sets a trap, leaving a long strand of hair across the top of the handle on the door to the incubator. The next morning the hair is gone and so is her fruit.

She is so angry she can hardly see. Going around the bench to Mark, she asks, "Will you eat with me today, just the two of us? I want to talk with you about something." Her gut says she can trust him.

"I'd be happy to, Harriet."

After they go through the line in the company cafeteria, she heads for a corner table with her tray. Mark sits down across from her.

"Is something wrong?"

"You remember when you helped me look for my missing apples and oranges? It happened again. I think someone is trying to sabotage my work."

His face grows redder than usual. "That's horrible."

"Do you have any idea who it could be?" Ever since she overheard Mark talking with Dr. Gallagher about Dr. Bryne's interest in their lab, her suspicions have focused on Bryne.

"I've seen Dr. Bryne in the lab during off hours lately."

Her hands clench into fists. "I bet Dr. Bryne's the culprit. He's had it in for me from the start." She's starting to despise him.

"Why would he have it in for you? You're a very reasonable person, Harriet."

"I'm the boss's daughter—I assume that's why." She considers how she might catch Bryne in the act, but that would require her to stay after work and make up some excuse to her father about why she wouldn't ride home with him. She'd rather not involve her father; she wants to solve her own problems. Taking a deep breath and then exhaling, she says, "I'm going to have to talk to Dr. Bryne."

"You should tell Dr. Gallagher. Let him handle it."

She shakes her head. "I think I should do this myself." She eats her salad while Mark tucks into his casserole. "I'll tackle Dr. Bryne on Monday. Maybe by then I'll be able to keep my temper."

∾

Harriet is not looking forward to the bridal shower that Ron's mother Betty is hosting for her. She knows she'll feel awkward having to ooh and ahh over presents from people she's never met. Fortunately she's attending the shower with her mother, her grandmother Abba, and her Aunt Edith. A couple of her mother's friends will be there too, and she knows Ron's sister, Dottie, who's a very quiet, sweet girl.

When Harriet arrives, Betty rushes over to her, shouting, "The bride is here!" She grabs her hand and pulls Harriet into the living room, where six other women are seated in a large circle.

She mumbles, "I'm not a bride yet."

"Nonsense," says Betty. "You're a bride until your first anniversary, and as far as Ronnie's concerned, you'll always be his bride. Now take this chair here."

Once everyone is seated, a maid comes around offering glasses of gin and tonic on a tray.

At the center of the room Betty stands in her flowered chintz dress with the rounded shoulders. "Isn't this a lovely morning? I am so pleased you all could join me here today in celebrating my soon-to-be daughter-in-law Harriet Sutton." She gestures toward Harriet, who rises to her feet.

"Thank you, Mrs. Wright."

Betty announces, "We'll chat for a while and then move onto the porch for lunch and the opening of our gifts for Harriet and Ron." She takes the empty chair next to Abba.

Harriet resumes her seat between Eleanor and Dottie. She's glad to be wearing the pretty silk dress her mother bought for her at Lord & Taylor last week. Everyone's summer frocks look brand new. Across the circle from her, Abba's in an ornate violet gown that's fit for royalty. Harriet's proud of how spiffy her mother looks too; she knows Eleanor had her hair done at the beauty parlor this morning.

The maid returns with hot cheese puffs.

Harriet turns to Dottie. "Do you know most of the ladies here?"

"Not at all," Dottie says softly.

Harriet thinks maybe Dottie is quiet because her mother is so noisy. "How did school go this year?"

"Fine."

"You're at the Country Day School, aren't you?"

"That's right."

Nearby a woman Harriet hasn't been introduced to says, "Did you read that story in the *New Yorker* about the Waldorf's having to get a huge Zionist flag made in just fifty-two hours because the president of the new state of Israel, Chaim Weizmann, was coming to stay there? It had to be twelve by twenty feet!"

Another woman tells the person on her right, "My daughter Gloria just bought one of those new Bikini bathing suits. They're named after the Bikini Atoll."

"Where's that?"

"In the South Pacific. It's the test site for our nuclear weapons."

Betty calls, "Harriet, tell everyone about the china and silver and crystal you and Ron have selected."

"Our china is Spode and the silver pattern is very simple . . ." Floundering, she looks to her mother.

"It's Reed & Barton."

"I want to hear about your wedding gown," Abba says. "Will you wear your mother's or buy something of your own?"

Harriet has no idea what Eleanor wore when she married George; she guesses this is a dig at her mother.

Eleanor replies, "Harriet and I plan to shop for her wedding dress next week."

"You're leaving it till then? I would have thought that would be the first thing you'd do once Harriet and Ron announced their engagement."

"We have plenty of time," Eleanor tells her mother-in-law. "Harriet insists on a simple cotton dress, though George would prefer her to wear something fancier."

"What about the men?" asks Abba.

"They'll wear blue-and-white seersucker suits."

"Seersucker? That's hardly appropriate, if you ask me."

It had never occurred to Harriet that they should have consulted Abba.

"It will be most appropriate for a simple summer wedding held outdoors," Eleanor states. "It's likely to be as hot as Hades in August."

"Humph." Abba turns to her neighbor and whispers something.

Suddenly it dawns on Harriet that her grandmother and her mother don't really like each other, and the realization makes her feel closer to her mother. Abba has never been particularly warm to Harriet, and she's pretty sure she knows why.

Betty moves everyone onto the three-season porch, where tables have been set up. Again Harriet sits between her mother and Dottie and doesn't say much other than "please pass the butter" as she eats crab salad, fruit, and hot rolls. Conversations about clothing, home decorating, and trips to distant places swirl around her. When the women move back into the living room, Betty directs Harriet to the chair next to a table that's been stacked with presents. She takes a deep breath.

Betty says, "I asked everyone to bring a favorite recipe too."

"That's a great idea," Harriet replies. "I want to learn how to cook. Your recipes will give me a head start."

"Rosalee does most of our cooking," Eleanor explains.

"As a chemist, I trust I won't find cooking too difficult." Harriet smiles gamely at the group.

Betty hands her a package. She pulls off a recipe entitled "Grapes in Sour Cream." She can't imagine ever preparing a dish involving grapes and sour cream, but she keeps her smile pasted on. She does not enjoy being the center of attention like this.

"Thank you. This recipe sounds interesting." The card is from Mrs. Eliot, and she's not sure which of these women she is. Inside the box she finds a Pyrex casserole. "I'm sure I'll use this. Thank you, Mrs. Eliot." She looks around for the donor.

Mrs. Eliot turns out to be the woman who must have had a permanent very recently, for her hair is tightly curled against her head. "I use my casserole every week. Gordon loves my chicken divan—it's the apricot preserves and French dressing that make it so tasty."

Opening presents and saying thank you goes on interminably. Harriet's cheeks hurt from smiling nonstop. She's twenty-nine years old and has never been a girly girl—she feels like a complete fraud in this setting. When Betty hands her the last package, a copy of *The Common Sense Book of Baby and Child Care* by Dr. Benjamin Spock, the ladies titter. Harriet feels herself blush. Everyone seems to assume that once she has a baby, her working days will be over. That is not what she wants.

When Harriet, Eleanor, Abba, and Aunt Edith finally get into the car to drive home, Aunt Edith asks innocently, "Did you have a good time, Harriet?"

"It was very nice," she responds politely. Actually she found the party excruciating. She hopes the wedding will be better than this.

ॐ

First thing Monday morning, Harriet marches into Dr. Bryne's office. She's wearing her most severe suit and her reddest lipstick. He sits facing the door, his suit jacket on the back of his chair. She closes the door behind her, but she doesn't take a seat.

"Someone is sabotaging my fungicide experiments." She pauses, waiting for his response. When he doesn't say anything, she moves forward.

"I don't know what you're talking about."

"Someone has been removing my apples and oranges from the incubator after I treat them." She's so furious her voice shakes. "Now, who do you think would want to undermine my work at Sutton?"

"Where's your proof?"

She points at him. "I want you to know that I have a very good idea who's responsible."

"What are you going to do?"

"Wouldn't you like to know!" She turns away. Grabbing the knob, she flings the door open and then slams it behind her. Let him worry that she might go to her father about this. Bryne doesn't know she solves her own problems by herself.

Once she's out of sight, she leans against the corridor wall, quaking. She has never exploded like this before. She just hopes she has managed to scare Bryne off.

∾

A padlock is installed on the incubator, and Harriet's the only one aside from Dr. Gallagher who knows the combination. Her apples and oranges stay put. All summer she refines the fungicide. Eventually she tries adding manganese sulfate to the dithiocarbamate, and the results excite her. After the apples and oranges sprayed with the newest concoction have been mold free for two weeks in the incubator, she takes one of each and races out of the lab and down the hall to the executive suite.

The door to her father's office is closed. She asks his secretary, "Is he in?"

"Yes, Miss Sutton."

She knocks on his door.

"Enter."

Nearly breathless, she says, "Father, I've found it! I'm pretty sure this latest solution will be a very effective fungicide." She sits in front of him. "I've been experimenting with different salts to make the dithiocarbamate. Manganese—"

"Spare me the details, Harriet. You say it works?"

"It certainly preserves the fruit. We'll need to test it for toxicity."

"We'll use an outside lab for that. I'm sure Dr. Gallagher has some names. Who knows about this?"

"I wanted to tell you first."

"Once we're sure this is our fungicide, I'll want you to write down the formula and give it to me so I can keep it in the safe. Actually, why don't you give me that information now—you'll probably be off on your honeymoon by the time we hear back from the outside lab."

"This is so exciting, Father!"

"Let's not count our chickens quite yet."

"I just have a really good feeling about this, Father."

∾

Then the big day is upon them. The wedding on August 21 passes in a breathless blur of images. Harriet sees herself standing in her white satin dress in front of the mirror in her bedroom, her mother at her side in a peach-colored frock and jaunty hat. Harriet refused to have anything to do with bows or ribbons or lace, so her gown is elegantly simple, tea-length, sleeveless, shimmery, and cut quite low in front. She's shaking.

Next she's aware of walking across the lawn down the improvised aisle defined by chairs on each side, her hand on George's tense arm. He's trembling, which catches her by surprise, but strangely his emotion calms her. While the string quartet plays Bach's "Air on the G

String," she floats toward Ron, feeling lovely for the first time in her life. Ron, remarkably handsome in his seersucker suit and bowtie, beams at her from the front. Nat is grinning, standing next to Ron's brother Mike and his buddy Mac. Susan, Dottie, and Judy, wearing different shades of the same cotton dress and straw hats with a band the same color as her dress, smile as she approaches. When she releases her father's arm and turns to him, she thinks it must be the music that's making his eyes glisten.

Then she's next to Ron, facing the minister, a friend of the family who speaks slowly in his deep voice. This helps to calm her, too. Ron places the wedding band on her finger and kisses her and then, as the musicians start playing the Brandenburg Concerto No. 5 in D Major, they're flying back down the aisle, hand in hand, while the photographer takes hurried shots.

Before they're surrounded, Ron puts his arms around Harriet and draws her close. "In just a few more hours, I'm going to ravish you."

She wants to melt against him, but not here, not yet. She leans back far enough to tap him on the chest with her bouquet. "I can't wait!"

They kiss for several long moments. His lips are so warm.

Abba stands nearby, waiting. Once they disengage, Abba seizes Ron's hand. "I like your bowtie, Ron—very dapper."

"Thank you, Mrs. Sutton." He ducks his head in a little bow. "I aim to please."

"I'd like to give you two a piece of property so you can build your own home nearby. Would that suit you?"

Smoothly, Ron grasps Abba's arm. "If you aren't the most generous lady I've ever had the pleasure of knowing!" He kisses her on the cheek.

Amazed by her grandmother's largesse, Harriet says, "I don't know what to say, Abba." She's not sure they'd actually want to live near her parents.

"Well, think about it."

Nat approaches the newlyweds. Her brother is even taller than the last time Harriet saw him. "Congratulations, you two! Isn't that what one is supposed to say? And such nice music!"

"Bach was one of the things I insisted on."

"Ron's a great guy, Harry. I'm glad for you." Nat grins.

"How are you, brother? We haven't had any time to talk since you got home. You're in a jazz group in Minneapolis now, aren't you?"

"It's so much fun!" Then his smile collapses. "If only Eddie were here."

"I know." Her shoulders slump. She stares at the crowd of boisterous people swirling around greeting friends, hoisting drinks, laughing, and eating. Then she hears her father speaking her name.

She edges closer. A drink in his hand, George looks relaxed and happy now as he speaks to his brother, Robert. Holding a glass of champagne, Abba stands between her sons. George says, "Harriet has managed to invent a coating for fruit that will open up a whole new line of business for us."

Her father is bragging about her!

Nearby Ron's father, Colin, says, "I can't believe those damned Soviets closed down the roads and rails so there's no entering Berlin from the West. How are we going to get food and coal to the people there?"

"I've heard the allies are organizing an airlift."

"It's only right that Germany and Japan were refused permission to participate in the Summer Olympics this year—the Austerity Olympics."

Dottie walks toward the house, and it looks like she's crying, so Harriet finds Ron and tells him to go after his sister.

Then Susan, still wearing her straw hat, comes up to Harriet. A pretty young woman with light brown hair and green eyes the same shade as her dress, Susan resembles her father, Uncle Drew, more than Aunt Jessica. "I was honored to be your maid of honor, Harriet. Thank you for choosing me."

"I'm happy you could be here. I didn't know whether you had a job that would make it difficult for you to come."

"I only graduated in June! I'm still looking around."

"Does Smith help you find a position?"

"I haven't asked the college for suggestions. I might work for my father."

"At his newspaper?"

"I think it'd be interesting. I like to write."

"Well, I can tell you it's a little tricky working for one's father. People might resent you."

Nearby Eleanor is talking to her sister, Jessica, who's wearing a fond smile. "And then Abigail had the nerve to say the men shouldn't be wearing seersucker. She drives me nuts!"

"Ellie, your mother-in-law simply wants to be included."

"You're right—of course you're right, Jessie. I don't know what I'd do without you to straighten me out." Eleanor glances at her wristwatch and then over at Harriet. "Time to cut the cake, dearie."

Harriet's next image is of handing Ron a piece of cake, which he pops into his mouth without spilling a crumb. She takes a small bite out of the piece he offers her, and that's enough—she's too excited to eat.

Then she's up in her bedroom changing into her going-away outfit while Eleanor hangs up the wedding gown. Once Harriet is dressed, she sits down on the bed. Her mother exits. Harriet sticks her nose into her bouquet. The white lilies smell almost peppery. Eleanor returns, holding a book. She sits down next to Harriet and hands her a copy of *Tales of the South Pacific* by James Michener.

Eleanor looks exhausted.

"Are you all right, Mother?"

"I'm a little tired. I got you something to read when you're on Martha's Vineyard."

"I don't think I'll be able to get through such a big book." Harriet hopes she and Ron will spend most of their honeymoon in bed, not reading. "I appreciate the thought, though."

"Take it. You never know, it might rain the whole time you're there."

"Thank you for everything you did to make this such a perfect day." She puts her arms around her mother and squeezes.

"I just want you to be happy, Harriet."

"I am very happy."

Her last image from the wedding is of launching her bouquet into the air, of the startled look on Susan's face as she catches it, and then of running down the stairs, hand in hand with Ron. As she glances back, she sees that her mother looks bereft. Then her father puts his arm around Eleanor, who hides her face in his shoulder while he pulls her close. Harriet's glad to see that embrace: she may be leaving home, but at least her parents have each other.

∾

Once they reach the hotel in Connecticut where they'll spend their wedding night, she's suddenly nervous. Putting on the new cream-colored silk negligee her mother gave her, which makes her feel sexy, helps. Ron is lying on the bed in his undershorts, having pulled back the bedding. She joins him. This is the first time they've ever been able to stretch out on a bed together. When he rolls on top of her, she hugs him tightly.

"You do realize I'm a virgin, don't you?" she says.

"I'll be gentle," he replies.

That's all she needs to hear. She relaxes, trusting that he knows what he's doing.

Before long he removes her negligee and his shorts. Then he kisses her eyelids and her lips and her neck and her breasts and all the way down to her toes. She's so excited and wet that she thinks penetration will be easy, but he has to push hard to get all the way in. That hurts.

The pain is fleeting, though, and he's so happy that she doesn't mind the discomfort.

The next night when they make love, she feels a little sore, but it isn't long before she's just as avid about going to bed as he is.

They have a wonderful time honeymooning on Martha's Vineyard, playing fierce rounds of tennis, lying on the sand, and swimming. The sight of Ron in bathing trunks, with his nice flat stomach and tight butt, does something wonderful to her insides—she loves to press herself against him. Ron turns out to be a very attentive lover who quickly learns how to drive her over the edge.

The only flaw appears their last night, when Ron becomes so drunk he can hardly walk back to their room.

∽

Now her lab coat no longer fits—it keeps riding up over her belly— and she tries to tug it down while the engineers, technicians, and sales manager surrounding her harass her with questions.

"If the fungicide works on oranges, what about lemons or limes or grapefruit? How about pears or grapes?"

"Is immersion the only way to apply the fungicide, or can the stuff be sprayed successfully?"

"How long does a batch of the fungicide last? Does it need to be applied as soon as you make it?"

"Will the fungicide keep if it's refrigerated? What if it's heated?"

She says, "I don't know what will happen if you heat the fungicide. That would probably destroy it."

"Does it rub off after a while?"

"Would you use a different strength of the fungicide on fruit with a thinner skin than an orange?"

"What's the lifespan of a product you've treated?"

Getting flustered, Harriet replies, "I don't know! We have a lot of questions to answer—we still have many tests to run. I need your help." Shouldn't they figure these things out for themselves? She did the tough work of inventing the fungicide, and now it's up to them to implement mass production and sales.

"How ripe are the fruits you start with?"

"I've been buying apples and oranges at the grocery store, so they're pretty ripe. We should find farmers to supply us as soon as they're picked."

"In our sales materials can we call this an 'edible' treatment to enhance the shelf life of foods?"

Mark, who has been assigned to the fungicide team, says, "Guys, let's break for lunch. We can get back to this afterward."

Gratefully, Harriet smiles at Mark. He's turned out to be her best friend at the company. She's relieved that she no longer has to report to Dr. Bryne, who left the company after George restructured upper management.

Too nauseated to eat, she sits back on her stool. She's curious now. What will heat do to her concoction? She leans forward and takes a test tube of the fungicide in one hand, then reaches for the Bunsen burner, but she can't quite get there because her stomach's in the way. Standing, she reaches over farther. Once the burner's on, she holds the test tube above it. Her stomach lurches. Is she going to throw up again? She feels so strange these days she hardly knows herself.

Taking a deep breath, she leans a little closer so the fungicide will start to boil. Suddenly the flame catches her hair, sizzling as it moves up the strands. Panic grips her. Immediately dropping the test tube onto the bench, she uses both hands to slap out the fire. The scent of singed hair is sickening. She turns off the burner and runs for the bathroom, her heart hammering.

After retching into the toilet, she moves to the sink so she can examine herself in the mirror. She lost only a little bit of the hair that hangs at her right shoulder. Swallowing hard, she moves back to the stall and sits. Placing her hands on her face, she bows her head and rocks in place while tears drip through her fingers. That was so close!

Eventually, she starts to think maybe it's time for her to leave Sutton Chemical. She doesn't want to give up working, but she's starting to realize that taking a product to market is not what motivates her. It was the experimenting that she enjoyed so much at Madison and in her first year at Sutton. Her father and Ron expect her to stop working once the baby is born—but maybe she should quit before then. The thought is strangely seductive. She's ashamed to think like this, but she's terribly tired now and awfully distracted by the changes going on inside her body. These days she spends most of each weekend resting, absorbed by the baby's movements, dreaming about who he or she will be.

She and Ron weren't using any form of birth control, but they certainly didn't expect her to become pregnant so quickly. Now when they're home together, she doesn't drink alcohol because she's nauseated much of the time, so Ron drinks alone while she sits by his side planning the house they're building on the land Abba gave them. She'd better talk with him about the possibility of leaving Sutton before the baby is born. Maybe a break would be wise. At the same time, she's very much afraid that this could be the end of her career as a chemist.

What should she do?

May 1949

WESTERN UNION

ELIZABETH NJ 450P MAY 20 1949

MR. NATHANIEL SUTTON

747 SE 4th STREET MINNEAPOLIS, MIN

BABY GIRL BORN THIS MORNING HARRIET AND BABY
WELL PLEASE CALL HOME COLLECT LOVE MOTHER

∾

May 31

My dear Nat,

Thank you for telephoning the other day so we could talk about the exciting news. Harriet and Ron have decided to name the baby Henrietta, which is a mouthful, but I think it's rather nice. Mother and daughter seem to be getting along fine. When I had each of you, my mother moved in with us for two weeks, but Harriet doesn't want that. She says we live close enough to see each other whenever necessary. Your sister is so independent she doesn't want any help with the baby. At

*least not yet. I know I can be overbearing, and Harriet told me
she doesn't appreciate unsolicited advice—she wants to figure
things out for herself—so I bite my tongue when I visit.*

*Your father and I are very pleased that you are taking a full
course load at the University of Minnesota. You surprised me
when you said you wanted to major in biology and minor in
music, but after you explained what good teachers the professors in the biology department are, it made sense. I wish I had
a better idea of what my major will be—I'll need to figure that
out if I'm ever going to graduate, and I do want to obtain a
bachelor's degree one of these years.*

*Here's an idea: How about we race each other to the finish
line? If you get your degree first, I'll give you $1,000. If I get
there first, you would owe me a bouquet of fresh carnations—
salmon colored to go with the new wallpaper in the dining
room. What do you say?*

Love,
Mother

∾

WESTERN UNION
ELIZABETH NJ 1105A JANUARY 23 1951

MR. NATHANIEL SUTTON
747 SE 4th STREET MINNEAPOLIS, MIN

BABY BOY BORN 4 AM TODAY HARRIET AND SON FINE
MOTHER

March 1951

Carrying baby Joey in her arms, Harriet follows her mother and little Retta into her parents' parlor, where the curtains are closed, the lamps are lit, and logs crackle in the fireplace. Retta, who has been walking for nearly a year now, is wearing the lovely smocked dress Eleanor bought for her. She holds her grandmother's hand tightly.

Harriet sinks onto the couch. "This is cozy, Mother." She unwraps the blanket around Joey and sets him on her lap facing the warmth of the fire.

Retta sits on the floor nearby.

Eleanor says, "I'll go get some drinks. Would you like a glass of milk, Retta, or perhaps some Ovaltine?"

Retta shakes her head, her curls bouncing with the movement.

"Will you join me for a cocktail, Harriet?"

"I'll have one. Maybe it'll help Joey sleep a little longer tonight."

While her mother is out of the room, she lifts up her blouse and starts to nurse. As she gazes down at Joey, she feels as if she could melt with love for her son.

Eleanor sets Harriet's glass on a side table and takes an adjacent chair. "I'm glad you feel comfortable feeding Joey in front of me. When I nursed you and the boys, it was always in the privacy of my bedroom."

Was this a criticism? Her eyes still on Joey, she replies, "I wouldn't nurse in front of Father." Then she looks up. "You've done something different with your hair, Mother. I like it."

Patting the sides of her head, Eleanor says, "I got Stella to give me a new look. Trying to cheer myself up a little."

"What's wrong, Mummy?"

"Oh, Harriet, I'm a little blue. Nothing's much fun anymore, and I don't seem to have any energy. I guess it's this long dark winter. But never mind."

She doesn't like the sound of this. "Do you want to talk about it?"

"No, it's boring." Her mother raises her glass and drinks.

"Then tell me about your coursework. I bet that's interesting."

"It is, but the class I'm taking now on the development of human behavior during childhood, adolescence, and aging is much more theoretical than I expected. I want to understand what it takes to motivate people to make changes in their lives."

"Hmm," she says, placing Joey against her shoulder and lightly tapping his back until a loud burp erupts. Then he spits up a little.

"May I hold him?" her mother asks.

It's a little hard for her to let go, but of course she wants her mother to get close to Joey. Then both women notice that Retta is fidgeting.

Eleanor points. "See that doll over on the shelf, Retta? You can play with her if you want."

Retta trots over to the shelf while Harriet rises to pass the baby to Eleanor. Her mother draws the baby to her chest. Harriet drapes an old diaper over her shoulder.

She resumes her seat, crosses her legs, and picks up her drink. Retta brings the doll over and sits at her feet.

"What do you like about psychology, Mother?"

"It's the science that can help us understand ourselves better."

"Can you really call it a science? It's not like chemistry or biology."

"I want to find something that will really engage me."

Hoping to be helpful, she says, "What about becoming a full-fledged nurse? You could do that—it's not too late. You loved your work at Halloran."

Her mother replies angrily, "I told you before, I'm not going to embark on a career at this age!" She gulps her Manhattan. "Enough about me, Harriet. Tell me, how do you enjoy being home with your children?"

She takes a sip of her own drink. "It's much more fun than I expected. I enjoy watching Retta's physical abilities develop, and I love to observe her mind at work. Joey's sweet and smiley. Plus, I've learned how much fun cooking can be."

"I suppose cooking is somewhat similar to making solutions in the lab."

"It's not the same at all."

Her mother flinches. She's really touchy these days. "You're so literal, Harriet."

"Okay, I guess I can see there are some similarities. Remember those recipes from the bridal shower Betty threw for me? That's what got me started on cooking. Ron says my coq au vin is the best he's ever eaten."

"Why don't you invite George and me over for supper? You could try your coq au vin out on us."

"I'd be happy to have you over. How about next Saturday?"

"That would be nice." Joey starts to wiggle. Rubbing his back, Eleanor says, "I just hope you won't regret stepping away from your profession, Harriet. It might be difficult to get back into it."

"Right now my job is to be the best mother I can. I'll return to work once the kids are more fully fledged—probably when they start school." She takes another sip of her drink. "I know Father doesn't believe women should work once they have children—which is infuriating—but I don't think I'd go back to Sutton Chemical anyway."

"Didn't you like working for the company?"

"It was fascinating to get to know Father as a businessman and watch him operate, but at Sutton I discovered that I'm not motivated by making lots of money as much as I am by doing research and learning new things."

"George was very proud of the work you did on fungicides, but I know he wasn't entirely comfortable with your working at the company."

"Because of the appearance of nepotism?"

"It's the fact that you're female."

"Did he say that?"

"He never said anything about it, but I'm familiar with his views on what is proper. George is a traditional man with traditional views."

"I know." Harriet turns her attention to her daughter, who is moving the doll's arms up and down as though she were marching. "You're a good girl, Retta." Then she takes another small sip of her drink. "Having children has made me think more about family." She sighs. "I wish I'd had a chance to know your mother as an adult. I don't remember her very well."

"Her death was such a shock—she was only seventy." As her mother's arms tighten around Joey, he starts to cry.

She takes back her son and soothes him. Once he quiets down, she says, "Do you know anything about my other grandmother—Henri's mother?"

"I met Irene once when Henri took me home. After the war I wrote to her but she never replied. I have no idea whether she survived the first world war, much less the second."

"Did you want to go back to France to look for her?"

"I thought about it, but I had you and the boys to raise, and then there was the next war."

She says, "I suppose if we wanted to find her, we'd need to go to the town where she lived and start asking questions. Maybe I'll do that one day when the children are older."

"I'm so glad you named Henrietta after your father."

"I know, Mother. You tell me that all the time."

"Really? Forgive me." She squeezes her eyes shut. "I try so hard to please you, Harriet, but sometimes you're not easy."

"I'm sorry, Mother. I just thought I was stating a fact. I don't mean to hurt your feelings."

"I'm just too sensitive these days."

That's true, Harriet thinks.

Retta stands and starts wandering around the room, touching the knickknacks.

She rises. "I should get these kids home, Mother. It's past Retta's supper time."

"George should be here soon."

"I'll see Father on Sunday when we come for lunch. Or maybe Saturday night—I'll let you know after I talk to Ron."

∿

It's late August at the family's summer house on the North Shore of Massachusetts when Harriet, her mother, and her aunt Jessica find themselves battling a monstrous storm that started rising early that morning. The radio issued warnings that this could become a full-blown Nor'easter, with heavy rain, gale force winds, and rough seas. Harriet and Jessica are upstairs stuffing towels at the base of the bedroom walls, which run with rain that's been hurled sideways at the leaky window frames while the wind howls outside. The cotton rag rugs are quickly becoming soaked.

Jessica says, "I can finish this if you want to check on your children."

"Thanks, Aunt Jessie." Harriet stands, stretches out her back, and then heads downstairs to the living room, which is the only room with a fireplace. Joey is crying in Eleanor's arms. Retta has covered her ears with her hands. Harriet reaches for Joey. Her mother rises and puts two more logs on the fire.

Eleanor says, "We need to go bail the sailboat. If we don't do it soon, it'll capsize and sink to the bottom."

This is a task the men usually handle, but Ron and George and Uncle Drew went back to their respective jobs two days ago. Calling up the staircase, she shouts, "Aunt Jessie, can you come down and keep an eye on my kids for a few minutes?"

Once they're outside, Harriet and Eleanor hurry to the edge of the rocks. Her mother quickly pulls the thrashing skiff in from its mooring and steps into it. Harriet follows, untying the painter rope as soon as her mother gets the oars in place. Gingerly stepping by her mother on the middle seat, she takes the back, facing forward. The waves heave the boat perilously close to the rocks, but Eleanor turns the skiff out into Ipswich Bay. The force of the huge surging waves is frightening.

Thinking about the line "those in peril on the sea," she sings "Eternal Father Strong to Save" under her breath while she places her hands on the oars to help her mother pull. This song she learned at school calms her a little as the wind whips the hood off her rain jacket and her hair is immediately soaked. She blinks rapidly to keep the water out of her eyes so she can see the way. So long as the sailboat doesn't take on too much water, it should be able to ride out the storm. But as they get close, the sailboat is bucking with the waves. They steer next to the stern, and then her mother leans to tie up the skiff while Harriet stows the oars under the seats. One after another, they move in a crouch, legs wide apart, carefully timing their jumps into the sailboat. The water is just over the floorboards. Eleanor pulls up one section and reaches in with the small bucket she brought with her. Harriet raises another and starts to bail out the boat. The wind subsides for a few minutes.

When they finish bailing, they move back into the skiff and untie it. Harriet sits down and places the oars back into the locks while her mother takes the middle seat again. The skiff rocks up and down and the wind rises again. She feels a shiver of excitement to be in the midst of all this unleashed power, but she's also scared enough to be very cautious as they row back toward shore. She's grateful her mother is so calm and capable! *This is what Mother is really like.*

Once they get close to land, Eleanor turns the skiff so that it's parallel to a huge chunk of granite they can step onto. Harriet watches her mother stand just as a wave breaks over the left side of the skiff and jolts the right side down to the edge of the water. Eleanor stares at the heaving gap between the boat and the rock and Harriet sees that her mother could easily slip into the gap and drown right here. Her mother pauses, watching the crests of water crash against the rocks—what is she thinking right now?

"Be careful, Mother!"

Slowly, taking the painter in one hand, Eleanor lowers her center of gravity as the skiff rocks back and forth, and then she leaps, aiming for solid ground. She barely makes it. She holds the boat while Harriet steps out. Then Eleanor ties the painter onto the running mooring and quickly pulls the skiff away from the rocks. Breathing hard, they head up the hill to the house.

Once they reach the open three-sided porch that overlooks the bay, Eleanor says, "That was exciting!"

"Scary too," Harriet agrees. "We'd better get some dry clothing on. It must have dropped twenty degrees in the last hour."

They hurry upstairs to their rooms. Harriet turns on a light, which flickers, and then the power goes off. Wriggling out of her wet clothing, she digs in the drawers for dry underwear and wool pants and sweater. A few minutes later, she feels her way down the stairs. Opening the door to the living room, she finds Joey on Aunt Jessie's lap.

"Mama!" Retta hugs Harriet's legs.

Eleanor appears with flashlights and candles.

Harriet disentangles herself from Retta so she can feed another log into the fireplace.

Eleanor says, "Isn't this fun, Retta? We're safe and warm. The storm can't get us in here, but we can watch it."

Retta nods her head in assent, but she looks dubious as she gazes at her grandmother.

Eleanor picks up Retta and holds her close. Then she moves to the window. Pointing, she says, "See our sailboat out there? It's bouncing up and down on the waves."

Retta slithers out of Eleanor's arms and leans against the window to look, her curiosity piqued.

The door bangs open to reveal Drew in a very wet raincoat and battered hat.

"Sweetheart, thank God you're safe!" Jessica cries, jumping to her feet.

"Oh good, reinforcements!" Eleanor remarks.

Once he closes the door and enters the room, Drew says, "I got here as soon as I could. Branches are falling all over the place. The roads are a mess."

Harriet says, "We may have lost power but we still have gas. I'll go heat up some soup." She feels energized by her encounter with the elements.

"I'll do it, Harriet," her mother says. "You've got your children to see to." She exits.

Aunt Jessie hands Joey to Harriet.

"Are the boats secure?" asks Drew.

Harriet replies, "I think so. Mother and I just finished bailing out the sailboat."

"Good for you."

She smiles. "If the storm keeps up, maybe you could go out later this afternoon."

"Will do." He sits down in an armchair facing his wife. "Everyone all right?"

Aunt Jessie says, "The children are a little frightened, but everything's fine."

After lunch Eleanor teaches Retta to play Go Fish. Harriet is really pleased to see her mother behave in such a grandmotherly way. She knows that her mother loves being at Sea View more than anywhere else in the world. For her entire life, except during the war years, Eleanor has spent every summer here with her own mother until she died, and her sister and their families.

Harriet has spent most of her summers here too. This ramshackle house, built in 1880, feels like home. It's not fancy at all, and they get to wear their most comfortable old clothes here. Swimming and sailing, playing tennis at the yacht club, digging in the sand and building sand castles, picking blueberries, taking naps and reading, and assembling simple meals make up their summer world. She knows she is lucky.

Around midnight the wind and rain die down. The power is restored soon thereafter.

෴

It's their last night before she and Eleanor head south to New Jersey with the children. After putting Retta and Joey to bed, Harriet joins her mother and aunt on the porch, where they watch the sunset together. The older women wear plain cotton dresses with cardigan sweaters, short socks, and leather loafers, while Harriet has on trousers and a sweatshirt. Cousin Susan and some of her friends play a raucous game of Monopoly in the living room.

They sit in companionable silence, watching the colors of the clouds change from pink and salmon and gold to gray as the light fades.

Her mother says, "I'm sad Nat couldn't join us here this summer. But that jazz band he's in plays at a supper club in Minneapolis every weekend. And he likes this group, plus he needs the money."

"Good for him," Aunt Jessie replies. "I know that's his dream."

"I'm just glad he's going to school as well. I challenged him to a race to see who finishes college first, though I'm really in no rush to obtain my degree. I just wanted to motivate him to finish up."

"I admire you for going back to school, Ellie. It can't have been easy to sit in a classroom with students as young as your children."

"I had to. I was having trouble finding a sense of purpose in my life."

"Has college given you that?"

"Not exactly. I feel a bit like a sailboat without a rudder, swinging every which way in the breeze. I'm still looking for my direction."

Harriet keeps her mouth shut. She's never heard her mother and aunt speak so candidly with each other while she was present.

Aunt Jessie cocks her head to the side. "How are you and George getting on?"

"You saw us over the Fourth. We're all right."

"You seemed very cautious with each other."

"I'm still furious at George for sending Eddie off to war. He says I'm obsessed with Eddie. It would help if I could talk about him, but George can't bear it when I do."

Harriet says, "I'd love to talk about Eddie with you, Mother."

"It's too late tonight."

"Anytime," Harriet reiterates.

Eleanor says, "I just can't find my way out of all this grief and anger and regret over the past."

"You've got to forgive George," Aunt Jessie says. "This is eating you up. You must forgive yourself too."

Eleanor's face crumples. "I don't know how!" After a long pause, she rises to her feet, swaying a little. "Back in a flash," she says, slurring the last word.

When Eleanor returns to the porch, she sits and raises her drink to her mouth. She says, "*You* could be a psychologist, Jessie."

Aunt Jessie crosses her arms against her chest. Gently but firmly, she says, "I'm worried about you, Ellie. You're drinking way too much.

Some mornings you don't even remember what we talked about the night before."

This is Harriet's opening. "I'm worried about you too, Mummy. I wish you'd stop drinking."

Eleanor closes her eyes. "It's not my fault that drinking is the only thing that makes me feel better. I've been trying and trying to find something else—what do you think the courses in psychology are all about? I'm looking for answers!"

"How can I help?" asks Aunt Jessica.

Eleanor shakes her head. "You're right, you're both right. I'll stop drinking for a week." She smiles tremulously. "And now, if you'll excuse me, I'm going to bed." She gets to her feet and walks carefully into the house.

Harriet looks at her aunt. "Do you think we were too hard on her?"

"No, I don't," says Aunt Jessie. "I've been worried for years."

"Me too," replies Harriet.

"I don't know what it's going to take for my sister to feel better."

October 1951

Nat is in his natural element, eyes closed as he blows poignant notes on his tenor saxophone behind the band's new vocalist, who is singing "In My Solitude" so soulfully that tears gather under his lids. This is one of his favorite tunes; he's been playing it for years. When the crowd applauds, he opens his eyes. Her name is Dorie something. Wearing a short orange gown and lipstick the same color as her dress, she raises her arms to the audience, welcoming their acclaim. This is the third song in the band's first performance with her at the Key Club near Seven Corners. The first two numbers were louder, faster swing tunes with an undercurrent of Dixieland, which always pleases the patrons here.

Dorie turns and looks intently at him. *What?* He glances down to see if his tie is askew. He doesn't think anything's amiss in his appearance. His suit coat isn't buttoned but it's easier for him to play his sax when he isn't constrained. He looks back at her and smiles slightly. Is she flirting with him? He has known so few girls of any kind that he really doesn't know. She nods slowly as her lips curve in subtle acknowledgment. She must have liked the solo he played. Then she lowers her gaze, suggesting she's shy, though he doesn't think that's true. She watched him closely during their rehearsals last week but kept her distance. She's so beautiful she scares him a little.

He examines his reed, scrutinizes along the length of his sax, and fingers his pads, preparing for the next song. After Ralph says "Four up front" and taps out a rhythm on his snare drum, they launch into "Blue Skies." Nat relaxes into the music, though at the same time his nerves hum with exquisite awareness of Dorie, who is moving with the music, swinging her hips briskly from side to side and then backward and forward. Mr. Snake starts to rise. *Not now!* Nat leans over a bit and positions his tenor in such a way that it hides the action in his trousers. For the rest of the set, he keeps his eyes away from Dorie, but he plays to her voice.

At the break, he puts his horn into its case. When he straightens up, she's right in front of him. He blinks a couple of times and steps back a pace.

She moves forward. "Nice blow, Mr. Sax-man. You were really cooking!"

Grateful for her opening, he says, "You have a fabulous voice. I loved the way you sang 'Memories of You.'" Then he's embarrassed that he'd just used the word *love*, so he looks at his feet. At least he doesn't have to worry about making small talk with her. They have music in common.

"Thank you. The crowd certainly seemed to enjoy that song. Can I call you Nathaniel?"

In his mind he hears his mother insist, "*May* I, not *can* I." He doesn't care about that. Raising his chin, he replies, "Nathaniel, Nat, whatever you like. Just don't call me Mr. Sutton—that's my father's name." Is he flirting with her now?

"Have you been at this for long?"

"I've played with the Aces since June when the Key Club opened, and from time to time I've been a sideman at some other clubs."

"I meant have you played professionally for long? You're awfully good." Her eyes are the color of melted chocolate.

He feels himself blush. "Well, thanks. I only started making some

regular money when I joined these cats. Most of the time I'm a student at the U—nights I wait tables at the Flame Room."

"Lucky you! You must get to hear fabulous bands there."

"It's a great perk. Of course, the hotel doesn't pay much, and they
can get away with that because staff like me just want to hear the
music while earning a few bucks."

He looks away when she straightens the shoulder of her dress so it
covers the strap of her brassiere.

After she's done adjusting her attire, he says, "What about you?
Have you been singing all your life?"

"I started singing solos in the church choir when I was a girl. But
I've got to go powder my nose now. Let's talk after the show."

When she returns, she moves sinuously among the music stands and
chairs on the stage to take her place in front. They have a super set. The
band gets even tighter, tossing the melody back and forth like a ball, improvising inventively, fingers flying, thrilling the audience. At the second
break, he finds the restroom, and then he is still so excited that he paces
up and down the hall. When he gets back to the stage, he sees Dorie sitting
cross-legged on her stool, gazing into the distance, energetically jiggling
her foot back and forth. He wonders what she's thinking about.

The last set is even better. When the band finally stops playing, he's
drenched in sweat. He pulls out a handkerchief to wipe off his face.
Then he notices that her face is shiny too, so he hands her his hanky.
Once she has finished using it, she tucks it away in her purse. After
everyone has packed up their gear, the guys leave while Nat and Dorie
move to a table.

She fiddles with a lock of curled platinum blonde hair near her
temple. "Aren't you a little old to go to school?"

"I started late, and I've had to work to pay my way, so it's taken a
while, but the end's in sight. I'll get my bachelor's degree in December."

"What's the point of school when you've got so much talent for
music?"

"I wanted to study music theory and music history, and then I got interested in biology. One of my professors wants me to apply to medical school."

"That's fascinating," she says pensively. "You want to become a doctor?"

"No, I want to make my living as a musician, but I realize that might not be easy."

"You can say that again! It's taken me three years of singing in bars around here to land a gig like this. But I have plans."

"You have such a fine voice, you could sing anywhere."

"You're nice, Nathaniel." She pauses. "Nathaniel's too formal. I'm going to call you Nate."

"Whatever you like." He's pleased that she has her own name for him.

She asks, "Where do you live?"

"I have a little efficiency in Dinkytown. Isn't that the silliest name?"

"Of course, you live near the university."

"I really like the way your dress cups your hips." He blushes again.

Leaning forward to place her hand on his arm, she says, "You're cute, Nate."

"Ah . . . no one's ever said that to me before."

"You are. You've got a good haircut and that's a class suit you're wearing."

"It's the only one I own."

Shaking her head with what appears to be wonder, she says, "I've never met anyone who talks like you."

He doesn't know how to respond to that. "Tell me about your plans."

She looks at the dainty wristwatch on her arm. "Some other time. I should be getting home. I need my beauty sleep, don't cha know."

He's startled, remembering that Emma, the one girlfriend he had for a couple of months, used to say "Don't you know." Is this an auspicious sign? Taking a deep breath, he asks, "May I see you home?"

"That would be swell."

"I'll get us a cab."

It turns out that she lives only five minutes away. When they reach her apartment building, he gets out behind her and walks her to the front door. Grabbing her hand, he says, "I'll be thinking about you." He can't possibly kiss her so soon, especially not with the cabbie sitting there. As he releases her hand, he exclaims, "I don't even know your last name!"

She smiles. "It's Larson. Good night, Nate."

The next night near the end of the first set, Dorie asks the group to play "The Way You Look Tonight." She moves over to the side of the stage, holding the microphone to her lips, and as she sings, she watches Nat with such a beseeching look and her voice reveals such longing that when the song ends, there's a hush. It takes several seconds for the audience to pull themselves together before they explode with applause.

At the end of the show, he offers to walk her home. His heart is beating fast. "I hope you don't mind walking. I can't afford a cab every night, and you live close by."

"That's fine," she says.

Outside, she takes his arm. He can't think of anything to say because he's thinking about kissing her. When they reach her door and turn to each other, he leans forward and gives her a quick peck on the mouth. This isn't the first time he has kissed a girl, but it's the first time he's kissed a woman.

She doesn't seem offended, but she does look a little surprised—at being kissed or because it was such a quick one?

Awkwardly, he says, "Well, good night."

She smiles. "See you soon."

❧

Two weeks later Nat is startled one evening when Dorie appears at the Flame Room while he's working. Wearing a sparkly dress and heels, she takes a seat at one of the small tables in the corner. He hurries over to her.

He grins. "What would you like to order, ma'am?"

She puts her gloved hands on the table and adopts a demure air. "I'd like a gin and tonic, please, kind sir."

When he returns with her drink, she says, "Can you sit down a minute?"

"The maître d' would frown if I did."

She shoves out her lower lip. "How long can we go on like this?" She sighs.

"What do you mean?" He's having a wonderful time making music with her and the Aces, dreaming about her at night.

"We never spend any time alone together. This is hard on me." She blinks rapidly.

Is she going to cry? He doesn't want her to cry—not here—not while he's working, because he wouldn't be able to do anything to comfort her.

"I just need to be with you, Nate."

What is she asking for? He's happy the way things are. He walks her home every night after their gigs, and their good night kisses are getting longer and deeper. "I don't have a lot of free time right now. We do our job with the Aces on the weekends, and I work here every night during the week. I'm at school all day."

"Can't you take some afternoon off? I get done waitressing at Peter's Grill at three."

"The afternoons I'm not in class, I work as a lab assistant for Dr. Schmitt."

"What about Sunday? You aren't at school on Sundays, are you?"

"That's the one day I have for studying and doing my laundry and buying groceries and taking care of things."

"I could help you do laundry and get groceries, and I'm a good cook."

"Okay, how about you come over to my place around three on Sunday?"

"It's a date," she replies, upending her glass.

Bowing, he retreats.

～

When Dorie arrives at his door Sunday afternoon, she has a package in her hand, which she thrusts at him. He pulls out a bag of peanuts and a bottle of Four Roses whiskey. Putting them down on a nearby table, he draws her into his arms. She is so petite that he feels quite manly as he envelops her. It feels so good to hold a girl again. This reminds him how much he enjoyed dancing with Emma. He should write a song about the dances at the girls' school. He could call it "Friday Night at Abbot."

He removes her coat. She's wearing a yellow dress with white buttons down the front. He puts his arms back around her.

"Your hair is like the color of gold."

"Thanks." She leans back as if to see him more fully. "I don't know what kind of whiskey you like."

"It doesn't matter." He kisses her hard, and as the kiss continues, he eases up a little.

She sags against him. "So sweet," she moans.

When he pulls away, he's breathing like a racehorse that's just finished the course. "You're so beautiful."

"So are you," she replies, running her finger down his cheek.

"I think about you a lot," he admits.

"You're always on my mind," she says.

"Shall we sit down?"

"I'd like a drink," she says.

She follows him into his tiny kitchen area and watches him put ice in two short glasses he'd bought at the five and dime store. As he pours a couple of fingers of Four Roses into each glass, she says, "Just a splash of water in mine."

When she sits on the bed, which is covered with a piece of fabric to make it seem more like a couch, he moves over to his record player. Taking a record out of its cover and sleeve, he places the disc on the turntable; then he delicately drops the tone arm down. The sound of stringed instruments fills the room.

"Nice sound," she says.

He sits next to her. After the first cut, he asks, "What did you think?"

"I thought the solo went on a little too long."

"Really? I thought the sax solo was the best part."

"Actually, Nate, I prefer ballads."

"I thought you'd like this album because most of the tunes originally included vocals, so they're songs you must be familiar with."

"What is this album?"

"It's *Parker with Strings*. You know Charlie Parker's music?"

"I don't think so."

"Charlie Parker is the most amazing musician I've ever heard. He's created a whole new kind of jazz, improvising over the chord changes around the melody. His flatted fifths and his speed and his ideas—he has such great ideas, he knocks me out!"

"The tune you just played was too speedy. It made me nervous." She kicks off her high heels.

"My sister says bebop is too fast for her too. You prefer swing?"

"Of course."

"Who are some of your favorite singers?"

"Billie Holliday and Bessie Smith. But enough chatter."

She moves her hand to the back of his neck and starts massaging the muscles there. He strokes the top of her thigh as they listen to the Charlie Parker album for a few more minutes. When Parker plays "April in Paris," she hums along. "I love that tune," she says. "Have you ever heard Billie Holiday sing 'April in Paris'?"

"Sure, but I'd like to hear *you* sing it."

She stands up. "Why don't you play too?"

He opens his case and pulls out his alto sax. He wets his reed, inserts it into the mouthpiece, and readjusts it. They start playing together. When she sings the line "What have you done to my heart," she reaches her arm out to him invitingly. He fumbles the next few notes but then recovers. They sound pretty darn good.

Suddenly he can see himself leading his own band with her alongside. *This is my dream—it's coming true at last!* He says, "We should work that up for the Aces."

"Yes, let's," she agrees. "A little later." She takes his saxophone away from him and places it back in its case. As she hums "I'm in the Mood for Love," she draws him back to the sofa bed. Sliding her arms around his shoulders, she kisses him softly and then with greater and greater intensity. Eventually, she pulls him over so they are lying next to each other. And after a while she repositions herself in such a way that he is lying on top of her. Mr. Snake is fully aroused, pressing down on her.

"Whoa," he says, scared he's going to lose control. He's never gone this far with a girl before. He rolls off her and sits up. He'd better buy some rubbers before next Sunday. He reaches for the package of Kent cigarettes in his breast pocket, places it on the table holding their drinks, and lights up.

Resuming her seat, she pulls her skirt down to cover her knees. "Boy, that was nice!"

Exhaling, he says, "I almost got carried away there." He crosses one leg over the other.

"That would be all right with me."

He clears his throat. "Would you like a cigarette? I've got this new brand."

"No thanks. The only time I tried a cigarette it hurt my throat and made me cough. My voice is the best thing I have going for me—I don't want to wreck it."

"You have a lot going for you, Dorie."

"Not really. My mother always told me that looks don't last."

"You haven't mentioned your mother before. Where does she live?"

"In Glendale, out in western Minnesota."

"Do you see her often?"

"I take the bus out sometimes when I'm between gigs. I send her money every week, though."

"Good for you."

"I have to. Mom's sick. She needs whatever I can do for her."

Touched by what a loving daughter she is, he crushes out his cigarette and turns to put his arms around her. "You're wonderful," he says, hugging her. "I'm so glad the Aces decided to add a vocalist. We've had to expand our repertoire, and that's been a little tough, but it's paying off. Our crowds get larger every week."

"Audiences like vocal music. It's easier to follow. Unlike your Charlie Parker."

From then on they spend every Sunday afternoon alone at his place together.

∾

By early December, Nat asks Dorie to come east with him to meet his family. They'll leave on December 21, the day after his commencement ceremony.

"I'd love to see New York! But what should I wear?" she cries.

"It doesn't matter. You're so beautiful that's all they'll see."

"I don't want to embarrass myself by showing up in the wrong clothes. Please come to Dayton's with me."

"I don't know anything about women's clothing."

"I bet you do."

When she emerges from the dressing room in one outfit after another, he's surprised to discover that he does have a pretty good idea which ensemble his sister would wear and which she wouldn't. He helps her pay for a few new things, using some of the money his mother sent him to fund his travel home.

The next Sunday afternoon as they sit on his couch, she plies him with questions about his family. She seems nervous but excited by the prospect of meeting them.

"Usually I get along with older men, but your father sounds scary."

He takes her hand. "Don't worry about him. I'm sure you'll charm everyone. Abba will love you—she's my musical grandmother. And I really want you to meet Peter, my best friend. He lives in New York City now. I hope we can see him while we're there."

∾

When Nat and Dorie enter the Café de la Paix at St. Moritz on the Park in Manhattan, the restaurant where Peter suggested they meet for dinner, he feels proud to have her on his arm. She's wearing a new black suit and a perky yellow hat that's perched on top of her head. He noticed all sorts of men giving her a second look as they walked along Sixth Avenue on their way here.

Scanning the room, he spots Peter waving from a table in the corner. Peter stands as they approach. He looks very snappy in a navy blue pinstripe suit, and he's taller and thinner than he was at Andover.

The men shake hands and then Nat turns to her. "Dorie, this is Peter Chase, my roommate at Andover. Peter, this is Dorie Larson, the greatest jazz singer in the Twin Cities."

"Nice to meet you, Peter," she purrs. "Nate never mentioned how handsome you are." She bats her eyelashes at Peter. His eyes are on Nat.

Nat pulls out a chair for her, and then he takes the place between them.

Turning to his former roommate, Nat grins. "You look awfully spiffy, Peter! It's been way too long since we've seen each other. You must have grown six inches since June '46."

Peter's thick brown hair is longer than most men wear, and he's sporting a surprisingly colorful tie with his white shirt and sober suit. He says, "You're skin and bones, Nat, but I can see you're happy now that you have a regular job playing jazz."

"I am happy. We're making hot music these days." He glances over at Dorie, who has picked up the menu on the plate in front of her. He turns back to his friend. "Your letters over the years have meant the world to me, Peter. You know me so well." So well that after he made it clear at Andover that he wasn't interested in anything physical with Peter, they actually grew even closer.

"We went through a lot together at school. There's nothing quite like that bond."

"We amuse each other," Nat says. He tells Dorie, "Peter's the cartoonist I told you about. He's the one who came up with a cartoon character named Sammy Phillips, a typical Andover student except that he wore a necktie for a belt."

Peter laughs. "Using a necktie for a belt was actually *your* idea, Nat."

"Really? I don't remember that."

Peter looks over to her. "Sammy Phillips was a slob, Dorie. He was a way for me to comment on the pretensions of Andover students."

She gazes at Peter with a blank look on her face.

Nat asks, "Are you still creating cartoons?"

"Not anymore. I took classes in figure construction and painting and composition at Cornell, and I really enjoyed learning more about drawing figures but found I have no aptitude for captions. Once I figured that out, I decided I'd better get serious about something that would land me a job."

"You were really talented!" Nat says. "I thought you'd be famous someday."

"I wasn't good enough," Peter replies.

"You would be if you kept at it."

"I don't think so. It was fun to draw cartoons when I was a kid, but I have to make a living now."

A waiter in a white shirt and black trousers appears to take their drink orders. Peter orders a Manhattan. Nat and Dorie ask for the same.

"When in Rome . . ." Nat remarks.

Dorie fingers the frilly material along the neckline of her blouse. Clearing her throat, she says, "What exactly do you do, Peter?"

Nat smiles inwardly. On the train into town, he encouraged Dorie to ask Peter questions instead of simply sitting back listening to the conversation that swirled around her, the way she'd been doing with his family. She's never been outside Minnesota before this trip, and he figures she must be intimidated by it all.

"I'm very lucky. I got a position as an apprentice of sorts to the curator of drawings at the Museum of Modern Art. I've been at MoMA for eighteen months now."

"That's really impressive, Peter," says Nat. "You must have been the top art major at Cornell to get an opportunity like that."

Peter turns back to Nat. "The art department at Cornell is first rate, and they have a gallery in Willard Straight Hall that features exhibitions of works by leading contemporary artists. Thanks to my professors, I was able to start understanding modern art."

Nat asks, "Who are your favorite modern artists?"

"Braque, Picasso, Mondrian. Most of all I like the paintings and prints of Klee and Miro—they're so whimsical."

Their drinks arrive.

She says, "What's it like to live here in New York City?"

"The city is fabulous!" Peter gushes. "There's more to see and do than I have time for. The shops and the restaurants are top notch, and the art scene is simply amazing—there's so much going on all the time, day and night."

Peter touches Nat's wrist and asks, "What about you, my friend? What are your plans now that you've graduated from college?"

"At last I can pursue my passion. Dorie and I are having so much fun playing with the Aces. We're thinking about starting our own combo once we've built up a nest egg. Dorie is such a wonderful singer; audiences love her. When we get back next week, I'll start hitting the clubs on Hennepin Avenue and the near north side of town to see where I can sit in with other groups. I know cats who work every night of the week, and I need to do that too."

She places her hand on his arm. She tells Peter, "Nate is a great improviser. Audiences go wild over his solos."

Turning to Nat, Peter says, "Nate?"

Embarrassed, he looks down for an instant. "That's what Dorie calls me."

Peter says, "I'm not surprised to hear what a good musician you are, Nat. I remember being floored by the job you did playing the piano for that Gilbert and Sullivan show at Andover, and you were just a junior then."

"I really enjoyed playing for *Pirates of Penzance*."

"I wish you all the luck in the world," Peter says, his face shining with sincerity.

Their food arrives. After tucking her napkin into her blouse, Dorie picks up her knife and fork. Nat almost says something about keeping her napkin on her lap, but he stops himself. They start to eat.

Once they've taken a few bites, Nat asks Peter, "Tell me more about your life here."

"I've made some real friends—guys who like many of the same things I do." He turns toward Dorie. "Nat taught me to appreciate

Gilbert and Sullivan. Now I enjoy the offerings on Broadway. I adore musicals. I saw *Guys and Dolls* recently, and last week it was *The King and I*, which was fantastic."

"Do you ever go to the jazz clubs around here? Nate tells me there's a whole lot going on around Fifty-Second Street and up in Harlem. I wish him and me could go hear what they're up to."

Nat flinches at her saying "him and me," but he's not going to correct her in front of Peter. She hasn't had the benefit of a fancy education like he did. "We've got to get back home after dinner. Mother's waiting up for us."

Peter replies, "I've tried a few clubs. I like swing music more than bebop."

"Me too," Dorie agrees.

Nat's thrilled to see his best friend and his girl getting along so well. He asks, "How are your parents and your sister?"

"They're fine. My parents are still up in Norwich, but sister Laura is here. She got married last summer to a good guy who's in advertising. They live in an apartment downtown."

Dorie is focused on her food, but when Peter adds, "She's going to have a baby," Dorie looks up.

Nat says, "It must be nice to have your sister nearby."

"It is. How is your mother doing, Nat? Has she gotten over Eddie?"

"I'm not sure she'll ever get over losing Eddie."

"I'm so sorry, Nat. I bet it's still tough for you too."

"Fortunately I have someone new to think about now." He takes Dorie's hand and gives it a squeeze, watching her intently. She smiles back at him. He turns to Peter. "And you, do you have a special friend?"

"Not yet, but I have high hopes."

Spearing a leaf of endive and lifting it toward his mouth, Nat says, "What do you think about the USSR's performing its first nuclear test this fall?"

"Terrifying. But I was interested to read in the *Times* about Walter

Zinn's experimental nuclear reactor for the production of electric power going live last week."

As the men carry on their conversation, Dorie doesn't say anything until she finishes her fillet of sole and mushrooms in choux pastry.

"That was the best fish I ever put in my mouth!"

Peter says, "I'm glad you liked it. This place is new, but the reviews have been fabulous."

"What's with your tie, Peter?" Nat chuckles so Peter will know he's teasing. "I bet you bought that tie knowing you'd spill on it, but with a pattern that wild nothing will show. Am I right?"

"Bull's-eye!"

"I know how you think."

"I'd love to show you around the Museum of Modern Art if you have time this week."

"Unfortunately we have to leave the day after tomorrow, but I'll count on a tour with you next time."

Over dessert, the men discuss former classmates and teachers from Andover while Dorie sips her coffee.

When the check comes, Nat insists he'll take care of it. He explains, "I won a big bet with my mother, and she paid me handsomely."

While they don their coats, Peter says, "What do you think of New York, Dorie?"

"I thought I'd like it, but this city is really noisy and dirty."

Peter laughs. "It is that!"

Outside the restaurant, he shakes her hand and then he turns to Nat. "Let's not let it be so long next time, my friend." He and Nat hug. Dorie turns away from them and stares at the street.

Once Dorie and Nat are walking along the south side of Central Park, he asks, "Did you have a good time?"

She takes his arm. "Why is Peter so possessive of you?"

"He's not possessive. We're just friends, the best of friends. *You're* something more." He stops walking. They turn to face each other, and he kisses her lightly on the mouth. Then he slides his arm around her waist and they continue down West Fifty-Ninth Street.

She says, "I could tell he doesn't like me. He hardly talked to me at all."

"Peter's shy around women. It has nothing to do with you."

"Hmm." She sounds skeptical.

∾

The next night as Nat and Dorie and George and Eleanor leave the dinner table, his father tells him he'd like to speak with him in his study. First Nat refreshes his mother's and Dorie's drinks and brings them to the parlor.

"I'll be back soon," he tells Dorie.

"Don't worry about ush," slurs Eleanor. "We'll have a nish chat here, jus ush ladiesh."

Nat heads down the hall, wondering, *Now what?* He opens the solid mahogany door to the room where his father usually chews him out.

Nat would like this room if it weren't for its unpleasant associations. Two walls are lined with books from floor to ceiling, windows without curtains look out onto the back meadow, and the fourth wall features a large fireplace and an oil painting of the ocean with two tiny sailboats in the distance.

His father stands behind his desk, looking down at some papers.

"Take a seat," he instructs Nat, gesturing to two old leather chairs facing the crackling fire.

Once they're both seated, George turns to Nat. "What are your plans, Nathaniel, now that you've attained your bachelor's degree? What's next?"

Nat leans forward. "One of my buddies in the Aces has a friend who has a friend in the recording business. If we get good enough, maybe we'll be able to make a record. After a while we might even come join the jazz scene in New York."

"Your mother would certainly like it if you were to move back to this area."

"Speaking of Mother, she's gotten loaded every night we've been here. I'm really worried about her. Is there anything we can do?"

His father shakes his head. "I don't know what to do. She stops for a while, and then she goes back to it with a vengeance."

"I don't even like to talk to her when she's loaded."

His father nods, a very sad look on his face. He pulls out a cigarette and lights up. "In the meantime, how do you plan on supporting yourself?"

"I'm going to go around to all the jazz clubs in the Twin Cities to see where I can sit in. Maybe there's a combo we can join that plays every night of the week, rather than just weekends, the way the Aces do. And of course there's my teaching at the St. Joseph's School of Music."

"How much do you get paid with the Aces?"

"Thirty dollars a week."

"What does your housing cost?"

"Seventy-five dollars a month."

"And food? Transportation?"

He starts to feel impatient with this line of questioning. Doesn't his father trust him to take care of himself? He's been managing on his own for four years now. "I'll figure it out, Father. I can always work more hours at the Radisson Hotel. I make enough money there. They like me a lot. My boss says I have good manners, and he can count on me to show up when I'm scheduled to work."

"I should hope so."

"They've offered me the position of host, but I don't want to commit to that. I mean to play sax every night of the week. Some jazz cats in town have that much work."

George crosses his right leg over his left. "What about Dorie? How long have you known her?"

"Three months."

"What are your intentions toward her?"

Sitting up even straighter, he says proudly, "Once I'm earning enough to support us both, I plan to ask her to marry me."

"That's what I was afraid of. I've seen how you look at her, Nathaniel. Don't let her trap you."

What is his father talking about?

"What happens if she gets pregnant?"

"We're careful."

"What kind of name is Dorie, anyway?"

"Her real name is Dorothy, but she never goes by that."

"Dorie is a looker all right, but she's not our kind."

Nat starts drumming his fingers on his leg "I know she's not sophisticated, Father, but she's a hard worker. She's very practical— salt of the earth."

"I mean she isn't bright."

Angrily, he replies, "She's very smart! Just because she didn't go to Smith doesn't mean she's stupid."

"She may have street smarts, but she didn't attend college."

"She had to go to work to help support her mother!"

"You would get bored with her before the first year is out."

Nat crosses his arms in front of his chest. "She's a talented musician. We share everything we care about."

His father shakes his head. "You're so smitten you can't even see straight. You don't hear a word I say."

"You're wrong about Dorie."

His father looks intently at him. "Please don't marry her, Nathaniel. You'll regret it for the rest of your life if you do."

His gut flinches, but he's used to disagreeing with his father. "You don't know me. You don't know what makes me happy."

"Oh, yes I do." His father sounds confident.

His voice low and furious, Nat says, "I'm nothing like you."

"Ha!" his father exclaims.

"There's no point in continuing this discussion. I just wish you could be happy for me. I'm finally happy!"

⟡

A few days after they get back to Minneapolis, Dorie appears at the Flame Room in the middle of the afternoon while he's at work. Wearing her new suit and hat, she smiles broadly at him as Nat seats her and takes her order for coffee and a piece of cake.

When he returns with her food, she says, "I have some news." Her eyes are shining. He thinks she must have landed them a new jazz gig. "We're going to have a baby, Nate."

His heart drops into his stomach. He sinks into the chair opposite her. This is way too soon! "How did you get pregnant?"

"How do you think?" She seems tickled by his question.

"But I thought you were using a diaphragm. We discussed that." He feels a momentary sense of panic, which he quickly dismisses. He loves her! It's just that this is going to complicate things.

She looks down. "Actually, I got fitted before we . . . went all the way. After a while I guess I must have gotten bigger down there, so it didn't fit tight."

Scrambling to think what to do, he asks, "How long have you known?"

"I suspected I was pregnant a few weeks ago. I went to see a doctor as soon as we got back from New Jersey. He confirmed my suspicions today. The rabbit died."

"What are you talking about?"

"They inject the woman's pee into a rabbit, and if the rabbit shows certain signs after a couple of days, they know the woman is pregnant." She starts tapping her index finger on the table. She has long red nails, which have always looked exotic to him.

"You're sure, then?"

"Yes!" she says fiercely. "Aren't you pleased, Nate?"

"Of course. You caught me by surprise, that's all."

"Well . . ." She looks expectant in more ways than one.

He takes a deep breath. "We'd better get married as soon as possible."

∽

WESTERN UNION

MINNEAPOLIS MIN 600P JAN 7 1952

MR. AND MRS. GEORGE SUTTON

1808 BRIARWOOD LANE PLAINWOOD NJ

DORIE AND I TIED THE KNOT TODAY AT MPLS CITY

HALL NAT

April 1953

"You're pregnant again?" Nat is beside himself with fury. "I thought we were going to wait until I have more steady club work!"

Dorie sits on the sagging sofa in their tiny furnished efficiency while he stands a foot away by their kitchen table. Baby Abby sleeps in her crib in the corner. WCCO radio is playing in the background.

"Well, you know how these things happen, sweetie," she says in a seductive tone of voice. She doesn't seem worried at all. "All I have to do is squeeze my muscles inside there and hold on while you're coming and . . . bingo."

"You haven't been using your diaphragm?"

"Everyone's having babies these days."

"We're not everyone."

"Abby needs a sister or brother who's close to her age."

"But we agreed!"

"We did not. You said what you thought. I never agreed."

"Are you sure you're pregnant?"

"I haven't seen the doctor yet, but I felt like this the last time I was pregnant."

"We don't have room for another baby."

"Babies don't take up much room. Besides, I like being pregnant. People treat me with respect when they see that I'm pregnant. Strangers open doors for me and ask me when the baby's due. Men take off their hats. Women tell me stories about their own experiences with morning sickness and weight gain and labor—usually ladies aren't that nice to me."

"We can't afford a larger apartment, Dorie."

Raising her right eyebrow, she says, "Maybe your parents would give us a loan."

"I am not asking them! Don't you understand? I've been preparing for a career as a jazz musician my whole life! I started playing music when I was five years old, and I wanted to go to music school right after Andover! But Father wouldn't let me. Wanting to play music led me to defy my father, and when he sentenced me to labor in that mill in Northfield, I vowed I would never ask him for help again. You know this!" Nat's voice has grown so loud that he's shouting.

Abby starts to wail. Rising quickly, Dorie goes over to pick up the baby.

He resumes speaking more quietly. "Do I have to fight you too? Now, when I'm finally making headway with the club owners in this town, you're telling me you're pregnant? Again!" He pounds the oil-cloth-covered table with his fist. Then he sits abruptly in one of the two metal chairs at the table. He has fought so hard for this dream, and she's not helping him move toward it. Dorie loves jazz, so he assumed she would embrace his dream along with him. He covers his eyes.

Dorie sways gently back and forth with the baby in her arms, humming softly, and soon Abby stops crying. After a couple of minutes, Dorie puts the baby back in her crib.

He says, "I don't see how we're going to manage."

"If you won't ask your parents, how about your grandmother? I bet she'd be happy to help us."

"Father would have my head if I asked Abba for money. Besides, Mother says Abba's not doing well."

Dorie comes over to him and kneels down. Putting her arms

around his back, she says, "It doesn't matter. I won't mind living here with two babies. We'll be cozy. This is our very own place—I've never had a place all my own. We'll be fine."

"I don't know." He feels nearly claustrophobic in their efficiency as it is—this apartment is so crowded with stuff he can scarcely breathe. Adding another baby and more bottles and diapers and clothing and toys? It's unimaginable.

Over the following months Nat hustles every club owner in town for more gigs, but he can't seem to get enough work to make a decent living. He starts to wonder whether he's been naïve. Perhaps he's not a good enough musician to play professionally—maybe that's why he isn't getting more jobs and a higher rate of pay.

To augment his income, he continues working as a lab assistant for his former biology professor Dr. Schmitt. The Radisson gives him as many hours of work as he can handle, but that's not a job that's going to get him anywhere. Dr. Schmitt thinks Nat should go to medical school. He did well in his biology and chemistry classes at the U, and he does enjoy having his brain engaged with scientific questions.

The idea of giving up his dream absolutely breaks his heart.

At the same time, there's the reality of a second child on the way, a wife, and a tiny apartment. He's twenty-five years old now. Perhaps he should consider a serious profession in which he can care for his family in a manner that's similar to his own upbringing. Doesn't he owe his children that much?

He decides it's time for him to become a man.

August 8, 1953

Dear Father and Mother,

I am writing to let you know that I have very reluctantly come to the conclusion that I have to give up my dreams of working as a professional jazz musician. Since graduating from the university I have pursued every possible opportunity to play sax in clubs around the Twin Cities. It seems a lot of the clubs aren't really interested in modern jazz; they prefer Dixieland, which is terribly disappointing.

I have done absolutely everything I can think of to get enough work, but I simply cannot earn enough to take proper care of my family. You see, we're expecting another child, and Dorie no longer sings in the clubs—she stays home with Abby. Dorie loves being pregnant, and she really wants to have a large family, which I can understand since she was an only child herself.

I am very sad to have to reach this decision, but it's something of a relief as well. I'm so damned tired of hitting my head against a wall. Ultimately I've come to see that my pursuit of music is self-indulgent. It's time for me to grow up and act like a responsible husband and father.

You were right, Father. I'll never make a living as a musician.

I want to do something that is needed, something that helps others. I want to acquire a body of knowledge that will really make a difference in the world.

The good news is that I've been accepted into the medical school here at the University of Minnesota. I just completed the final prerequisite this summer, a course in organic chemistry. Harriet would be proud—I aced it. Minnesota's medical school is absolutely top notch—the world's first successful open-heart surgery was performed here at the university last year. I'm very excited that I got in. And once I'm a full-fledged physician, I won't ever have to worry about being able to earn a good living.

Father, I imagine you're wondering how I can afford to go to medical school when I have a family to support. I will continue to play my sax for paying gigs where I can—I won't give up music entirely! I'll keep working at the Radisson as much as possible. I will work as a lab assistant for my biology professor Dr. Schmitt, and I've applied to the medical school for financial aid. I get a break on fees since I'm a Minnesota resident. With classes and studying and working I'll be awfully busy—fortunately I don't need much sleep.

Dorie and I live very modestly in a $75/month efficiency apartment, which is adjacent to the campus. We don't own a car. Sometimes I'm able to bring home leftover food from the Radisson, which helps. We eat a lot of peanut butter and soup.

Mother and Father, I am writing to you now with my hat in my hand. Would you be willing to invest in my education as I work my way through medical school? Fees for the first year are $736, which includes a one-time charge of $300 for a microscope. I would pay you back as soon as I start earning a decent salary. I don't know exactly how much money I might need to borrow because I don't know how many hours I'll be able to work once I'm immersed in medical school.

Please telephone once you've had a chance to consider my request.

Love,
Nathaniel

The following Sunday, the phone rings on the kitchen counter in their apartment. Dorie answers.

"Hello. Yes, Father Sutton. He's right here."

Nat takes the receiver. "Father?"

"Nathaniel. Your mother is still at Sea View or she'd be in on this call as well. I am proud of you for getting into the university's medical school, and most of all I applaud your decision to become a physician. You've finally chosen a path that makes sense."

Briefly he bridles at his father's words, but he keeps his mouth shut.

"Of course we will help you financially."

"Oh, Father, thank you. That's such a relief!"

"Your mother will be delighted to hear that another grandchild is on the way. With two children, you'll need a larger place in which to live, so you should move as soon as you can. You'll need some kind of car too. We'll figure out the financial details after you send me a budget detailing your income and expenses."

Before he can finish reiterating his thanks, his father hangs up in his usual brusque manner. Putting the receiver back in its cradle, he grabs Dorie and dances her around the room. "We're going to be all right, Dorie!"

An hour later his mother calls. "Nat! Your father just read me your letter over the phone. I am so happy Abby will be getting a sister or brother—that's grand news! And I couldn't be more pleased to hear you're going into medicine."

"Thank you, Mother. I'm glad too."

"I guess you take after your old mother after all. Though I always thought you were the spitting image of your father."

"Really?" He's like his father? "How are things at Sea View?"

"Fine, everyone's fine. When do I get to see you? Can you come home for Christmas?"

"I don't know. I'll have to see what sort of flexibility I have once I'm in med school."

"I'll send you money for airplane tickets."

"That would help."

"When is the baby due?"

"Sometime in January."

"Dorie can't fly that close to her due date. Let's plan on the next year then."

❧

WESTERN UNION

ELIZABETH NJ 430P MAR 13 1954

MR. NATHANIEL SUTTON

825 FOURTH STREET SE MINNEAPOLIS MN

MY MOTHER HAD A STROKE AND DIED LAST NIGHT NO MEMORIAL SERVICE PER HER INSTRUCTIONS FATHER

❧

January 23, 1956

Dear Nat,

I miss you. I wish you could see my children—Retta and Joey are growing so quickly! Retta loves numbers and jigsaw puzzles. And Joey can already read. It was great to see you and Dorie and Abby and to meet Ned for the first time when you came home for Christmas last year. I wish you'd bring your family to Sea View so our children can get to know each other better. Even if you can't come yourself, why not send Dorie with Abby and Ned? We would take good care of them.

Mother reports that you're working your fanny off at medical school. I hope you're glad to be on this path now. I must

admit that I feel envious—I would love to be learning about the latest discoveries in science and medicine.

It's been nearly seven years since I stopped working. After staying home to raise my children, I'm beginning to feel my brain atrophy. I want something more than just taking care of my husband, children, and home. Retta attends school seven hours a day now, and Joey will start first grade next fall. It's time for me to get out of the house and do something really challenging. I'm ready to become a member of the workforce again.

I wouldn't go back to Sutton Chemical. I was trying to fill in for Eddie by working for Father, but I really couldn't take his place. Besides, I learned that making money for the company didn't provide me with the sense of satisfaction that I had doing research at Madison. I guess business isn't my cup of tea. I might have been happier working at the Rockefeller Institute when I had the opportunity, but that's all water under the bridge now.

I've started to wonder about teaching chemistry in one of the private schools nearby. Perhaps Hartley could use a new science teacher next fall, or maybe your alma mater would.

When I told Ron I was thinking about going into teaching, he raised all sorts of objections. He works hard at his office in Manhattan, and usually he doesn't even get home before seven—he's ready to put his feet up as soon as he gets here. He likes to find his martini ready and dinner in the oven so we can eat together as soon as the children are in bed. He doesn't want to have to wait. Only one of the wives in the couples we're closest to has a job, and Ron looks down on her husband for allowing that. He feels it reflects badly on the husband's ability to provide for his family. I pointed out that being a teacher would give me much the same schedule as the children, with weeks off at Christmas and Easter, and the whole summer free.

Before I agreed to marry Ron, I made sure he felt comfortable about my continuing to work. I don't know whether he's changed his tune based on what he sees his peers doing or whether he wasn't quite truthful during our courtship.

I don't know what more I can say to convince Ron that this would benefit our family because it would be good for me. If I have to insist, I will.

Am I thinking straight, Nat? Being a mother seems to have softened my mind. I believe I need to do something with my life beyond simply being a wife and mother. I want to try something new—make a fresh start—and I think teaching might be just the ticket. I'd really like to hear your thoughts.

Please get in touch, Nat.

Lots of love,
Harry

∾

February 1, 1956
Dear Harry,

You would make a GREAT teacher! When we were together last Christmas, I admired the way you were constantly explaining things to your children as well as to mine. You asked lots of questions, making the kids observe and think, and you stimulated their curiosity. You're so much more patient with them than Dorie is.

Yes, you should definitely become a teacher! I can't wait to hear more.

Love,
Nat

September 1958

Harriet was thrilled when she was offered the job to teach general science in the middle school at Hartley, the day school she attended as a girl, for the '56/'57 school year. Last spring when Hartley's upper school chemistry teacher retired, she'd applied and was hired for that position. She'd spent the summer preparing for her new classes.

Now it's after ten at night. Harriet and Ron sit on each end of the sofa in their living room. Harriet is reading the *New York Times* while Ron looks at *Forbes*. The children are asleep in their rooms.

Ron gets up and stumbles a bit as he heads toward the bar on a table in the corner.

"Please don't have another drink, Ron. Let's go to bed now." She stands and puts her arms around his shoulders. "I'll give you a treat if you come with me now." Usually this works. They make love frequently, with great satisfaction. Aside from their children, sex is their strongest bond.

This time, he extricates himself from her hold. "I'll be up soon."

Although she's tired, she sits back down. She's glad to see he poured himself only half a glass of Scotch this time.

She says, "I think we should lock up the liquor from now on. I don't want Retta and Joey experimenting when we're not around."

"They're way too young to get into anything like that."

"They're growing up quickly." *If the bottles are out of sight, maybe they'll be out of Ron's mind.*

"Go ahead, if you wish."

"I'll take care of it."

Once they're under the covers, he says, "I might be late tomorrow night. The partners are throwing a little retirement party for Tim Mulcahy. He didn't want a splashy event, so spouses aren't included."

"That's fine—I'll be busy grading lab reports."

"You're always busy, Harriet."

"I love working, Ron. You know that." Is he trying to get her to quit her job?

"It just doesn't reflect well on me. People could think you have to work because I don't earn enough money."

"Why would you care what people think?"

"I have to look successful to attract new clients."

"Don't your new Cadillac and fancy suits and membership at the country club convey success?"

"To become a senior partner at Smith Barney, I need to bring in more business than I have lately."

"You will, Ron. You listen really well, you respect your clients, and you're completely ethical. You just have to be patient." Patience isn't one of his strong points. She believes that because success came so easily to him at school and in sports, he hasn't acquired much grit. She isn't worried about his success in his profession—he's smart and he's charming and he really likes people.

"I need to find a huge new account."

"Thanks for letting me know you'll be late tomorrow. Usually you don't warn me ahead of time, so when you're not home by seven thirty, I just go ahead and eat supper by myself. That's been happening a lot recently."

"You know I need to entertain my customers and friends at the club."

"I know."

"Maybe I should join Rotary. That might bring in some new contacts."

"Good idea."

∾

The next night, it's one in the morning when Ron finally drives into their garage. Waiting in the living room, Harriet rises after a few minutes and goes out to see why he hasn't come into the house yet. The Cadillac is running and the garage door is still open. He's slumped forward over the steering wheel. She opens the car door and leans over to turn off the ignition. She shakes his shoulder.

"Come on, Ron, wake up. You need to come inside."

He lurches back against the seat.

"Come on, I'll help." She pulls him out of the car and then puts his arm around her so she can help support him into the house. She tries to be kind, but she really hates it when he gets like this.

∾

A month later, Harriet hurries home from the weekly after-school staff meeting at Hartley to relieve her mother, who picks Retta and Joey up from their schools every Wednesday and feeds them at her own house before driving them home. Eleanor claims to have more fun alone with her grandchildren than when their parents are around. Ron is out of town on business.

When she gets into the house, she finds her mother in the kitchen at the stove heating milk. Setting her books and papers on the counter, she asks, "Where are the kids?"

Eleanor murmurs, "They're upstairs in your bathroom. I've just been cleaning them up." She won't look Harriet in the face.

Harriet moves in close. "What happened, Mother?"

"We had a little accident on the drive over here."

"What!"

"I ran into a truck. We weren't going fast. I'd just turned my attention away for a second to look at what Joey was doing."

"The children were hurt?"

"Retta has a gash where her head banged into the dashboard, but she doesn't need stitches. You know how those head wounds bleed!"

"Joey?"

"He says his shoulder has 'an owie' but I couldn't see anything when I removed his shirt. They're both going to be fine."

Harriet leans in even closer to her mother. "How much did you have to drink before you drove my children over here? I can smell booze on your breath."

"I only had one drink, Harriet."

She doesn't believe that. "Mother!" she explodes. She's so furious she's shaking "How could you endanger my children like that!"

"I'm sorry. I'm so very sorry. I won't drink when I'm around the children. I'll quit drinking entirely."

Turning away, Harriet races up the stairs.

ᐭ

Once the children are in bed asleep, Harriet telephones Nat to tell him about the accident.

"The kids are all right, but we've got to do something about Mother's drinking. Does medicine have any answers for this?"

"I'll make some inquiries," Nat says. "We should talk to Father too."

"I'll telephone him tomorrow at the office."

ᐭ

Two weeks later, Harriet tells her mother she'd like to stop by before lunch on Saturday. After she picks Nat up at the Newark airport, they drive to their parents' house, where George awaits them.

When she and Nat walk in the front door, she calls, "Mother, where are you?"

"We're in the parlor, dearie."

Silently Nat follows Harriet down the hall and into the parlor.

"Nat!" exclaims Eleanor. "I didn't know you were coming for a visit." She rises from the couch and goes over to hug him.

"I'm not here for a visit, Mother."

"Then what are you doing here?" Her surprise quickly fades to a look of fear. "What's going on? I thought Harriet was coming over to tell us that Retta and Joey could expect a new brother or sister before long."

Harriet says, "I'm afraid that's not what this is about, Mother."

"What *is* this about?"

Her father looks at Nat and Harriet, then at her mother. "Sit down, Eleanor," he says. He sounds grim.

Taking a chair, Eleanor asks, "What's happened?"

"Nothing . . . yet," he replies.

"What? What is going on?"

George says, "We're here to talk with you about your drinking, Eleanor. It has gotten completely out of control. You aren't yourself any longer."

Eleanor crosses her legs and wraps her arms around her chest.

He goes on. "You embarrass me in front of our friends. You're more interested in your next drink than in anything else. Booze has gotten to be more important to you than your family, your husband . . ."

Harriet interrupts. "The accident you had with Retta and Joey was the last straw, Mother. I can't trust you with my children. I hate to have to say that, but it's true. I can't let you endanger the lives of my children." She's on the verge of tears but she controls herself.

Eleanor leans forward intently. "I know, Harriet. I'm sorrier than I can ever say. I told you I promise not to drink when I'm around them."

George clears his throat. "You've made promises and quit drinking dozens of times, Eleanor, but it never lasts."

She's fidgeting now with what looks like shame.

Nat says, "There's a residential rehabilitation center in Minnesota that specializes in treating people who drink too much—it's called Hazelden. They've had great success since they started ten years ago in helping problem drinkers get sober."

"You've been discussing me behind my back. You're ganging up on me!" Angrily she adds, "You're calling me a drunk. I am *not* a drunk!"

Nat continues calmly, "Hazelden has recently opened a facility just for women, called Dia Linn."

"Eleanor," George says, "your children and I are asking you to go to Dia Linn. We believe this is the only way we can recover the woman you used to be, the woman we love, the woman we miss."

Harriet has never heard her father say the word *love*.

"I'll be damned if I'll go!"

Harriet says, "Please, Mother." Now her voice quavers with emotion.

"I can't stand the idea of being shipped off to some residential place, interrupting my life, people knowing I have to go somewhere to take care of some problem. What about an outpatient program? There must be something like that around here."

George replies, "Dr. Barnett is worried about your liver, Eleanor. He thinks Dia Linn is a good idea. It might save your life."

She turns to Nat. "'Et tu, Brute?' Do you think I need to do this?"

His mouth turns down in a deep frown. "I'm afraid I do, Mother. Dia Linn has the best plan of recovery available. We want you to get well."

She stands abruptly. "I need to go to the bathroom." She hurries out.

Harriet looks to her father. "Should I follow her?"

"Yes," he replies.

Her mother has shut the powder room door. Harriet hears her open a cabinet and then, after a pause, a gurgle and a sigh.

"Mother, what are you doing in there?"

"I'm busy."

"I'm coming in." She tries the door but it's locked.

"Leave me alone!"

After Eleanor flushes the toilet, opens the door, and exits, Harriet walks into the little room. She opens the cabinet under the sink and finds a bottle of Old Grand-Dad stashed next to a bottle of Listerine. *This is not good.* She closes the cabinet.

Back in the parlor, her mother stands facing her husband and son. George says, "Eleanor, please sit down."

Her mother says, "I can't go anywhere right now. Agnes and I have been planning the auxiliary gala for months—I couldn't possibly go before the gala is over. The hospital needs the money we'll raise for the physical therapy department. Agnes counts on me."

George uncrosses his legs. "You and Agnes have done yeoman service for the hospital over the last few years—starting the auxiliary, organizing volunteer committees to run the welcome desk and delivery services, the library cart, the gift shop. But now"—he leans forward—"we can't afford to put this off. Nat made a reservation for you to start at Dia Linn tomorrow. You'll fly to Minneapolis with him this afternoon and Nat will drive you to Dellwood tomorrow morning."

She closes her eyes tight. "Please don't make me do this, George."

He comes over to her. Reaching out, he takes her hands in his and pulls her up. "We wouldn't ask it of you, Eleanor, if we didn't believe this program was absolutely necessary."

Tears start to roll down her face. "I don't want to do this. I'm so frightened. What will I do when I'm dying for a drink? Will they put me in a straitjacket? Lock me up?"

Desperately, she scans the faces of each of her children. Finally, she says sadly, "I can't fight all of you."

George puts his arms around her. "You'll get through this, El. I know you have the strength. I'll be here waiting for you to come home." Then he releases her.

Nat sighs.

Harriet jumps to her feet. "Come on, Mother, I'll help you pack."

On their way up the stairs, Harriet says, "I'm sorry to be so tough on you, but I can't cope with having both a mother and a husband who drink too much. Maybe you'll learn some things in Minnesota that will help Ron too."

November 1958

November 10

Dear Harriet,

The first week at Dia Linn was hell. My hands shook terribly and my skin screamed for the soothing effects of booze while my stomach kept threatening to rise up into my throat. It's still nearly impossible for me to stay seated during the interminable meetings with the group of women I've been sentenced to associate with. Everyone is supposed to spill their guts about the heinous things they've done under the influence. I don't belong here with these alcoholics. There's no one at Dia Linn that I have anything in common with.

Has Alice telephoned you? What are my friends back home thinking about my sudden absence? Have they heard the truth about where I've been forced to go? Everyone knows that women drunks are even more despicable and morally depraved than men who drink too much.

I hate everything about Dia Linn, despite the lovely grounds, the tall pines and walking paths, and the beautiful facilities. The place feels like a sanatorium for crazy people, though the doors aren't locked, the windows aren't barred.

I received your letter and letters from Nat and Jessica. George actually sent me a dozen red roses with a card saying

"Thinking of you." That's a first! When each of you children were
born, he gave me a new silk bed jacket. It's almost as though I'm
in the hospital recovering from a serious operation, but what
I'm going through here hurts worse than that, and there's no
one who'll give me morphine or anything else for the pain. I feel
as though I'm a raging beast trapped in a cage.

> *I'm not a degenerate, I am not a bum on Skid Row.*

> *Then what am I?*

> *That question makes me cry. I never meant to drink too*
much, but it's the only thing that makes me feel calm. I need
alcohol to muffle all the horrible feelings swirling inside. I've
been swallowing my grief for so long that it sits like a rock at
the bottom of my gut. My heart hurts so much. If Eddie had
lived, he'd be thirty-three years old now—he'd probably be mar-
ried with children, grandchildren I'll never know. There's no
way to escape my losses now. I just have to sit and cry and cry
and cry. And then at the end of the day, when the light fades, I
long to be home with George.

> > *I want to come home.*

> > *Mother*

∾

November 23

Dear Harriet,

> *I'm still here at Dia Linn.*

> *Every day I'm required to attend three daily lectures on the*
Twelve Steps along with the other patients, but I can't stomach
the steps because they're all about God. I'm supposed to turn my
will and my life over to him, to admit to God the exact nature
of my wrongs, to ask him to remove my shortcomings, to pray
for knowledge of his will for me. I've never been comfortable

with God. I believe in morality and integrity and the Golden Rule, but not in God. Nothing in my life has ever led me to believe in him.

When I complained to my counselor Jane, she asked, "Do you believe in anything greater than yourself, Eleanor?"

Without pausing to think I answered, "Yes, love is greater than anything."

Jane replied, "All right then. Simply substitute Love for God in your mind. When you recite the Twelve Steps silently, use the word Love instead."

This sort of works. Once I started asking myself what Love would have me do with my life, I had something meaningful to think about.

I am beginning to understand that everyone at Dia Linn struggles with anger and fear and grief and shame about their drinking. Finally I am coming to acknowledge that I am just like the others here: I am an alcoholic. We all suffer from the same affliction, while many of the women here have much tougher situations to deal with than I do. That helps me acquire some perspective.

My twenty-eight days in the program will end right after Thanksgiving—I can go home on Saturday, November 29, but I think I'd better stay a few days longer to make sure I'm strong enough to return.

When I get home, I want to start learning everything I can about grief.

Love,
Mother

January 1960

Harriet's very grateful that her mother hasn't had a drink since she came home from Dia Linn. Now Eleanor is involved in a weekly grief group that she started at Plainwood Hospital; she helps to facilitate it along with a licensed social worker, and this seems to bring her a lot of satisfaction. Her father is in the process of seeking a buyer for Sutton Chemical. At age sixty-six, he tells Harriet he wants to set up a philanthropic foundation with the proceeds from the sale.

Retta, eleven years old, is happy to attend the school at which her mother teaches, and Joey is working hard to master his multiplication tables at Warden, the boys' school.

Harriet enjoys teaching chemistry more than she ever imagined she would. Ron seems to be getting on too. He was named a junior partner at Smith Barney a few months ago. The only problem now is *his* drinking. He gets loaded almost every night. After struggling with her mother over alcohol, it seems unfair that she would have to face the same challenge all over again with her husband.

She doesn't wait up for him, but tonight when she hears the garage door open but then no other sounds, she goes down to investigate.

The car is still running but he has passed out.

She turns off the car and reaches in to get him. When they move into the kitchen, he collapses, slamming his head on the ceramic tile floor.

She kneels quickly and tries to rouse him, but he doesn't respond. Terrified now, she leans down to make sure he's still breathing. Then she races for the telephone.

When Eleanor answers, she cries, "Help, Mother! Ron is unconscious—I can't wake him."

"What happened?"

"He just came home really drunk. He fell, hit his head. I've got to get him to the hospital."

"Should I call an ambulance?"

"You'll get here faster. Father can help me move Ron into the car. You stay here with the kids."

"Of course. We'll be right over."

"Please hurry, Mummy!"

After opening the front door, she returns to Ron's side. She takes his hand and squeezes. "I'm here, sweetheart." He reeks of booze. She used to love the smell of his sweat, but she hates this stench of alcohol. *When was the last time he smelled good to her?* Tears threaten to fall but she blinks them back. She needs to stay strong.

When her parents finally arrive, she makes way for her mother, who squats down. Eleanor takes Ron's arm to feel his pulse. Then she slaps his face. No response. She slaps harder. His eyelids flutter.

"Ron," she says, "you need to stand up."

"Wha . . . ?"

"We'll help you to your feet. Come on."

Eleanor and Harriet grab his arms while George puts his hands underneath Ron to lift him up. They walk him out to the Lincoln in the driveway.

George speeds off to the hospital with Ron and Harriet in the back seat. In the emergency room the physician tells Harriet that Ron will need to spend the weekend in the hospital. They'll watch him for signs of concussion.

As she and her father drive back to the house, Harriet says, "It's a relief to leave Ron in a doctor's care for a couple of days." Days she won't have to worry about his drinking. "I don't want the children to see him in this condition."

"That's understandable," George replies.

The next day when she visits Ron in his hospital room, a different physician pulls her aside. "Mr. Wright doesn't seem to have suffered a concussion, but you'll want to pay attention to any symptoms of delirium tremens after he leaves here."

"What symptoms?"

"Tremors. Agitation. Confusion."

"Is there some treatment for DTs?"

"We prescribe paraldehyde or some other sedating medication." The doctor consults Ron's chart, then looks up at her. "How much does your husband drink on a regular basis?"

"He has a few cocktails every night. I think that's all."

"Hmm." He sounds skeptical.

That night after the children go to bed, she enters Ron's study and looks around. When she opens the door to the closet, expecting to find office supplies and old jackets, she discovers more than a dozen empty bottles of Scotch that he has hidden there. *This is much worse than she realized.*

Is it her fault that Ron has been drinking so much? He must be unhappy. Is there something he needs from her that she's not giving him? But this doesn't make any sense. They have a great life together— wonderful kids, jobs they enjoy, family nearby, friends.

She needs to talk with her mother—maybe her mother can help her understand more about Ron's drinking.

On Sunday night when she brings Ron home from the hospital, he says, "I am so sorry for what I put you through, Harriet."

"I was really scared when you passed out."

"I swear that I'll never get drunk like that again." After looking her in the eyes as he solemnly makes this promise, he hangs his head.

"I'm counting on you to keep your word."

"I will."

"Ronnie, I've been thinking, from now on let's do more of our entertaining at home rather than at the club." *That way she'll be better able to monitor how much he consumes.*

"Whatever you want, Harriet."

"I was thinking I'd like to take some cooking classes in French cuisine. Then we'd have something really special to offer guests."

Gamely, he replies, "That sounds good."

"Mother suggested that I go to some Al-Anon meetings."

"What's that?"

"It's like AA, only it's for family members of an alcoholic."

"I'm not an alcoholic."

"I wasn't thinking of you. Mother's an alcoholic, even though she's sober now. I was raised by an alcoholic. Mother says alcoholism is a disease. It's not about a lack of willpower or weakness or moral depravity. It's a disease that impacts the entire family."

Ron says, "I don't believe it's a disease. That's just an excuse."

"Well, I'm going to see what Al-Anon is like."

❧

At Al-Anon meetings Harriet learns that she cannot control Ron's behavior, or the actions of anyone else, for that matter. She can only govern herself. She signs up for cooking classes, and they're fun; she becomes proficient at making French onion soup, duck à l'orange, cassoulet, and crème brûlée. They host dinner parties in their home, and it seems that Ron is drinking less.

One night, two hours after they turned out the light, she awakens to see that Ron's no longer in bed with her. She gets up and walks around the house looking for him. He's not in his study or anywhere else. After another hour, she hears the front door open and close quietly. She hurries downstairs.

"Where have you been?"

He grimaces. "Country club." Clearly he doesn't want to be having this conversation.

"Why did you go over there at this hour of night?"

"Buddies, see my buddies." He's loaded.

"Well, come to bed now. It's almost midnight."

Suddenly, he pulls off his winter coat, throws it on the floor, and runs to the bathroom. He vomits. Then there's a pause. More vomiting. She goes in to see if he needs help. The toilet bowl is filled with red.

She hurries to the phone. "I'm sorry to call so late, Mother, but Ron's vomiting blood. What should I do?"

"Call an ambulance. Your father is away in Wilmington on business, but I'll get there as soon as I can."

She telephones, unlocks the front door, and then she starts to shake. She gets Ron to sit on the floor in the living room with a bowl between his legs. Then she runs upstairs to put on some clothes and check that the children are still asleep.

Her mother is entering as she descends the stairs.

"Znot blood," Ron slurs, "izz tomahdo jews."

Eleanor leans over the bowl and sniffs. "It's not blood," she agrees, "but you're drunk, Ron."

The medics appear and quickly move Ron into the back of the ambulance.

Harriet says, "I'm going to follow in my car. You'll stay?"

"Of course."

"Thank you, Mother. I'm so glad I can count on you again."

After putting on her coat, she grabs her purse. Before she heads out the door, she turns around and informs her mother, "I can't stand to see him like this. It's too terrifying. I will never go through this again. When Ron sobers up, I'm going to tell him, never again. He can keep his bottle or he can keep me—but not both."

Eleanor gives her a quick hug. "I'm so sorry, Harriet. But don't worry, I'll be here."

March 1966

After a few years of turmoil, Harriet's life has settled down into a comfortable routine. She lives alone with her children in the house she and Ron built, and he has moved to San Francisco and started a new family.

Today the girls in the Advanced Placement Chemistry class are fidgeting—they can hardly hold still, for spring break starts right after this class. Perched on their stools, ten juniors wearing navy blue jumpers and pale blue blouses, pencils in hand, take notes as they lean on the soapstone counter, their books shoved in between the Bunsen burners, sinks, and goosenecked water faucets. They're asking Harriet questions that arose while they prepared their homework assignment.

She knows that girls expect chemistry to be hard. Math and science courses can make students feel really stupid because the answers are either right or they're wrong, so she works to make her classes fun. Since reading and learning strictly from books was difficult for her when she was a student, she uses lots of demonstrations and experiments in her teaching.

Walking back and forth in front of the long counter, she answers their questions about air pressure. Then she dangles a conversational gambit before them. "For a scientist, girls, nonconformity is an essential attribute. I know at your age conformity has a distinct appeal—most of you don't want to stick out from the crowd—but I can assure you that thinking for yourself is terribly important. A scientist must be curious about whether what we actually see is what we seem to see. We must analyze every observation, open it up, turn it upside down, inspect every facet. You must not make assumptions."

A student replies, "But if you're a nonconformist, won't people think you're a difficult person?"

"You're absolutely right, Anna. Scientists don't typically have the best social skills. We can be awkward around people who don't think like us. It's not easy to swim against the tide. But enough lecturing. I have a demonstration for you. Please clear the counter."

While the girls move their books and notebooks to the floor, she opens a cupboard and brings out an empty beer can. She hands it to Cathy, who sniffs the can and upends it to see whether there's any beer still left inside. The other girls titter.

"Rats," she jokes, "it's really empty."

"All right. I want you to put a small amount of very cold water into the can. Jeanne, you fill a bowl with two to three inches of water and set it aside."

Jeanne gets off her stool and goes to the cupboard for a bowl, which she fills from one of the faucets. Cathy runs the water a minute before putting the can under the tap.

"Now get some tongs, Cathy, and hold the can over a Bunsen burner. You'll need to heat it for several minutes."

The girls are quiet while they observe Cathy. Harriet checks her watch. The Bunsen burner hisses.

"Mrs. Wright," asks Cathy, "how long do I need to keep doing this?"

"Be patient. Watch for steam to exit the can."

"I don't see anything."

Ally asks, "Is it going to blow up?"

White steam rises from the hole in the can. The girls move closer.

"Thirty seconds more," says Harriet. A long pause. "Now, quickly invert the can into the bowl of water, making sure the hole in the top is immersed. That seals the can and starts it cooling."

Cathy flips the can into the bowl.

The other girls step back. A few giggle nervously.

Bang! The can crumples with a sudden sound that's almost as shocking as a gunshot.

Ally screams.

Harriet takes the tongs from Cathy and lifts the can out of the water. It looks as if it's been crushed. She says, "The can collapses inward because suddenly it doesn't have any water vapor inside. It implodes."

"That was exciting!" says Ruth.

A quick knock on the door to the classroom heralds the appearance of Miss Braun. She looks to be in her early fifties, though her hair is completely white. "Is everything copacetic here?"

"Of course. We've just imploded a can."

She nods. "Please stop by my office before you leave today, Mrs. Wright." Then Miss Braun exits.

Ally says, "Uh oh, Mrs. Wright is in trouble now if she has to go to the principal's office."

Harriet's glad Ally feels comfortable enough to tease her. "I'm not worried," she says.

Nina, the AFS student from Germany, says, "Miss Braun's name means brown but her hair is all white."

"Isn't that ironic?" Cathy remarks. "People say her hair turned white when she saw her fiancé's plane crash in an air show."

Harriet says, "That's enough now, girls. You're dismissed."

As they troop out, the girls thank her for the fun demonstration and wish her a good break.

Despite what she said, she does feel a little anxious, wondering what Janice Braun wants to discuss with her.

ᦉ

She enters the principal's spartan office. Although Miss Braun has been the head of Hartley School ever since Harriet was a student here, there are no photos or personal items around. The room gives nothing away about Miss Braun's life outside the school.

She stands in front of the desk. "You wanted to see me, Janice?"

"Take a seat, Harriet. I have a proposition for you."

"Oh?" Sitting, Harriet pulls her A-line dress down toward her knees, which she presses close together. The short skirts on dresses nowadays certainly look good, but they are not the most comfortable. She wears modish clothing and straightens her wavy shoulder-length hair purposefully so the girls see that a science teacher can be feminine and stylish too.

"Miss Bryan plans to retire in June. I would like you to consider taking her position as director of the upper school."

She's startled. "Why me?"

"You have the respect of the faculty, you're an excellent teacher, and you know what good teaching entails."

She has a sinking sensation in her stomach. She knows she should be grateful for the opportunity to move up an echelon at her school, and if she wants to please her boss, she should probably say yes.

"I'm honored that you thought of me, Janice, but I really like teaching the girls. I learn so much from them. I love their questions."

"You could continue to teach one course each semester. I think you'd find this job in administration would give you an opportunity to look at the bigger picture for our school and to see where private education is headed."

"What exactly would the job entail?"

"You would be responsible for the upper school faculty and curriculum. That means hiring, evaluating, and if necessary, firing teachers who don't make the grade."

Harriet doesn't think she would enjoy that part. She likes her colleagues, but she's younger than most of them. On the other hand, in the three years she's been at Hartley, only one teacher has left and been replaced.

"I'd also like you to make sure the sequence of courses in each subject area makes sense, so they build appropriately upon each other and there aren't any major gaps in what the students learn. You would work with your colleagues to implement improvements."

"That part sounds interesting. But as you know, I am divorced with two children at home. Having my summers off is important to me."

"You could take the whole month of July every year."

"I'll have to think about it."

"Of course there would be an appropriate increase in your salary."

"Thank you for the offer, Janice." Rising from the chair, she says, "I'll get back to you in a few days with my decision."

"Excellent."

ॐ

The next day is surprisingly warm for late March, and Harriet can't wait to get outside and take a long walk. Retta is off playing tennis with a schoolmate, and Joey took the train into the city for a program at the Museum of Natural History. Usually the children spend a week during spring vacation in San Francisco with their father, but not this year—Ron's young wife has just had another baby, so he asked Harriet to keep the children with her until June, when they'll go to him for a month.

She strides quickly along the trail through the woods near the house she and Ron built, enjoying the songs of birds and the start of springtime. Is that a red-winged blackbird she's hearing? She'll have to look at the bird book when she gets back home. She's wearing a jacket, a long-sleeved blouse, and lime-green short shorts, which make her feel attractive because she knows she has nice legs, just like her mother. Not that she's trying to attract anyone these days. She is so completely occupied with her job and her children and her family that she doesn't have time for a man. That's been true ever since she and Ron split up, when she couldn't allow herself to give in to her feelings. She had to be tough—she had a family to raise! Anyway, at this point she's probably too independent to take on the role of wife ever again.

Which job, is the question. She loves teaching chemistry to the bright young ladies at her alma mater, and she's grateful that Retta can attend this school too. As a teacher at Hartley she doesn't have to pay tuition for Retta or for Joey at Warden, Hartley's "brother" school, so long as her children maintain an average of B or better.

This is not an easy decision. She believes she'd be happy to spend the rest of her working life as a chemistry teacher. On the other hand, she has seen problems that need to be fixed. The sequence of science courses should be rearranged, and the labs need to be scrutinized. She's completely overhauled the instruction and instrumentation for the chemistry labs; she guesses biology and physics could use updating as well.

As director of the upper school, she could probably make more of a difference to the quality of the education Hartley girls receive, and it might be a good way to employ her bossiness. The business courses she took at Madison would probably come in handy too. And a larger salary would certainly help. Retta will be going to college in another year, so that expense is looming.

Thinking she probably shouldn't turn down an opportunity like this, she starts walking faster. As soon as she gets home, she'll telephone her parents and invite herself to lunch. Since selling Sutton Chemical to Dupont, her father has joined several boards, and he is on Warden's board of trustees now. He's sure to have some thoughts about this.

Right now the sun warms her back as she strides along. The buds on the trees are swelling, and green shoots have started emerging from the forest floor. After the cold, dark winter, this feels like the resurgence of life itself—a new beginning.

∽

Harriet joins her parents for lunch. They sit at the dining room table, glasses of lemonade at their places. Eleanor hands her the platter of egg salad sandwiches.

Her mother chuckles. "After eating eggs constantly during the war, I never thought I'd ever serve egg salad sandwiches again."

Harriet says, "I remember that you came up with the strangest concoctions to use eggs in new ways—your eggs in noodle nests were memorable."

"With all the chickens we were raising for the war effort, I had to do something! Eggs were coming out of our ears."

"You were very creative, Mother."

"Thank you, dearie." She takes a bite of her sandwich, then says, "What do you hear from Ron? I hope he's still attending his AA meetings—it's the only way to stay sober."

Harriet rankles at the implication that she should constantly monitor Ron's behavior from three thousand miles away. On the other hand, she knows she needs to be aware of anything that impacts her children's safety when they are out in California with him and Shelley.

"I don't know about Ron. I want to talk with you about a proposition Janice Braun put to me."

Her father raises his eyebrows.

"What did Janice propose?"

"You know her as Janice?"

"We're on a committee together."

"I didn't know that. Anyway, she's asked me to consider becoming director of the upper school at Hartley."

"That's very exciting," her mother says.

"It's scary too," she replies. "I love teaching. This job would be mostly administrative, and I'd be working eleven months of the year. That's an even bigger commitment of time."

Her mother asks, "What does your gut tell you to do?"

"I feel flattered and interested but also cautious—what if I hate it?"

Her father clears his throat. "I think you should take the position, Harriet. This is a critical juncture in the history of both schools. Janice and I are on a confidential committee of top administrators and board members from Hartley and Warden who are meeting to discuss the possibility of merging the schools into one coeducational institution."

"Whoa! I had no idea."

"As I said, this is confidential." She can tell he's proud to be involved in this.

"A merger would change everything!" She doesn't like the idea at all.

"It would indeed. I expect we'd get a lot of pushback from alumni."

"I really liked going to a girls' school and a women's college!" She's surprised by how vehemently she feels about the matter. "I know what it's like to be in a class with both men and women. At Madison the men totally dominated classroom discussions—we could hardly get a word in edgewise. When they're adolescents, girls can be intimidated by boys in the classroom."

Then it occurs to her that if a merger is implemented, she could lose her job. This could be another reason to take the job as director of the upper school—she'd be in a better position to fight against the merger.

Her father pulls a cigarette out of its package and lights it. "We have to be practical, Harriet. With declining enrollments and rising costs, many of the single-sex schools are facing the same questions. Can we afford to maintain and operate two parallel sets of facilities? And there are questions about whether it's even wise to keep boys and girls segregated from each other. Some of the studies suggest that children learn more adaptive social skills if they're taught in mixed classrooms."

"The girls wouldn't have a chance to be heard!"

"They'd have to learn to speak up for themselves. I should think you'd want that, Harriet."

She has to laugh. "Good point, Father."

"Take the job, Harriet. We'll have fun working together again."

"It would be interesting to participate in high-level deliberations about the future of my school." Her stomach feels tight: is it excitement or fear that she could find herself at odds with her father?

⁓

Months later, the family's summer house is filled to the brim with children and adults when the whole Sutton gang spends the first weekend in July together at Sea View. Sandy beach tools, buckets, and pails litter the porch, along with packs of playing cards, paperback books, magazines, a cribbage board, and glasses with the dregs of milk or Kool-Aid. It's midmorning, and Nat is busy in the living room with all four of his children and Harry's two; they're practicing a song Nat has written, which they plan to perform for the family tomorrow night. Both Harriet's daughter, Retta, and Nat's daughter Abby play guitar. Nat's son Ned is a drummer, and of course, Nat has his saxophone. The younger children are there too. Harriet can hear the excitement in her brother's voice as he takes them over the musical phrases again and again.

She sits with Eleanor and Dorie in adjacent chairs on the porch while George is back at the dining room table with his newspapers. Dorie, still in her bathrobe, listlessly turns the pages of *Ladies' Home Journal*. Eleanor is reading *Man's Search for Meaning*. Harriet's legs are crossed, and she's jiggling her foot back and forth.

Eleanor says, "I love this book. Viktor Frankl is so wise."

Dorie asks, "Who?"

"Viktor Frankl is an Austrian therapist who survived the Nazi concentration camp at Auschwitz, where he lost his family and the manuscript of a treatise he'd written. His experience led him to develop a new approach to healing patients—he calls it logotherapy. Frankl says, 'The striving to find a meaning in one's life is the primary motivational force in man.'"

Harriet puts both feet on the floor. "That's what *The Feminine Mystique* is about too!"

Dorie sighs. "What's *The Feminine Mystique*?"

"You should read the book, Dorie. Betty Friedan talks about the yearning in women who are expected to find all their fulfillment in the home, the women for whom simply being a wife and mother is not enough."

"With four kids, I don't have time to read books," she tells Harriet. Dorie returns her attention to her magazine.

Eleanor riffles through Frankl's book, then stops near the end. "This statement hit me like a ton of bricks: 'Suffering ceases to be suffering . . . at the moment it finds a meaning.' That's exactly what happened to me."

"What do you mean, Mother?"

"Eddie's death nearly killed me. It wasn't until I started wondering what I could do with my experience of suffering that I started to find my way. Helping others deal with their own grief is where I found the meaning for my life."

"I'm so glad, Mother."

"It's made all the difference."

Actually Harriet thinks it was treatment at Dia Linn that was most helpful in getting her life back on track. "How is your grief group managing without you this summer?"

"My co-facilitator keeps it going when I'm away."

Ten-year-old Ernie emerges from the living room. "I'm hungry," he tells his mother.

Dorie looks up. "It's not time for lunch. I'll make sandwiches in a while."

"Peanut butter and fluff?"

"Sure."

Ernie heads back into the living room. The screen door slams behind him.

Harriet says, "I'd be glad to make Ernie a sandwich now, Dorie."

"I can't be giving the kids food every time they ask for it. If I did that, I'd be in the kitchen all day long. We eat three times a day—that's it."

"Okay," Harriet replies. "I'll go see how the musicians are doing." Her children returned from California just two days ago, so she craves the sight of them.

When she enters the living room, the music stops.

With mock fierceness, Nat says, "You're not supposed to be in here! Our songs are meant to be a surprise." He looks stern but he's teasing her, at the same time making a big deal of this for the children.

"Sorry."

As she retreats, she hears, "All right, kids, from the top. 'Let's not put the boats away. Maybe we'll stay for one more day.'"

Dorie gets up from her chair. "I'm going to lie down for a while."

Eleanor asks, "Are you feeling all right, Dorie?"

"I'm just tired, Mother Sutton."

Once she is out of earshot, Harriet says, "Dorie gets up late, takes naps during the day, and goes to bed early. What's going on with her? She wasn't like this last summer."

"Perhaps she's pregnant again. Or she could be depressed," Eleanor says.

"What does she have to be depressed about? She's got four fine children and a wonderful husband who's doing very well professionally." Harriet can't believe what just came out of her mouth. She must feel a touch of envy that Dorie doesn't have to work; at the same time, she'd never want to be in her sister-in-law's shoes.

"Come on, Harriet, you know better than that."

"Of course I do. I don't understand why I judge Dorie so harshly. It's difficult to feel like I know her. She doesn't open up with us."

"I suspect she doesn't feel she fits into our family, though of course she *is* part of this family."

"I just can't seem to warm up to Dorie. I'd like her a lot more if it looked like she was making Nat happy."

"Let's try compassion," says Eleanor. "It's not Dorie's fault that she isn't sophisticated. She never went to college. She doesn't have any brothers or sisters, so she doesn't have that experience in getting along with others. She might feel intimidated by us."

"I suppose so. I'll see if I can draw her out when she gets up."

〜

After dinner that night, the children race around the outside of the house, playing Capture the Flag, while the grownups sit on the porch.

George proclaims, "I'm glad President Johnson is sending more troops to South Vietnam. If we don't push back the Red Chinese, they'll take over the Far East."

"I don't know why we're even in Vietnam," Harriet replies. "What business is it of ours? If this keeps going and they institute a draft, Joey could be shipped over there."

Fervently, Eleanor says, "I hope to God that never happens!"

"We've got to be realistic," George replies. "In the last war we had a great lesson in man's capacity for evil. I don't think the Communists are any better than the Nazis."

Watching the sun descend over the bay, Nat turns around to interject, "I hate all this killing: JFK, Malcolm X . . . What's next?"

Harriet says, "At least we got the Civil Rights Act passed. That's *some* progress."

"Speaking of progress, Harriet," George says, "have you had a chance to read the financial study the Taylor, Lieberfeld, and Heldman research firm prepared?"

"I've skimmed it, Father. I've got other things I need to study to prepare for my new position."

"What are you talking about?" asks Nat.

George answers. "Warden and Hartley are considering a merger. Coeducation has become a national trend for many independent schools. Both Warden and Hartley have declining enrollments, especially in the lower schools. The financial study shows that both are running deficits that are barely covered by their annual fund campaigns. The schools rely much too much on annual giving for their operating budgets. They've got to merge if they're to survive."

"But single-sex education is so much better for the development of confident girls with a sense of their own autonomy. I keep telling you that, Father!"

He says, "Boys and girls should go to school together so they can prepare for life in a world that is coeducational."

Harriet crosses her legs. "It sounds like you've already made up your mind."

"It's up to the boards to decide."

"I hope you'll seek input from the administrators and faculty of both schools."

"We'll see."

Eleanor puts her knitting aside. "Tell us what's going on at the university, Nat."

Dorie, who's now wearing a faded housedress, gets up from her chair and leaves the porch.

"As I've said before, I was very fortunate to have a fellowship at the Variety Club Heart Hospital under Doctors Walt Lillehei and Richard Varco. Now, unfortunately, the funding for that cardiovascular training grant from the National Institutes for Health is about to end."

"Is that so?" says George.

Harriet can tell that wheels are starting to spin in his brain.

"We've learned so much about how to repair the heart. The surgery itself is relatively simple. The trick was to find a safe way to slow the heart down long enough to fix it without depriving the body of oxygenated blood. First they used hypothermia, and then they developed the heart-lung machine, but a lot of patients developed 'heart block.'"

"Tell me again what that means," Eleanor says.

"It means their hearts stop beating during or after the surgery. So Lillehei and an electrical engineer named Earl Bakken developed an electrical pacemaker to make the heart start beating again."

George leans forward. "I was glad you told me about Bakken when he took Medtronic public. My stock in that company has done very well."

"There have been lots of refinements in the pacemaker since the one Dr. Lillehei inserted into the first patient's heart muscle in 1957. Now we have much smaller ones." Nat pauses.

George says, "Go on."

"Well, the fellowship program has attracted physicians from around the world, and they're taking what they learn from the pioneers in the field back to their home countries. I don't know what will happen when the funding ends."

"How much money did the NIH grant provide?"

"I have no idea, but I can find out. Are you thinking the Sutton Foundation might be able to help?"

"Possibly."

Nat's youngest, Violet, runs onto the porch, crying. She climbs onto her father's lap. The other children follow close behind.

"What's wrong, Vi?"

"I tripped and hit my chin."

He inspects her chin, licks his finger, and wipes the dirt away with his saliva. "It isn't bleeding, pumpkin." He looks at the kids. "How about we go to the Little Red Store for some ice cream?"

"Yeah, sock it to me!" cries Joey.

Retta grabs Violet's hand.

"Wait," Harriet says to Retta. "Give me a hug before you go."

Retta complains, "Oh, Mother," but she hugs her quickly, then takes Violet's hand again.

While Nat leads the children away, Eleanor rises. "I'm ready to head up to bed. George?"

"I'm coming."

Harriet stays on the porch. She wasn't able to get Dorie talking, and she's worried about what kind of home she and Nat are providing for their children. Not that it's any of her business. But as their aunt, maybe it *is* her business.

♻

Later that evening she tracks down her brother, who's sitting in the living room. "What are you up to, Nat? It's nearly midnight."

"I'm making copies of the lyrics to my new song so everyone in the audience tomorrow night can follow along."

"I hadn't realized you've been writing songs again."

"It's what I do when I wake up in the middle of the night and can't get back to sleep. I was writing songs about Andover, but now I've started writing about Sea View."

"That is so cool, Nat! Do you want help copying the lyrics?"

"No, I can finish this later."

"Let's get a drink. I'd like to talk with you."

They go into the pantry and pour themselves short glasses of whiskey with water.

Back in the living room, she goes to the sagging sofa. "How are you, Nat?"

He takes a nearby cushioned chair. "Work is great—very challenging and endlessly fascinating."

"I'm really glad to hear that. Do you miss working as a musician?"

"I play music in my free time."

"Retta and Joey certainly enjoy making music with you. You kept the kids occupied much of the day."

"We have fun together. I'm pretty happy with the songs we're getting ready to perform. Do you want to hear one?"

"Of course I do."

He rises to pick up Abby's guitar, which is leaning against the wall. Standing, he strums a few chords and then he sings:

Let's not put the boats away!
Maybe we'll stay for one more day,
Cook out once more and watch the sun
Setting red and gold in Sea View Bay.

"That's great!"

He grins. "You'll have to wait till tomorrow night to hear the rest of the tune."

"You really love music, don't you, Nat?"

Placing Abby's guitar in its case, he responds, "Always have, always will. Music helps me stay sane."

"How are things at home?"

Slowly, he sits back down. "The kids are growing like weeds."

"I see that. Abby must be five inches taller than she was last summer."

"She towers over Ned now. He doesn't like it one bit."

"Are you thinking of sending him to Andover when he's old enough?"

"No. Both Abby and Ned attend the University High School on campus. It's first rate and they like it a lot. Students have to demonstrate academic excellence to get in and it's quite affordable, with tuition around $200 per student. The school is filled with faculty brats."

She's going to have to be more direct. "I've noticed that Dorie seems pretty withdrawn."

"She's depressed. I've tried to get her to go see someone about it, but she refuses."

"I'm sorry, Nat."

"Me too." He sighs. "How about you, Harry? You were getting pretty hot under the collar while you and Father talked about that merger."

"I'm convinced it would be bad for the girls."

"It's not pleasant to disagree with Father, is it? I'm trying to figure out how to tell him I can't serve as medical advisor for the foundation."

"He asked you to do that?"

"Yes, but I can't possibly leave the kids alone with Dorie over a whole weekend. I'd need to come east for meetings."

"It's that bad?" As she imagines what his life at home must be like, she reaches over to put her hand on his arm.

Then she wonders why their father hasn't asked *her* to play a role at the foundation? She knows that he's still in the throes of getting organized, establishing an office for the Sutton Foundation, applying for a 501(c)(3) tax determination letter from the IRS, hiring an assistant, and setting up the business and accounting systems for his nonprofit organization. She tries not to feel too hurt about this. She refocuses on her brother, who's gazing at his knees.

"Is Dorie pregnant?" If she is, that would explain a lot.

"Absolutely not. She couldn't be."

Realizing what this likely means, she feels even worse for him. "I'm sorry, Nat. Is there anything I can do?"

He shakes his head. "Nope. I made my bed. Now I get to lie in it."

February 1967

It's well after dark when Nat arrives home from the hospital. The outside light is on, illuminating the white stucco façade and the double windows on both sides of the front door, though it barely grazes the twin dormers in the roof or the desiccated hydrangeas leaning against the foundation. A swing, hung from the large cottonwood tree, moves eerily with the wind, as though some invisible person were riding it.

He likes everything about their house in Prospect Park, and it's close enough for him to walk to work if he has the time, though that's rarely the case.

Opening the front door, he's met with a blast of heat and sound. Abby, Ned, Ernie, and Violet are seated around the dining room table, plates of food and glasses of milk at their places, while Dorie looks on from the end of the table. There's nothing in front of her except a glass of water.

"Daddy!" cries Violet, jumping up from her chair and running over to him. As she embraces his legs, she says, "You're home!" He can hear the relief in her voice. "Ernie's being mean to me!"

Violet's so skinny, her arms and legs look almost like sticks emerging from her old pajamas, which clearly she outgrew some time ago. Suddenly it occurs to him that she looks malnourished—but that's impossible—they have enough food. "Wait a minute, Vi. I can't hear myself think."

The other kids are shouting over the song "Somebody to Love," which is booming from the kitchen. He charges in to turn off the radio. He's had enough noise for one day after attending to the ceaseless paging of physicians and code blue announcements at Variety Club Heart Hospital.

Violet stands in the doorway.

He gets down on his knees so he's level with his nine-year-old. "Okay, pumpkin. Tell me what happened."

Her lower lip trembles. "Ernie took my favorite paper dolls, and he cut them into little tiny pieces. They're ruint!"

At eleven, Ernie shouldn't be acting like this.

"Don't worry, Vi. We'll get you some new paper dolls."

"But I liked the ones I had!"

He wonders why she would care so much about paper dolls—isn't she a little old for this? "You and I will go to the store this weekend and see what we can find."

"Thank you, Daddy."

Rising from his crouch, he pats her on the top of her head. She heads back to the table while he picks his way through toy cars and trucks and dolls and crayons and Lincoln Logs strewn across the floor of the living room. He stuffs his coat into the crammed front hall closet and returns to the dining room.

The children are eating macaroni and cheese with peas once again. He turns to Dorie. "Can't you fix them a decent meal with meat? Growing kids need protein. Hot dogs and beans? Surely you can manage something like that."

Slumped in her chair, Dorie says, "I'm not feeling well. Abby made dinner."

He feels sick. This happens almost every night.

Sweating now, he moves over to check the thermostat, which has been pushed up to seventy-five degrees. He turns it down. Then he takes the vacant seat at the dining room table. Inhaling and exhaling deeply, he tries to contain his frustration.

"So, tell me about your days. Vi, you go first."

Bouncing in her seat, Violet's golden curls jump as she exclaims, "I got one hundred on my spelling test!"

"Good for you, Vi."

Ernie chimes in: "My trumpet teacher said I did a really good job on the piece I learned for my lesson today."

Ned, who's been shoveling noodles into his mouth, looks up from his plate and says, "It sounded like screeching when I heard you practicing." Nat is startled once again by how much his thirteen-year-old son can eat.

"I got better," Ernie replies. "Dad, I want to play the bass."

"We can think about that."

Vi stabs one pea and puts it in her mouth. The mound of macaroni on her plate looks untouched.

Nat's worried about Vi's health, and his fury at Dorie for not feeding her better rises higher. "Have some noodles, Vi. You can't just eat peas."

Violet shakes her head. "I'm not really hungry."

"Would you like a piece of cheese?"

"No thank you, Daddy."

Giving up on this for the moment, he looks over at his oldest. "How about you, Abby?"

"We finished *Bellum Gallicum* in Latin class today. We start reading *Fabulae Faciles* next."

"You're moving right along."

Abby brushes back the hank of hair that's fallen across her eyes. "Would you like the rest of the macaroni and cheese, Dad? I can warm it up for you."

"How about you, Dorie—do you want some?"

Staring at the wall behind him, she says, "No."

He turns back to Abby. "In that case, I'll finish it off. Thank you, sweetheart."

Dorie adds, "I had peanut butter on saltines a while ago."

"Then why didn't you give the children some peanut butter?" he mutters under his breath.

❧

Later that night after he has checked everyone's homework and brushed teeth and tucked the younger children in, and the house has grown quiet, Nat goes into their bedroom, where Dorie lies under the covers in her nightgown. Her face looks puffy.

He sits next to her and takes her hands in his. "Dorie, why don't you sing around the house anymore? I always loved hearing you sing while you went about your chores."

"I don't know, Nate. I don't feel like singing. Maybe I would if I had a gig to prepare for, but that'll never happen now. I don't have any time for myself."

"You must admit, it's not Abby's job to make dinner and look after the other kids. She's only fifteen."

"It's too much. I don't know how to do it all. I didn't have brothers or sisters to take care of. I never babysat—I was busy taking music lessons and singing in the church choir."

"I've heard this before."

Defensively she says, "I handle the driving, get groceries, and take the kids to all their lessons and doctor's appointments."

"You need to feed our children. Violet looks like she's starving to death!" He's nearly shouting now. "What do you actually *do* all day?"

"I just don't have the energy for everything."

"We can't go on like this." He sighs deeply. In a quieter tone of voice, he says, "Do we need to hire someone to help out—a housekeeper or a cook?"

"No."

"Why not?"

"I don't want someone in my house looking over my shoulder."

"Would you like to take a class at the university? Or you could teach singing to kids in some school."

She shakes her head despondently.

"Then what are we going to do?"

"What about me? I'm stuck here by myself all day. I never get to go out with my friends and just have fun."

Nat has never met any of those supposed friends. "You've *got* to make an appointment to see Dr. Mason."

"I'm not crazy!"

"Of course you're not. But I think he could help you feel better." As her husband, he's torn between anger and pity. As a physician, he's frightened by the state she's in.

"I'll try harder."

"That's not good enough. We've had this conversation too many times over the last few years. I want you to get help. You need help."

"If only I could have another baby, then I'd feel better." Tears start leaking out her eyes and down her cheeks.

He groans as an image of a pregnant Dorie wearing one of her checked maternity smocks, looking terribly proud, assails him. "Dorie, you can't have another baby."

Her face turns red. "I know. And you had no right to tell the doctor to tie my tubes after Violet was born!"

"During that C-section you were out, so I couldn't ask your permission, but it was the right thing to do. I could see you were barely managing to care for the children we already had."

"You had no right," she says angrily. She sits up. "You're just like your father, making decisions about my life the way he did to you."

Clenching his fists, he stands and walks away from her. The thought that he could in any way be like his father appalls him.

Chastened, he returns. "I may have been a little presumptuous, but

I was thinking of the welfare of our entire family. We don't need any more children."

"I can't talk to you." She slides back down under the covers and shuts her eyes.

Years ago, as he got to know Dorie well, he became deeply discouraged to discover that their making music together was simply not enough. Sometimes he still feels brokenhearted at the death of the life he thought they would have together. Once in a while, late at night while he sits alone with a drink and a cigarette, he feels as if his heart will burst with how much he wanted a different outcome. His father was right. He never should have married Dorie. He is so lonely with her.

That summer, instead of going to Sea View, he takes his family to a cabin on Lake Superior for vacation, hoping a change will cheer Dorie up. It doesn't work.

ᘒ

At the staff Christmas party in early December, Nat stands with his back against a wall, watching Dorie, who is holding court, surrounded by a group of nurses and the wives of his colleagues. Last week he suggested she buy herself a new outfit for this occasion, and she chose well. The pink crepe dress becomes her, though she's put on a lot of eye makeup. Holding a cocktail in one hand, she gesticulates with the other, and he's glad that she seems to be having a good time. He's reminded of what she was like when they first met. She comes alive in front of an audience. Maybe she should go back to singing in clubs?

Down the hall, he hears a woman protest, "No! Take your hands off me." A door slams. One of the senior cardiologists emerges from the hallway, his face flushed.

What just happened? A few moments later, Lucy Anderson appears, her eyes more sparkly than they should be. Has she been crying?

He moves over to her. "Are you all right, Nurse Anderson?"

"Please, Dr. Sutton, I'm Lucy outside the hospital."

"I'll call you Lucy if you call me Nat."

Smiling, she sticks out her hand. "It's a deal."

As they shake, Nat becomes aware of how warm her hand feels.

"Was Dr. Howard bothering you?" He and Lucy have worked together at Variety Club Heart for a few years, but he's never directed a personal comment to her before.

"Yes. I guess I'm fair game since I'm not married. But *he* is. And I wasn't flirting with him."

"I'm sorry he treated you badly. Should I speak to him?"

"No! I don't want to make trouble. But tell me, Dr. S . . . Nat—why do so many married men assume that because I'm a widow, I must be dying for a roll in the hay with them?"

She is so real and honest and direct. She reminds him of his first girlfriend, Emma, who was like that. He could tell Emma anything, and she would laugh when he hoped she would, and she always seemed to understand what he was saying. He felt sad when she didn't return to school at Abbot the next fall. Now he tells Lucy, "I didn't know you'd lost your husband. I'm sorry."

"We've never discussed anything except the patients."

"That's true. I guess I'm pretty focused on work."

"As you should be. Heart surgery is a matter of life or death. Each operation is very high risk."

"You're right."

"Well, I should get back to the ladies. I don't want another encounter with you know who." She grins meaningfully at him before going over to take a vacant seat in the circle around Dorie.

He watches Lucy lean forward and ask his wife some question, which Dorie proceeds to answer at length. As he gazes at Lucy, he feels so much longing that he has to shut his eyes. He can't allow himself to feel this way. He turns and heads toward the bar.

∾

One afternoon two weeks later Nat is bent over a patient's chart. The patient in the bed, a small boy with lips that are tinged blue, gasps for breath. Lucy takes the boy's pulse.

"I'm afraid this ventricular septal defect is large enough that we'll need to operate. What do you think?" He passes Wilbur Wagner's chart to her, inadvertently brushing his hand against hers.

"What did you say?" She sounds startled.

Jolted by touching her, he clears his throat. "Um. Ah. I was asking your opinion."

"I've never had a physician do that before," she states, her blue eyes twinkling.

"I guess I'm not typical."

"That's for sure! It's too bad there aren't more docs like you."

He blushes.

She goes on. "Wilbur is cyanotic. Look at his skin, his fingernails. He's tiny for a four-year-old."

"Sewing up the hole in his septum shouldn't be complicated. Let's get him scheduled for tomorrow morning."

As she nods, a fetching tendril of strawberry-blonde hair comes loose from under her white cap.

Moving toward the door, he says, "Did you hear about the heart transplant that guy performed in South Africa last week? What was his name? Christiaan Barnard. He trained here a few years ago."

"Was it successful?"

They pause outside the room.

"So far. It's terribly exciting to think about all the new developments in heart surgery. Just a couple of weeks ago René Favaloro performed the first successful heart bypass surgery at the Cleveland Clinic."

She asks, "What does bypass surgery involve?"

"It's complicated. Maybe I could explain over a drink sometime."

"Really?"

"Are you available later today? I should be done with my work at the clinic around five-thirty."

She looks up and down the hallway, which is momentarily empty. "I suppose I could." She sounds a little nervous.

"I just want to talk with you."

"All right."

∾

When he gets to the Triangle Bar, he walks around until he spots Lucy sitting in a booth far from the front door. Is she afraid to be seen with him?

As he sits down across from her, he says, "That's a nice blouse."

She stands up. "It's actually a dress, the style is called a shirtwaist. I went home to change out of my uniform and get my daughter some dinner."

"I didn't know you have a daughter. How old is she?"

A waiter appears to take their orders. Lucy asks for a beer, Nat a Manhattan.

"Olivia is fourteen."

"When did your husband die?"

"Five years ago. Bert was going to see a client in South Dakota when his plane crashed."

"That must have been a terrible shock."

She looks right into his eyes. "Yes. I had to reconsider my whole life." *She's so strong*, he thinks.

She pauses, picking up the round cardboard coaster in front of her. Then she goes on. "Having to stop and consider what matters most to me led me to leave orthopedics. I moved over to the heart hospital, where patients and their families are especially vulnerable and the stakes are high. I feel I can make more of a difference here at Variety Club. Every day I'm floored by the patients' courage and the love of their families."

"I want to make a difference too."

Wordlessly, they beam at each other.

When the waiter arrives with their drinks, Lucy takes a sip of her beer. "You said you'd explain heart bypass surgery to me."

"Right. To treat a blocked coronary artery, Dr. Favaloro cut open the patient's chest. Then he took a blood vessel from the patient's leg and grafted it directly onto an artery, thus bypassing the blockage and creating a new route for the blood to reach the heart. He did this while the heart was still beating."

"Wow!"

"I expect we'll see many more of these procedures in the years to come." He lifts his glass and swallows. Then he pulls out his cigarettes. "Would you like one?"

"I'd love a cigarette, but after Bert died, I knew I'd better give them up. With only one parent, Olivia needs to be able to rely on me."

"Good for you." And he needs to be the parent his kids can count on. "I know I should quit—I have asthma, after all. I've tried to give up smoking, but it's not easy, especially these days."

She inclines her head. "These days?"

He pauses a moment, then decides to answer honestly. "My wife is having some trouble with depression."

"I'm sorry."

"Her depression is dragging me down too. And there have been so many changes at the hospital. I enjoyed working with Walt Lillehei. I understand his leaving Minnesota to head the surgery department at Cornell Medical Center, but I miss him. And with Dr. Wangensteen's upcoming retirement, I'm afraid the culture of the hospital will change. Dr. Wangensteen created such a great atmosphere of open inquiry, where every question is welcome, every serious hypothesis worth testing. That's critical in a research hospital."

"Hopefully Dr. Wangensteen left enough of an impression on you and the other surgeons that you'll continue along the same lines."

"What got you into medicine, Lucy?"

"I always knew I wanted to help people, so nursing was the obvious choice for me. I grew up in Rochester around lots of docs from Mayo and St. Mary's—fathers of my friends, customers at my parents' supper club. I saw arrogant doctors who thought they were next to God and others who cared about healing others. I knew doctors who treated nurses like slaves and others who respected nurses and worked with them."

He wishes he could sit here all night talking with Lucy, but he has to glance at his wristwatch. "I should get going pretty soon. I've got to see to my own children."

"Tell me about them."

"Abby, the oldest, is fifteen, and then there's Ned at thirteen, Ernie's eleven, and Violet is nine. They're all budding musicians. I'm very proud of them."

"Music runs in the family?"

"Their mother was a singer, and I played sax in jazz clubs."

"Do you still play?"

"I don't have time to be in a group, but I love to make music with my kids. Fortunately they don't notice that I've gotten a little rusty."

She smiles.

He observes, "Our daughters are almost the same age. What is Olivia like?"

"She's very creative. She wants to be a writer when she grows up, and she's a pretty good student too. She's a huge Beatles fan."

"So is Abby."

"I kind of like their music myself. But if I sing along with their songs, Olivia cringes. These days she seems to find everything I do incredibly embarrassing."

"She's a teenager."

"Exactly."

He finishes his drink. "I really must go now. But I've enjoyed getting together so much."

She looks down. "Me too—very much."

"Can we do this again sometime?"

"That's probably not a good idea, Nat." Now she looks sad.

"Why not? Can't we be friends?"

"I don't know. That's the question. You're married. I'm not."

"I understand." He's disappointed, but he doesn't feel rejected exactly, because he senses her regret. Placing a twenty-dollar bill on the table, he rises.

She pulls on her coat and hat. "Thank you, Nat. It's been lovely."

They leave the bar together and move in separate directions to their cars.

March 1968

The next year Nat accepts his father's offer to serve as medical advisor to the Sutton Foundation, which means he has to fly east for the board meeting in mid-March. He's dying to get away for a few days. Dorie will simply have to cope with the children on her own. He doesn't plan to say anything to his parents about his troubles at home, but he can't wait to see his best friend. They talk to each other on the phone pretty often, but there's much he can't say when he could be overheard by his wife or one of his children.

At Peter's suggestion, they meet for dinner at the Oyster Bar in Grand Central.

Nat likes the feeling of warmth in the brightly lit windowless restaurant on the lower level of the train terminal. It feels very private.

Peter is already seated at a small table in the corner. When he sees Nat, he stands. He's wearing a light tan suit with an eye-popping navy tie featuring gold bursts behind little navy squares.

"Wow, Peter, you look so spiffy you could be in a Courvoisier ad!" Nat leans forward and fingers Peter's tie. "Silk!"

As they shake hands, Peter replies, "You look very cool yourself, Nat." He signals to a passing waiter.

Sitting, Nat jokes, "Would you believe I can finally afford more than one suit? I actually have two now, one for summer, one for winter.

Of course I don't wear them at the hospital—I'm in scrubs most of the time."

The waiter comes over. Nat orders a Manhattan. Peter orders another martini—the one in front of him is half gone.

"Your sideburns are so long, Peter!"

"As an employee at the Museum of Modern Art, I must show that I am *au courant* when it comes to fashion." He raises his eyebrows in a characteristic show of self-deprecation.

"I suppose if we were at Andover now, you'd draw your Sammy Phillips cartoon with sideburns down to his jaw."

Peter chortles. "I'm so glad to see you, friend. No one else remembers my cartoons."

"I *loved* your Sammy Phillips!" Nat tells him.

"You've come east for some sort of meeting?"

"Father created a philanthropic foundation with most of the money he made selling Sutton Industries two years ago. He's still figuring out the foundation's priorities for funding, but one of them is medical research. I'm here to help him define those parameters."

"Interesting."

"It is. He's getting advice from all sorts of people. I believe the arts is another one of his focus areas."

"Tell him I'd be happy to talk with him about art any time he wants."

"I will."

Nat's drink arrives and he takes a sip. It's a little stronger than the ones he gets in Minneapolis. Then he takes a closer look at his friend, who has crow's feet at the corners of his eyes and long lines that dent his forehead. He looks older than thirty-nine.

"How are you, Peter?"

"I'm fine. But I can't believe what's going on these days. It seems like the world is going to hell in a handbasket. The assassination of Martin Luther King in Memphis two weeks ago by some unknown white guy. How hard are the police actually trying to find King's killer?"

"It's such a tragedy for all of us."

"And the war in Vietnam. I'm dying to take part in anti-war demonstrations, but I'm afraid to. As a homosexual, I've got to be completely circumspect about what I say and do and where I'm seen, or I could lose my job."

Nat says, "I've never heard you use that word before."

"We danced around it at Andover, but you knew I swing that way."

"Of course I did. And I remember telling you that I don't."

"I'm following the black power movement too. I know what it's like to be discriminated against."

"I don't know much about the Black Panthers," Nat admits. "But tell me, how is your work going?"

"I love it! Right now I'm working on a fabulous exhibit of pieces from the Paul J. Sachs Collection called *The Taste of a Connoisseur*. We're showing drawings from Pollaiuolo's *Fighting Nudes* and even Ben Shahn's *Sacco and Vanzetti*."

Nat grins. "I have no idea what you're talking about."

"That's okay." Peter finishes his first martini and moves on to the second. "How about you, Nat? How's everything in your world?"

"Awful, frankly. My marriage is a mess. Dorie is so depressed that she can barely function, and I don't know what to do. I've read up on depression and learned that sadness and fatigue can be symptomatic of hypothyroidism, especially in women, so I got her to go to our family physician, but apparently that's not the problem—she doesn't have an underactive thyroid. I think she needs to find a psychiatrist she likes, someone she can talk to, but she refuses to seek one out, even though I've given her the names of three who've been recommended to us. I can't *force* her to call them."

"How bad is it?"

"Really bad."

"I'm sorry, Nat. I was a little surprised that you married her—"

"I had to! The truth is she trapped me. She became pregnant before

I'd even gotten to know her properly." He feels terrible revealing this—
he's never said such a thing before to anyone else, but it's the truth
and he trusts Peter completely. He knows Peter won't betray his confidence. It feels good to admit the truth, however embarrassing it is. He
should have been smarter.

"Oh, no," Peter groans.

"Now it's as though she's paralyzed. I don't know how to move her
out of the state she's in."

"Maybe you should offer to go together to a marriage counselor. If
you were there too, it might be easier for her."

"That's an intriguing idea."

"Worst case, there's always divorce."

"Oh no. We've never had any divorce in our family. It's frowned
upon. I have an aunt and uncle who stay married, living together in
the same house though they haven't spoken to each other in decades."
He pauses. "At least we hadn't had any divorces until Harriet and Ron."
For the first time it strikes him how difficult breaking up with Ron
must have been for his sister.

"Well, why don't we order? I was thinking we could go down to the
Village Vanguard and hear some music after dinner."

"That would be great! What do you hear from our fellow classmates?"

∾

Two hours later Nat and Peter sit at another table in the basement
nightclub on Seventh Avenue South listening to the mellow sounds of
the Bill Evans Trio.

"That's some mural," Nat says, inclining his head toward the poet
running with quill and paper toward a naked woman sitting at a table,
her legs crossed, with greenery decorating her lap.

"It's silly but fun," Peter says. "A guy named Petroff is the artist."

Cautiously, Nat asks, "Are you seeing anyone, Peter?" He has never asked Peter about his love life before, but the atmosphere of this club feels so intimate that it seems like an appropriate question here.

"I'm living with a fabulous guy I met last year. Stephen is a set designer for Broadway plays. He gave me this tie you like."

"I'm glad you have someone."

"I am too." He takes a sip of his martini. "It's easy to meet people in this city. It's not so easy to settle down with one. You have to be really committed."

Nat sighs. "Marriage certainly is a commitment."

They listen for a while. Then Nat says, "I like this music. It's cool. And it's easier to talk over than bebop, though I wonder how these cats feel about being talked over. I never liked it when I was playing."

"I bet the band is used to it." Peter leans forward a little. "I get the feeling you haven't told me everything, Nat."

"You know me so well." He takes a sip of his Manhattan. "There's this nurse at the hospital, Lucy Anderson. We work together, and one time about a year ago we went out for a drink. I'm so attracted to her I can hardly stand not touching her, but I know I can't act on my feelings."

"Because you're married."

"Right."

"What's Lucy like?"

"She's very caring and compassionate with our patients and with everyone, really. She's smart and she's funny. She lost her husband a number of years ago. She has a daughter around Abby's age."

Peter puts his hand on Nat's. "She sounds like a nice lady."

"With Dorie the way she is, I don't know how long I can hold out in this marriage. I'm almost tempted to start something with Lucy to see what's there."

"Maybe you should. It might clarify things for you."

"But I can't have an affair. You remember years ago when I told you I was sure Father was having an affair? I never knew the other woman's name, but I saw how Mother suffered. I can't do that to my wife. I can't do that to Lucy either. She deserves to be with someone who is free to love her."

"What about trying for an open marriage? Lots of couples seem to be doing that these days. You'd be free to experiment."

"Open marriage seems like it'd get very messy."

"What are you going to do?"

"I don't know." He pulls out a cigarette, lights up, and exhales. "I must say, Peter, it's a huge relief to be able to discuss my problems with you."

"Call me anytime. If I'm not in the office, our secretary will take a message."

"Thank you. I'm sorry Dorie doesn't have a friend like you."

❧

One afternoon a few weeks later while he's in a patient's room at the hospital, Nat hears, "Calling Dr. Sutton, Dr. Sutton, urgent. Pick up the phone."

His heart seizes with fear. Has one of his children been hurt? He reaches for the telephone on the wall. The hospital operator answers.

"This is Dr. Sutton."

"Hold on, I'll connect you."

A moment later he hears, "Nat, it's Alice next door."

"What's happened?"

"I just wanted you to know I have Ernie and Vi with me. When they got home from school, they couldn't get into your house. They rang the doorbell again and again, but Dorie didn't answer. They came over to our place. When I tried telephoning your wife, there was no answer. I hope everything's all right. I'll keep the kids here with me until you come and get them."

He glances at his watch—it's three-thirty.

"Thank you, Alice. Could you keep them with you a little while longer? I'll be there as soon as I can."

He's relieved that there hasn't been an accident, but what's going on with Dorie? Has she done something to herself? As soon as he can get another doctor to fill in for him, he races home.

Turning his key in the lock, he's a little afraid of what he'll find inside. Hurrying through their home, he discovers Dorie sound asleep in their bed. His feeling of relief quickly turns to exasperated fury.

Shaking her shoulder, he says, "Dorie, wake up! What are you doing asleep at this time of day?"

She pulls herself into a sitting position. He sees that she's wearing her nightgown. Vaguely, she says, "What time is it?"

"Four o'clock. Ernie and Vi have been home for an hour. They're next door with Alice because you locked them out of the house. Alice called me at work. This is outrageous, Dorie! And where are Abby and Ned?"

"I don't know. At school, I guess."

"I want you to get dressed and go over and bring the kids home. Apologize to Alice. It's not up to her to take care of our children!"

"You get them. I'm too embarrassed."

"This is *your* responsibility."

Grumbling, Dorie climbs out of bed and pulls on some old clothing. Nat goes down to the kitchen to see what they have for dinner. The refrigerator is practically empty.

As he drives to the grocery store, he's grateful this incident didn't occur when it was twenty below. Then he realizes he can't take any more chances; his children simply aren't safe when Dorie's in charge. The kids need to be able to come home to someone who will be there to let them in. A nice, reliable woman who cooks. He'd better cut back his hours in the clinic, focus on research, which will give him greater flexibility so he can be home more of the time.

Later that night, he stands over Dorie, who's back in bed. "Today was the final straw, Dorie. I'm going to hire a housekeeper whether you like it or not."

Weakly she replies, "Please don't." Tears start to dribble down her wan cheeks. "I'm sorry about what happened today, but don't bring in some other woman. I don't want somebody watching me in my own house."

"I don't trust you to attend to our kids."

She dashes the tears away. "I refuse to let another woman in to rule my home."

"Then I will leave and take the children with me."

He's frightened that it has come to this, while at the same time an exciting sense of liberation is rising in him. The love he once felt for Dorie is long gone.

"You can't do that. I live for the children!"

"I have to do this." He'll need to find a furnished house and a house-keeper as soon as possible. Fortunately he can afford to buy another place. When his father sold Sutton Chemical, George gave him and Harriet $100,000 each.

But how is he going to explain moving to his kids? He aches for them when he thinks about how unsettling this change will be for them. He can't tell his children he doesn't trust their mother without damaging their sense of being safe when they're with her.

He'll have to allow them to spend some time with Dorie, but he'll want to be the one who drops them off and picks them up again so he can monitor Dorie's behavior. This could get really ugly.

May 1968

On her way to the faculty room for a quick cup of coffee, Harriet notices that the door to Janice Braun's office is closed. She stops, startled, for she's never seen it shut before, though she realizes it must be from time to time. She hears people talking inside. Is that her father's voice? She knocks briskly.

"Yes," Janice replies. "Come in."

As she enters, her father and Janice, who are seated close together at a small round table in the corner, jerk apart. Janice blushes. She's wearing a ruffled pink blouse Harriet has never seen before. Come to think of it, Janice has worn all sorts of new blouses with her suits lately.

"Hello, Father, I didn't expect to find you here."

Janice laughs. "George is here all the time." She sounds a little flirty.

What is going on? The atmosphere in the room is positively electric. She doesn't like the energy she senses between Janice and her father.

Calmly, he replies, "We're discussing the merger."

"What? The merger! You're going ahead with it?" She's shocked. She hasn't heard anything about a merger in months. She assumed the financial problems that led the boards to consider merging had faded away. The general economy is certainly booming.

Sitting back in his chair, her father says, "Of course we are."

Her stomach tightens. "Why didn't you tell me?"

"I knew you'd be angry."

She *is* angry, but she's just as mad at herself for being so willfully blind. A while ago when her mother remarked that her father was rarely home because of all the meetings he had to attend, she never asked questions. How could she have been so stupid? Her conviction that the merger should not proceed caused her to ignore any indications that the process was indeed moving forward.

Her heart starts pounding in her ears. "But you didn't give the faculty a chance to offer their ideas for saving Hartley." This is so unfair! She looks at Janice and then George.

He leans forward. Speaking slowly, emphatically, he states, "It doesn't matter what the faculty think. It's up to us with the fiduciary responsibility for the schools to make this decision."

Now she's trembling inside, but she takes a tight grip on herself. "It seems to me . . ."

He cuts her off. "It's our responsibility to determine what's best for both institutions." The arrogance in his voice makes her think her father considers this his own personal responsibility.

She turns to her boss. "Janice. How could you let this go ahead?"

"We have to accept the inevitable, Harriet. Our students will have a better educational experience once we work everything out."

"I don't believe that," says Harriet. "Hartley's curriculum is much more rigorous than Warden's. Their upper school chemistry course is anemic compared to ours."

Janice says, "Is that true?"

"You're telling me the final decision has already been made? But girls thrive in schools for girls! I would never have developed any confidence in my intelligence if I hadn't attended a girls' school and women's college." She's absolutely convinced that this is the case.

"We'll be announcing the merger in June, after the school year is over." Janice looks down at her hands resting on the table. How can she be so passive?

"I see," Harriet says. "You're presenting a fait accompli at a time when the parents and students stop thinking about school for a few months."

Glancing at George, Janice says, "We can't disrupt the end of the school year or distract students from their final exams, and we certainly hope to minimize any opposition."

Harriet can scarcely breathe. Is there anything she can do to stop this juggernaut? She's so lost in thought that she absentmindedly sits down at the table with them. She could quit her job in protest. "What's your timetable?"

"We'll start the fall with the new school operating on both campuses."

"That soon?" Then she understands: if she were to resign, her action would have no impact all. Her stomach twists until it's as taut as a drum.

"The sooner the better," says George. "Like tearing a bandage off a wound, it's best to do it quickly."

This is awful.

Looking hopelessly around the room, she cries, "Why aren't Mr. Stryck and Dr. Edie here with you?" What is going on?

Her father says, "Walt Edie is retiring. James Stryck has a very busy law practice. While he attends meetings of the board and the merger committee, he doesn't need to get involved in the level of detail that Janice and I are addressing."

"Will Janice head the new school?"

Janice replies, "The merger committee believes we need to find a new head—someone who isn't associated with either institution—to lead the new school."

"Then what will your role be?" Harriet realizes she's treading on ground that is none of her business, but she feels that Janice is more of a colleague than a boss.

Her father says, "That remains to be determined." Harriet doesn't believe him. She thinks her father knows exactly what Janice will be doing in the new school.

Janice smiles. She doesn't seem nervous at all.

As Harriet considers the implications of the impending changes, she starts to feel nauseated. She asks, "Will people lose their jobs?"

"Perhaps a few," he admits. "After all," he adds defensively, "we're looking to operate more efficiently."

"Who will make the decisions about staff?"

His eyes dart over to Janice and then back to Harriet. "That's enough, Harriet. This is confidential information—I trust you to keep it under your hat."

She glances at her watch. "I still have one class I'm responsible for—I need to go teach now."

As soon as she closes the door, she leans back against it and inhales deeply, exhales slowly, and inhales again, trying to calm herself before she has to face a room full of students who have no idea what's coming.

❧

As soon as the school day ends, Harriet hurries over to her parents' house in hopes of finding her mother there. Joey is at practice with his tennis team, so she doesn't have to pick him up until five.

Once she and her mother have settled on the porch with glasses of iced tea, she asks, "Did *you* know the merger is going forward?"

"Yes, I did. I'm sorry I couldn't warn you. George asked me not to speak to you about it because he wanted to tell you himself."

"They're moving so fast!"

"Apparently many schools around the country are looking at consolidation. The times are changing. Sometimes it seems that everything is changing."

"What if I lose my job? Father suggested there'll be some streamlining, which must mean fewer administrative positions." Clenching her fist, she says, "I'd hate to lose my job, Mother!"

"I know, dearie. Perhaps you could return to teaching. You loved that."

"I did love teaching, but if I became a full-time teacher again, wouldn't it feel like going backward? I enjoy being head of the upper school—I'm learning a lot, and I think I've done good work." She *knows* she's done well. She really liked working with the faculty to integrate the science and math curriculum into a much more logical sequence of courses, and she enjoyed being greeted by students in the halls.

"From all I've heard, you've done a super job, Harriet. You're supremely capable at everything you do." She pauses. "Would you ever consider teaching at a college?"

"I might need a PhD to do that, and I'm much too old to go back to school now."

"You aren't even fifty yet. That sounds young to me!" Eleanor smiles fondly.

"I'll be fifty in a few more months." Harriet extends her legs out in front of her, finally relaxing a little.

"True enough." Eleanor raises her glass and squints into it. "I seem to have missed some of the lemon seeds."

"I love your iced tea, Mother. The mint makes it especially good."

"Thank you." She takes a sip. "When does Retta get home from Mt. Holyoke?"

"Joey and I go get her this weekend. I can hardly wait."

"She likes college, doesn't she?"

"It's been a while since I've had a letter from her, but she sounds happy. She appreciates the variety of courses and outside lecturers she has access to through the five-college consortium." It's a relief to think about her children instead of Hartley for a few minutes.

"Bring Retta and Joey over for dinner once you're back from Northampton. I'd love to hear all about Retta's first year, as well as Joey's plans. Has he started visiting colleges?"

"Not yet. As soon as the kids get back from California, we'll begin looking at the schools he's interested in."

"I hope you'll be at Sea View for the Fourth of July."

"Of course we will." Harriet finishes her tea. Crossing her legs, she asks, "Has Father said much about Janice Braun? It seems the two of them are spending an awful lot of time together." She doesn't want to alarm her mother, but she feels uneasy about them.

"I'm aware that they see each other with great frequency these days. I warned George not to let himself get too close to Janice."

Harriet's glad to hear this. Should she tell her mother that Janice seemed positively flirtatious with her father?

Eleanor adds, "We don't need any more problems like that."

"What are you talking about?"

"We had some trouble during the war. Your father became involved with the woman who headed the Jewish Refugee Resettlement Committee, where he served as chairman of the board, and it took me months to realize what was going on. It wasn't until I saw them together at a gala fundraiser that I understood he had fallen in love with Miriam. I pretended I didn't know, hoping it would blow over, but even then it took me a long time to confront him."

"I'm really sorry, Mother. I had no idea."

"You weren't meant to know. I felt such anguish about his affair that I couldn't face it."

Her father had an affair! That must have been *terrible* for her mother. "I'm *so* sorry."

"I pretended nothing had happened, but I drank more and more, and you know where that led. Sobriety required me to get honest with myself and with others. I've learned how important it is to speak with your husband about everything—even the tough stuff he may not want to hear."

She nods, wondering how her mother managed to live with his betrayal.

"I'm going to get some more tea. Would you like some, Harriet?"

"That would be great." She hands her empty glass to her mother.

While she waits for her mother to return, Harriet starts thinking about her own life. If she'd been honest with Ron early on, making it clear how she felt about his drinking, would they still be married today?

∾

Early in June on the day after graduation, Janice asks Harriet to come to her office.

When she arrives, she taps on the open door.

Seated at her desk, Janice says, "Come in, Harriet. Please take a seat."

She sits in front of the desk.

Looking down, Janice appears nervous as she fusses with some papers. Finally she slides them over to the side and looks up.

"I have to inform you that I've been selected to serve the new institution as director of the upper school. I regret that this means you will no longer hold that position. We'll do a search for a new head of the school."

"You're taking my job?"

"I'm sorry, Harriet."

Desperately, she says, "I could teach chemistry again!"

"Mr. Hodgkinson and Dr. Gepner aren't going anywhere."

"Oh." She starts to sweat. Drops of perspiration run down her back.

"You will receive six months' salary as severance and a letter of reference detailing your stellar performance."

She can't speak. How could they do this to her? She has worked so hard for many years. She's done everything the school asked of her—she even accepted Janice's request that she leave teaching to become director of the upper school, and now they're taking that away from her?

Feeling wobbly, she stands and grips the front of the desk. "I've loved working at Hartley." She's about to lose control.

"I know you'll land on your feet, Harriet. For now, I advise you to take some time off. Think about what you want to tackle next. You can do anything you set your mind to."

When Janice stands, Harriet turns to leave.

"I wish you well, Harriet."

The hell you do. You're glad to have my job, she thinks angrily.

Back in her office, she starts throwing her books and papers into one of the boxes she brought for her end-of-the-school-year stuff. Now it turns out she needs to take *everything* home with her. She pulls the posters from the Museum of Natural History off the walls and rolls them up. She refuses to cry, though her eyes feel hot. On the way out to her car with the first box, she glances into the chemistry lab, but her stomach clenches at the thought of going in there one last time, so she heads toward the door instead. She'll miss so much about this place, even the smells of floor wax and dusty radiators. She's glad Retta and Joey have already left for California; when she gets home, she'll be able to sob without upsetting them.

At the house, after she puts her boxes down on the kitchen counter, she moves into the living room and sits. Rocking back and forth, back and forth, she isn't able to cry. She's too hurt and scared. She returns to the kitchen and picks up the phone.

"Mother, can I come over right now?"

"Of course, dearie."

ॐ

She rushes into her parents' house, letting the door slam behind her.

"Mother!"

"I'm in the kitchen."

Eleanor is boiling a pot of eggs. It's at least ninety degrees and so humid that her hair curls wildly all over her head.

"They axed me! Janice is taking my job for herself." Tears start to stream down her cheeks.

Her mother quickly turns off the flame under the pot. "Let's go out to the porch where we can talk. It's stifling in here." She pours two glasses of iced tea, and they start down the hall. Looking over, she says, "You go ahead and cry your eyes out, Harriet. It'll be good for you."

Once they're seated, Harriet puts her face in her hands. Eventually she looks up, pulls a Kleenex out of her pocket, and blows her nose. Finally she can speak.

"I'm terrified, Mother. What if I can't find another good job that's interesting and challenging, and that pays enough? I've got to be able to cover Retta's college tuition. I've been making $8,000 a year, and Retta's tuition is $3,000. And Joey, I might have to pull him out of Warden—or whatever the new school is going to be called—his senior year. He'd hate that. What am I going to do for money?"

"You have the money George gave you a year ago."

She shakes her head decisively. "I can't touch that money—it's my nest egg for when I'm old."

Eleanor reaches out to touch her arm. "We can help if you're really strapped for cash, dearie."

"But I shouldn't need to ask my parents for financial assistance at my age. I should be able to cope on my own."

"Please feel free to ask anytime."

"I know this isn't really rational, but I feel as though Father fired me. It's his fault I lost my job."

"Feelings are facts, Harriet. Don't deny them."

"My job is my life!"

"You do have your children."

"I know, but they don't need much from me now." She feels panicky. "What am I going to do, Mother? My whole world is falling apart."

"You should let yourself grieve, Harriet. Take the time to really give in to your pain and fear and sorrow. The children are with Ron this month, so you have an opportunity now to really dive into your suffering. I don't think you've ever allowed yourself to feel sad over the demise of your marriage."

"I couldn't afford to." She didn't have any choice but to focus on caring for her children.

"You need to *grieve* now. Let yourself feel everything."

The idea frightens her, for it means losing control. "That doesn't sound like fun at all."

"Once you get through it, you'll feel so much better and stronger than ever."

"Hello," George calls. "Where are you?"

Eleanor replies, "We're out on the porch."

Harriet lurches to her feet. Her face flushes; she wants to scream at her father.

Her mother puts her hand on Harriet's leg. "Don't go."

George appears with a short glass of neat bourbon in his hand. He sits. "It's a real scorcher out there."

Scowling at him, Harriet says furiously, "I will never forgive you for taking my job away from me."

She expects him to bluster but instead he says quietly, "I take it Janice has spoken with you."

Her voice quivering, she says, "You betrayed me, Father. You're the one who encouraged me to take the upper school job. I could still be teaching chemistry if you hadn't done that. And then you drove the merger through, which meant that I lost my job. This is all your fault."

He lights up a cigarette. "Actually, Harriet, I did not intend for you to lose your job. I wanted Janice to be named head of the new school, and you could have been director of the new upper school. But I didn't get my way."

Surprised but undaunted, she says, "You've always pursued your own interests instead of looking out for me. I told you I wanted to work for Sutton Chemical once I got my master's, but it was months before you offered me a job." She knows she sounds childish, but she needs to say these things to him for once and for all.

"I wanted you to keep your options open in case you got a better offer."

"My goal all along was to work for you! Don't you understand?" She's near tears.

"Then why didn't you come back to work for me once the children were in school?"

Taking a deep breath, she calms down a little. "I realized that money didn't motivate me, while making lots of money is what drove you."

He taps the end of his cigarette into the ashtray. "Businesses must make money if they're to survive."

She looks at her mother. "Frank was right," she says. "I should have taken the research job at the Rockefeller Institute."

"I thought we had a good time working together at the company, Harriet. You learned a great deal there."

He actually sounds hurt. Touched, she says, "That's true. I learned how to deal with a lot of different people." She pauses a moment as her anger rekindles. "But now because of you, I have no job! I need a job. Independent women work. I don't know what I'm going to do."

"Relax," he says, smiling. "I have other plans for you."

"Like what?"

"I'm not quite ready to say more yet."

Although a wisp of hope starts rising, Harriet is still furious enough to doubt whether she can trust her father to consider her well-being.

"I'm somewhat surprised by the resistance we're getting to the merger," he says. "One of the upper school teachers at Warden claims he can't work for a woman, so he quit. Another teacher complained that girls use up all the oxygen in the room, and boys need more oxygen than girls, so the boys will suffer. Can you believe that!" He lifts his glass to his mouth.

Eleanor snorts. "Outrageous!"

"It's a man's world," Harriet says. "Men expect preferential treatment and they always get it. Women as a class are disadvantaged."

George raises his arms, and after hooking his fingers behind his head, he leans back in a cocky pose. "It turns out that we have a serious problem with the differences in salaries at the two schools. Teachers at Warden have always negotiated their salaries, whereas teachers at Hartley are paid on a stepped system based on years of experience and academic degrees."

"It won't be easy to resolve those differences," remarks Eleanor.

"And then we're going to need more bathrooms at each campus for members of the opposite sex."

"You asked for it," says Harriet.

She rises to her feet. "I've got to go. Thanks for the tea, Mother." She glances at George, neither smiling nor nodding, though her fury is abating. "Father," she acknowledges.

Eleanor jumps up and embraces her with such a warm hug that she feels comforted. Then her mother says, "I'm sure everything will turn out well in the end, dearie. You'll see."

ॐ

She decides to follow her mother's advice. She spends the next three weeks by herself, walking and weeping and sleeping and thinking. She misses Ron. He was so much fun at parties and on the tennis court and in bed, and he was sweet with her and the kids. She questions everything. Did she neglect Ron? Is that why he turned to alcohol? Was she so caught up in the children that she didn't give him the companionship he needed? Maybe she shouldn't have delivered the ultimatum that he had to quit drinking or she'd leave their marriage.

Regrets gnaw at her, but it's too late to change anything. She cries a lot. Was it her bossiness that drove him away? Should she have deferred to him more? She has always tried to be a strong woman, but maybe she went too far. Did she simply become too independent in determining her own priorities without heeding his? This question makes her cry some more.

Now she's got to find a new job. She knows she'll find something, but what's it going to be? She's embarrassed that she hasn't stayed in any position for longer than a few years. It makes her look flighty. She's much more serious than her track record suggests.

Now what?

June 1968

Lucy is already sitting in what has become their usual booth at the back of the Triangle Bar. It's been a few weeks since they started seeing each other, right after Nat moved out of the house he'd shared with Dorie. Now he and the children live in a bungalow not far from the place that's now Dorie's.

As he hurries toward Lucy, his unbuttoned blazer flapping, she spots him and smiles broadly. Her eyes look positively sparkly. He quickly removes his jacket and places it on the seat before he sits down.

Seeing that she has a beer in front of her, he says, "I hope I haven't kept you waiting long."

"Not at all. I've only been here a few minutes."

As he slides into the booth across from her, he says, "I really appreciated your help this morning."

"The poor woman panicked when you told her about the lesion in her daughter's heart. It took both of us to convince her that Stacy would die if you weren't allowed to operate."

"They both seemed pretty calm when I checked on them before coming over here."

"I'm happy to hear that."

He waves a passing waitress over. "Could you get me a Manhattan with just a whisper of vermouth?"

Lucy leans forward and touches his hand. "How is it going, Nat?"

"There's a lot to adjust to."

"I can imagine."

"I met with an attorney a couple of days ago to start divorce proceedings. He said the only way I can get sole custody is if I document Dorie's negligence. I need to get a statement from the neighbor who called me when Dorie locked the kids out of the house. I'll talk with their teachers to see what they've observed. And the court will likely appoint a psychologist to interview the older kids. I don't like this going around behind Dorie's back, but I have to protect my children."

"It's none of my business, but I'm curious." She hunches her shoulders slightly. "How do you take care of four children while you're at work?"

"I've hired an older lady to come in afternoons, oversee their homework, and start supper. Once school ends for the summer, she'll be there all day to drive them to their lessons and other activities. We'll see how she works out."

"Do you trust her?"

"She comes highly recommended. She's a young grandmotherly type with lots of energy."

"I bet she'll need it."

He pauses, worried suddenly by her response. "Are you daunted by my having four kids?"

"Not at all. I'm the oldest of five. I helped raise my brothers and sisters, so I know what it takes. Actually, I always hoped to have a big family myself, but after Olivia I wasn't able to get pregnant again."

It's such a relief to hear this! Much more relaxed now, he muses, "I was terribly young when I married Dorie. Innocent. I'd known few girls of any kind. I had no idea what I was getting into."

"It takes a long time to learn what somebody's really like."

"That's for sure. I suppose I'm still young in some ways."

"I like catching glimpses of the boy in you."

The waitress returns with his Manhattan. He raises the glass. "To the future."

Lucy picks up her beer. "To the future."

Staring into each other's eyes, they each take a drink.

Once he puts his glass back on the table, he asks, "What is Olivia up to this summer?"

"She's going to Girl Scout camp for a week in July, taking swimming lessons, and reading lots and lots of books. What about your children?"

"I'm taking them East for a couple of weeks to our family's summer place."

"That should be fun."

"I wish you could come with us."

She shakes her head. "Oh no, Nat, I couldn't do that. I haven't even met your children."

"Oops," he says. "I guess that was premature." He doesn't mean to pressure her, but he's sure she's the one for him. She's so warm and caring, honest and direct. "Well, someday soon I'd like them to meet you."

She sits up straighter. "We'll have to think about the best way to handle that. How are your children dealing with being separated from their mother?"

"I think they see this as a temporary adventure, though I certainly get a sense of relief from Abby. She hasn't said anything—she's not going to bad-mouth her mother."

"Of course not."

He takes a drink of his Manhattan. "Do you need to hurry home, or do you have time to eat something?"

"Olivia's at a friend's house for the night, so I have all the time in the world." His heart speeds up. Is this an implicit invitation? He remembers the time he met her here right after Bobby Kennedy was shot. He was so upset by the assassination that he wanted to rush into her arms, and while she stood facing him with her arms folded tight against her stomach, it almost seemed as if she was holding herself back from hugging him. They've barely touched each other—so far. He says, "Let's order then. I could do with a hamburger and fries."

"That sounds good."

After they place their orders, he can't think what to say next. He is so drawn to her he can hardly think. He wants to kiss her, but if they start, will he be able to stop? If they get too involved and Dorie finds out, he's sure she'd use that against him.

Lucy asks, "Do you know why it's called the Variety Club Heart Hospital?"

"No, I don't."

"Would you believe that the money to build the hospital was raised by people in the *entertainment* business?"

"No way, Jose."

"Dr. Morse Shapiro, who ran a children's rheumatic fever clinic, and another physician who specialized in tuberculosis convinced the local chapter of the Variety Club that there was an acute need for a special heart hospital for children that would be part of the university hospital."

"Really?"

"Since members of the Variety Club are part of the motion picture industry, they decided to make a movie, and they got actor Ronald Reagan to urge audiences to make donations toward the fight against heart disease."

"This is a great story."

"When it opened in 1951, it was the first hospital in the country just for heart patients."

"I knew it was the first but not how it got started."

"I'm interested in history so I read a fair amount."

She's not a showoff. He admires that.

"I know you're worried about the future of heart surgery at the U. Did you consider going to New York with Dr. Lillehei?"

"He asked me to come with him, but I wanted to stay here. I really like living in Minnesota."

Their food appears.

After they start eating, he says, "You're into music, aren't you?"

She swallows before answering. "I *love* music, especially live music. Must be because I spent so much time at my parents' supper club. I got to hear lots of different bands playing swing, jazz, even rock."

He thinks, *We have so much in common!*

He asks, "What's your favorite kind of music?"

She puts her hamburger back on the plate. "I like choral music, like Bach's B Minor Mass, and jazz and folk. I really like the Beatles. They're amazingly creative. When you think how far they've come in four years, it's unbelievable—from singing "I Want to Hold Your Hand" on the Ed Sullivan Show in 1964 to coming out with *Rubber Soul* and *Revolver.*

"They've written some great tunes."

"I have all their albums." She picks her hamburger back up.

He moves his head from one side to the other, as though he's trying to see behind her. "What's that you've done with your hair?"

"It's called a French twist." She turns so he can see the back of her head.

"Very elegant. Makes me think of Audrey Hepburn."

Blushing, she looks down for a moment. "Thank you." When she raises her eyes to him, she says, "You have no idea how long I've been watching you, wanting to get to really know you."

"How long?" he teases.

"Years!" Her eyes are so shiny he almost thinks he sees tears at the corners.

He reaches his right hand out to her. "Well, I'm finally free."

She takes his hand and squeezes it, then pulls hers back. "Not completely," she says.

"Close enough. There's no way I'd ever go back to Dorie."

She stares into his eyes. "Are you sure?"

"Absolutely."

"In that case," she says, grinning, "would you like to come over to my place for a drink?"

"Would I! I'll call Mrs. March and see if she can stay with the kids a while longer."

He stands and fumbles in his pocket for his wallet, releasing scraps of paper that flutter to the floor.

She picks one up and reads.

Red suffusing blue,
Granite's gray;
One last ray, through orange clouds, breaks through
As we say, "Goodnight, Sea View."

"What is this?" she asks.

"Just some lyrics for a song I'm writing for my family."

"I'd love to hear it sometime."

"You will," he promises.

∾

Nat follows Lucy's car along West River Road to a white stucco house in South Minneapolis. As soon as they get inside and Lucy shuts the door behind them, he turns to face her.

"May I hold you? I'm much more interested in holding you than having a drink." He opens his arms.

She walks into his embrace.

He sighs. She feels so good. When he moves his head to sniff her neck, he catches a whiff of lavender soap. Sighing again, he draws her closer. They're still standing in front of the door.

She pulls back and grasps his hand. "Let's move over to the couch where we can be more comfortable."

She leads him around a coffee table covered with books and sits down. He settles at an angle to her. She turns toward him as he leans forward to kiss her. Her lips are soft and warm.

He puts his arms around her as their kiss continues. He wants to sink into her. After a few more breathless moments, he says, "Would it be all right if we lie down?"

"Oh yes."

He takes off his blazer while she removes her green cardigan. When she loosens the clip holding her French twist in place, her honey-colored hair tumbles to her shoulders. Then they stretch out facing each other. The couch is flat all the way across the seat—Nat can stick his feet off the end. Arms around each other, they touch the entire length of their bodies. As they rock gently back and forth, their heat rises. Lucy snuggles in even closer. She presses against Mr. Snake, who is very excited.

He moans, "So good, Lucy."

"Would you like to go to bed?" She seems a little shy asking this.

"We should wait till we're not so pressed for time. When I make love to you, I don't want to be in a rush."

"You're right," she agrees. "Let's not rush. It feels so wonderful just to be held. Let's savor this now."

He says, "We'll find a time to spend the whole night together. Soon!"

❧

Early in July, Nat brings his children to Massachusetts for two weeks, pleased by the prospect of a family vacation at Sea View without the burden of Dorie weighing him down. As he drives from the Boston airport toward the North Shore, he realizes that he feels free for the first time in years. He's so light, he could almost fly. When the car rises up the lift bridge onto Cape Ann, he suddenly hears the first line of a new tune in his head—both words and notes. The line is "Sea View, summers spent at Sea View." Humming it quietly to himself, he thinks about additional lyrics to complete the song. He has a good group to work with: his daughter Abby and Harriet's Joey on guitars, Harriet's Retta on flute, his sons Ned on drums and Ernie on bass, with Vi on vocals. The summer before last, Abby and Joey were a great team helping him polish the lyrics and tune for "Let's Not Put the Boats Away."

When they arrive, the rest of his family streams out of the house. His father and mother greet the kids while Harriet, Retta, and Joey help carry their luggage inside. The children chatter among themselves as they haul the instruments into the living room. A snare drum and one hi-hat sit in the corner where Nat left them before. Joey's guitar case, covered with multicolored Flower Power stickers, and a small amplifier rest nearby.

"Hey kids," he says, "you want to work on more songs this summer? I've started a couple of new ones."

Joey exclaims, "Groovy!"

"We can put on a show the last night we're here together."

"That would be so cool!" says Retta.

His sister's kids are looking more like hippies this summer. Retta's dark brown hair is long and straight, held back from her face with a bright orange headband, and Joey's wearing a tie-dyed T-shirt with red sunbursts all over it. Of course, his own kids are younger; they live in the Midwest, and perhaps they've been sheltered more than Harriet's East Coast kids, who also spend time on the West Coast with Ron. He should ask Retta and Joey what it's like for them to have parents who are divorced, if he can get them alone. Perhaps he'd learn something that would help in his own case. His kids don't know yet that his divorce is underway.

Before dinner the first evening, the older folks sit on the porch with their drinks while the younger ones play a game of Monopoly in the dining room. A cool breeze is blowing in from the ocean. Both his mother and sister wear sweaters. Harriet's is the same purple color as her slacks. Eleanor, in a denim skirt, dons pants only for gardening. He dressed in long plaid pants to please his mother—otherwise he'd be wearing blue jeans. His father is attired in his usual white shirt, dark trousers, and sneakers.

Eleanor says, "It's wonderful to have you all here at last!" She looks at Nat, squinting a little. Does she need new glasses? "What's the news on Dorie?"

He quickly glances around to make sure his kids are out of earshot. "She's very depressed, and she continues to refuse to see anyone about it. She's living in our house, and I've rented a bungalow nearby so the kids can walk back and forth."

"That's good," says his mother.

He goes on. "I met with a divorce attorney last month. He's drawing up the papers to grant me sole custody of the children, but he cautioned me that it would be very unusual for the courts to give custody to the father. As I've told you, I can't trust Dorie to be responsible for them any longer. My attorney says I'll need to provide documented evidence of her unfitness as a mother. We'll probably get a hearing in front of a judge."

Eleanor replies, "I'm very sorry, Nat. This must be extremely difficult for you."

"No fun at all."

"Before you go to court, I hope you'll get your hair cut and sideburns trimmed."

"Mother! Everyone's wearing their hair longer these days. I'm finally in style along with everybody else."

Harriet laughs. "That's true, Nat. It's a first for you."

His father is sitting to the side, staring out to sea, but Nat knows from the way his head is cocked that he's listening.

His sister turns to their mother and speaks quietly. "You were right, Mummy. I feel a lot better now that I've done some grieving."

"I'm very glad to hear that."

"It helped to say everything I did to Father. I guess I had a lot to get off my chest."

Nat says, "Thanks for your recent calls, Harriet. What's next for you?"

"I don't know yet. I've got some feelers out."

Joey emerges from inside. "I'm out of the game—used up all my money."

"Come join us if you like," Harriet says.

Joey takes an empty chair near Nat. "What do you think of The Byrds, Uncle Nat? Do you like their music?"

"I'm not familiar with them."

"Their 'Turn, Turn, Turn' and 'Mr. Tambourine Man' blow my mind. I can play one of their albums for you later if you want." Joey looks at him expectantly.

"You have a record player here?"

"I brought mine from home."

"I'd like to hear The Byrds and anything else you want to play for me."

"I'll play you my Country Joe and the Fish album too."

Harriet says, "Blowing one's mind makes me think about a situation we had in May with a senior who was seen smoking marijuana behind Hartley at the end of the school year."

George turns around to hear better.

She continues, "Of course, there's nothing in the handbook yet about smoking marijuana, though consuming cigarettes or alcohol in or near the school and at school functions is forbidden. Anyway, this senior was near the top of her class, her grades qualified her for the Cum Laude Society, and she'd been accepted by Wellesley. I thought long and hard about what kind of punishment would be appropriate. We could deny her membership in Cum Laude. We could suspend her for a few days, but then she'd miss her exams, which would mean she couldn't graduate. If we expelled her, it would be even worse. Any punishment for her at the end of her senior year could ruin her life."

Nat says, "What's the big deal? I smoked Mary Jane in my jazz club days. I was an early beatnik—I guess."

Eleanor exclaims, "Mary Jane?"

"Pot, Mother."

Joey's watching his uncle closely, a dreamy smile on his face.

Harriet says, "I didn't believe we should simply ignore her bad behavior. It sets a terrible precedent. Everyone knows what's going on in a small school like ours."

"Aren't you being a bit prudish, Harriet?" says Nat.

"The rules should apply to everyone."

George asks, "What did you do?"

"Janice gave the student a stern talking to. That was it."

"We'll have to make sure the new student handbook addresses marijuana use," says George.

Joey gets up and goes back into the living room. A moment later, they hear him tuning his guitar.

Harriet sits with her legs crossed, swinging the top leg back and forth, gazing at the ocean.

Saying, "I'll just check on the casserole," Eleanor heads into the house.

George says, "Harriet?"

She turns to look at him.

"What would you think about working at the foundation? I need someone to manage operations, and I think you'd be great."

"Really? Is this what you meant when you said you had plans for me?"

"Yes."

"Why did you wait? Why didn't you tell me when I lost my job at Hartley?"

"I thought you should take the summer off."

"I would have enjoyed myself much more if I'd known about this job possibility."

"With all your experience in research and administration," says Nat, "you'd bring a lot to the foundation, and we'd get to work together on the advisory committee."

George says, "Let me know if you want it, Harriet."

∾

Later that evening, Nat sits drinking with his father. They're alone on the porch. The older kids are back in the living room, and everyone else is in bed. In the relative quiet, he can hear the frogs in the lily pond behind the house croaking loudly.

His father asks, "Do you want to try to reconcile your differences with Dorie?"

"I can't imagine ever getting back together with her. What complicates the situation is that I've fallen in love with someone else."

"You've been having an affair?" His father sounds surprised.

"Not exactly. I've known this woman for years—we work together—and we didn't start spending time together outside the hospital until after Dorie and I separated. It just feels a little like an affair since technically I'm still married."

"Is this other woman the reason you and Dorie split up?"

"God, no. There are a million reasons we split up. We're completely incompatible."

His father nods agreement.

Is now the time to confront his father after all these years? He puts his hands on his upper thighs. "I know *you* must have had an affair, because I saw you with a dark-haired woman at the Three Deuces jazz club one night during the war. I lost a great deal of respect for you at that time."

George bends forward to touch the flame from his lighter to the tip of a cigarette. After exhaling some smoke, he admits, "Yes, I did have an affair then."

"I knew it! I was so angry at you, Father. I couldn't believe you would do that to Mother." He lights a cigarette too. "What ever happened to that woman?"

"Miriam ended it after a year."

"Have you had any other affairs?"

"I was always dutiful until Miriam came along. Then I completely lost control of myself. It was some sort of compulsion that I was unable to resist."

"Since then?" He knows he's probably going too far by asking this question, but he suspects he'll never have another opportunity. How much like his father is he, really? Is he guilty of adultery too?

George replies, "That was the only time I acted on an attraction to someone other than your mother. Since then," he chuckles, "she wouldn't let me get away with it." Does his father count on being kept in line?

His situation is different. "I don't think I could ever give Lucy up."

Smiling ruefully, his father says, "I do know the feeling." He crushes his cigarette out in a nearby ashtray.

Nat takes one last drag of his own cigarette. "We've never had a talk like this before."

"That's true. All I can say is that I hope you manage to free yourself from Dorie. She was never a good match for you."

"Thanks for understanding, Father. It's my kids I have to look out for now."

"Indeed."

During their time at Sea View, everyone enjoys the usual swimming and sailing and games, eating favorite meals, talking and laughing and hanging around with each other. Late afternoons while dinner is being prepared, Nat and the children work on their songs. Making music with his family like this—he couldn't be happier as they prepare to perform for his parents and sister. With Abby and Joey's assistance, "Sea View, Summers Spent at Sea View" has become a delightful song.

On the day before he and his children have to return to Minnesota, while they're rehearsing for their show later that night, he receives a frantic telephone call from Dorie's mother.

"Dorie's in the hospital, Nathaniel. She's in rough shape. You've got to come back right away!"

"What happened?"

"She tried to kill herself! Last night I found her sitting in the bathtub covered with blood. I cleaned her up as best as I could and drove her to the emergency room. They admitted her into the hospital and put her in a special ward."

"Oh God. No." He's been kicked in the stomach.

"She needs you!"

"We're flying home tomorrow, Mother Larson. I'll come to Glendale as soon as I can get someone to cover for me on Monday."

"Hurry! I'm so worried, Nathaniel."

He won't tell his children about their mother yet, but the joy he's felt these past two weeks is gone. He gets the kids to help setting up the porch for their performance, pushing the chairs around and arranging the instruments and music stands in a row across the back. He doesn't say much while this is going on.

At one point Abby comes over to him and asks, "Are you all right, Dad?"

"I'm just a little distracted. Getting psyched for our gig tonight."

He starts to feel better once he's standing with the children, ready to start their show. He's wearing his first pair of bellbottoms and a flowered shirt.

Harriet has dressed up in an attractive short dress with big blobs of strong color, which she told him was Marimekko, whatever that means. Joey's wearing another sunburst T-shirt and jeans, and the rest of the kids are wearing the best clothes they have with them. Eleanor has a striped dress on, and George has donned his navy blazer. Nat's pleased by all the attention his "band" is attracting.

Once they start playing "Sea View, Summers Spent at Sea View," the girls singing the tune, he's able to stop thinking about Dorie. At the end of the first song, the audience claps loudly. He breathes in deeply, glad it's going well. After "Let's Not Put the Boats Away," they conclude with "Goodnight, Sea View."

When they finish, Harriet stands and whistles. Eleanor cries, "Encore!" George appears to be dashing tears from his eyes before he starts to applaud. Nat bows and then recognizes each member of the band individually. Then they perform "Let's Not Put the Boats Away" all over again. He wishes Lucy were here with them.

Harriet says, "Abby, why don't you play something we can all sing together? How about 'We Shall Overcome'?"

Abby brings her guitar over and sits next to her aunt. Abby says, "You too, Joey. I'll tell you the chords."

While they all sing "We Shall Overcome" together, Nat's eyes start to water. He doesn't want to think about what he has to face at home.

∾

After seeing Dorie in the locked ward at the Glendale Hospital on Monday afternoon, Nat drives back home. The concern he felt for her is starting to curdle. She boasted about how many stitches it took to stop the bleeding from her wrists, but he knows she would have needed to cut much deeper if she'd actually intended to die. This was clearly a call for attention. When she claimed she has nothing to live for, he reminded her their children need her. She said they have him. The only good news is that her physician has put her on antidepressants and is keeping Dorie in the hospital for at least a week.

November 1968

A lthough Harriet and Gus have been seeing each other for only three months, he's the first man she's been serious about since she and Ron divorced seven years ago. She can tell he's intent on being with her. It might be a little early to bring their children together for Thanksgiving, but the kids all know each other to some extent. Retta was at Hartley with Gus's girls, Nelly and Cathy, though they were in different grades, and Joey is at Warden in the same class with Gus's son, Andy. Not only that, but Nelly was a student in Harriet's chemistry class her senior year.

Now Harriet looks around her dining room table with some nervousness and lots of hope. Her best linen tablecloth, crystal glasses, silver, and wedding china grace the table. She smiles at Retta, home from Mt. Holyoke for Thanksgiving break, and Joey, who will be graduating from Warden School next spring. The turkey sits on a platter in front of Gus, who carves it into slices. His children watch her. This is the first time in years she hasn't celebrated Thanksgiving with her parents—who've taken the train to Minnesota to be with Nat and his children.

She says, "I'm glad you all could join us for dinner today. We don't say grace at our house, so why don't you start passing the mashed potatoes, Nelly?"

The platter of turkey, the gravy boat, a dish of peas, and a basket of rolls begin to circulate around the table too.

Nelly helps herself to a dollop of potatoes and then passes the dish to her sister. "I have to say, this is a little weird, Mrs. Wright. I'm sorry, but you were my teacher and now you're dating Dad? Mom only moved out to Chicago a few months ago."

"*Six* months ago," Gus clarifies.

"Nelly, please call me Harriet."

"I don't think I can do that. You're Mrs. Wright to me." She shoves her spoon into her potatoes and pours gravy into the indentation.

"How long have you and Dad been seeing each other?" asks Cathy. Her mouth looks as though she's tasting something bitter.

"Your father called me this summer and asked me out to dinner, and I've enjoyed getting to know him." How can she show his girls she genuinely cares about their father? "He's even gotten me into playing duplicate bridge. He's quite a competitive guy, isn't he?" Looking down the table, she winks at Gus. The light fixture above the table shines on the top of his bald spot.

"Yep!" says Cathy.

"How do you like Barnard?" Harriet asks her.

"Well enough. There's a lot to do in Manhattan."

Harriet raises her eyebrows at her daughter. *Help!*

Retta turns to Nelly, who's sitting on her right. "I hear you have a job in the city?"

"I'm in the commercial training program at Bankers Trust."

"You must be good with numbers."

"Since I have an economics professor for a dad, something must have rubbed off on me."

"Yeah," Retta replies. "Mom told me he's teaching at Rutgers."

Harriet grins at Gus. He's been very helpful to her as she comes to grips with the intricacies of charitable finance rules and regulations that pertain to her new job at the foundation.

Joey and Andy sit across the table from each other. Joey says, "I'm totally bummed about Richard Nixon. Aren't you, Andy? Gene McCarthy would have gotten us out of Vietnam."

Andy says softly, "I don't know who I would have voted for."

"Don't you care about the war?"

Andy asks, "Where do you want to go to college next fall?"

"I don't know," Joey says. "What about you?"

"I'm going to Harvard."

"Huh." Joey spears a piece of meat and puts it in his mouth.

As she gazes at Joey, she notices that the curtains behind him look terrible. She hasn't done much cleaning lately. It's not pleasant to be at home since Joey was suspended in September for smoking pot at school. She's been on high alert ever since. She'd grounded him for a month and explained how humiliating it was for her, a former teacher at the sister school, and for her father, a current trustee at the newly merged school, that he'd behaved so badly, but he never did apologize. He was very angry about not being allowed to rehearse with his band, and she worries about him all the time, wanting to know where he is and what he's doing. Her mother is very concerned as well. Eleanor told Harriet that she knows from her AA meetings that marijuana can be the first step on the road to heroin and other hard drugs. Harriet would hate to admit it to anyone, but she can hardly wait until he's safely off at college. His grades have been slipping, but she hopes he'll be accepted somewhere.

"Cathy," Harriet tries again, "what are your favorite courses this year?"

"Physics and anthropology," Cathy replies. She returns her attention to her plate.

"I bet you're doing well in physics. You were one of my best chemistry students."

Cathy mumbles, "Thanks."

The conversation feels so awkward, Harriet can hardly stand it. She looks hopefully at Gus.

"What about you, Retta?" he asks. "What are your favorite classes?"

"I like anthro too. And music."

"Your mother tells me you play the flute very well."

Retta bobs her head. "I enjoy it."

"Which musicians do you follow?"

"Joan Baez, and Peter, Paul and Mary."

He nods. "Would you sing something after dinner?"

Good question, Gus, Harriet thinks.

"Okay," she says reluctantly.

Harriet stands and starts clearing the dishes. Retta and Joey jump up to help. Once the apple pie has been served, they sit down again.

Gus says, "I hear you're a musician too, Joey."

"I play electric guitar—especially 12-string."

"That's cool. Who are your musical heroes?"

"The Doors. The Byrds. Jefferson Airplane. Jimi Hendrix. The Who."

"I heard Steppenwolf playing at the Fillmore East last weekend," says Nelly.

Joey says, "I'll play something for you, Mr. McDonald, if you want."

"Great."

Joey sprints up the stairs. He comes running back down with his acoustic guitar, sits on a chair away from the table, and tunes for a moment before he plays something that sounds Spanish to her. At the end of the song, he drops his hands.

"Very nice," says Gus. "You've got a lot of musical talent, Joey."

He beams. "Thank you, sir."

Gus clears his throat. "Did any of you hear the speeches and prayers on Friday honoring Dr. Martin Luther King?"

Joey replies, "Convicting James Earl Ray to ninety-nine years isn't enough."

Harriet agrees. She's glad that she and her son share some values.

Once they finish the meal, Joey says, "Andy, want to come up to my room to listen to some music?"

"Ah." Andy looks at his father. "Are we staying?"

"Go ahead, Andy. We don't need to leave until three."

Harriet senses that Andy is reluctant to go off with her son. Why is that? Her anxiety rises. Maybe they shouldn't have forced these kids together quite so soon.

"How about a game, everybody? Do you want to play charades, or we could get out a crossword puzzle?"

"I'm going upstairs," Joey says. "Andy?"

Andy follows him out of the dining room.

Retta, Nelly, and Cathy clear the table.

Once Harriet and Gus move toward the living room, he pulls her close. With frequent physical gestures that aren't seen by anyone else, jokes, and allusions to experiences they've shared, he lets her know he's always aware of her when they're together. She likes having this ongoing conversation with Gus that no one else is privy to.

"I think that went well," he says.

"Really? This is harder than I thought it would be."

◌◌

That evening, Harriet telephones her brother. "Happy Thanksgiving, Nat. How did it go introducing Lucy to Mother and Father?"

"Very well. They seemed to like Lucy and Olivia. Lucy came over early to cook the turkey at my house, and Abby and Olivia baked brownies."

"Does Lucy enjoy entertaining a mob?"

"She loved it—she's from a big family, and she's thrilled to become part of ours."

"When will your divorce be final?"

"My lawyer thinks another couple of months. Lucy and I will marry as soon as we can. I hope you'll come, Harriet. It'll be a very small wedding."

"I'll be there. How do your kids get along with Lucy and Olivia?"

"I think they're glad their life isn't so chaotic anymore. What about your family and Gus's?"

"Gus's children are not happy their father has taken up with another woman so soon, even though their mother took off with the man she calls her 'soul mate.' Retta and Joey seem fine with the situation, but they've had lots more time to adjust to their parents' being divorced."

"I guess that's understandable."

"How is Dorie doing?"

"She's better. The antidepressant she's taking helps."

"That's good. This morning, Nat, while I was getting everything ready, I suddenly remembered that Thanksgiving during the war when we had to slaughter all those turkeys we'd raised. What a disgusting job!"

"I think that experience must have desensitized me to the sight of blood. We've both come a long way since then."

"Especially you, Nat. Who would have thought you'd become this big heart surgeon?"

"Music was the only thing on my mind back then."

"Retta and Joey really love making music with you at Sea View."

"I do too. It's more fun than anything."

∾

Late one Friday afternoon in January, Harriet is finishing her review of the foundation's financials when she receives a call from Janice Braun.

"You've got to come get Joey, Harriet."

"What happened?"

"On the bus back from their basketball game at Lawrenceville, Joey told the boys he'd just swallowed a tab of acid. Andy reported it to me."

"No," she moans. She's been afraid of something like this. She almost expected it.

"We must expel your son, Harriet."

"His senior year?"

"We really don't want to expel him, given your history with the

school and your father's role on the board, but we must uphold the
rules. We have no choice."

"I understand that, but what school will take him now?"

"I regret that we have to do this."

"Oh God, he could get drafted—sent to Vietnam!" He could die in
the war, just like Eddie. Her throat tightens.

"Joey's starting to act flaky. How soon can you get here?"

"I'm on my way."

"He'll be in my office."

Harriet grabs some papers off her desk, shoves them into her briefcase, and hurries out the door.

When she gets there, Joey is sitting in a chair with his head craned
back, staring at the ceiling.

"I'm taking you home, Joey."

"Far out." He doesn't move.

"Come on, let's go." She doesn't know what her son is experiencing
right now, so she's not quite sure how to handle him. Taking his arm,
she tugs gently on it.

He stands and looks around the room as if he doesn't know where
he is.

"I'm sorry, Janice. I can't tell you how sorry. Joey, please apologize
to Miss Braun for all the trouble you've caused."

"Sorry, sorry, so sorry."

She grasps Joey's hand and pulls him out the door. Once they're
sitting in her car, she says, "Where in the world did you get LSD?"

"Oh wow, the colors, they're dancing!"

She realizes now is *not* the time to have a conversation with him.
She takes him home, and after offering him food and water, which he
refuses, she tells him to stay in his room. Then she calls Ron to ask
if he can come East and help her figure out what they're going to do
about Joey. He claims he can't possibly free up his calendar for at least
a week.

Then she calls Nat. "Is Joey's life in danger while he's tripping?"

"Just make sure he stays safe at home—don't let him leave the house. He should come down after about twelve hours."

Then she calls her parents. Her father is not at all pleased by the news, but he says he'll see what he can do to find Joey another school.

Her mother says, "Would you like company, Harriet?"

"No thank you, Mother."

"This is not your fault, Harriet. Joey's probably just experimenting. I only hope he doesn't end up taking after me!" Eleanor says.

Oh good, something else to worry about.

Gus calls. "Andy told me about Joey. Is he there with you?"

"Yes, Janice had me pick him up from school."

"Do you want me to come over?"

"Thanks for offering—that's very kind of you." She'd like his company but she's too ashamed right now. "You need to stay with Andy."

She sits up all night, drinking coffee in the living room, fearful and worried as she listens to loud music pounding through the floor from Joey's room. Is he going to climb out the window and jump? Run away? Why did he do this? Is his behavior somehow her fault? He's from a broken home, and he probably needs more of a father than he has in Ron. According to Joey, Ron hardly notices him when he and Retta are there in California.

Is this her fault for getting divorced? Maybe she should have figured out how to stay with Ron and make him get sober. But how could she have accomplished that? Tears start leaking down her cheeks. She feels so much guilt for allowing her family to break apart. No one in her family had ever gotten divorced until she did.

She'd been taught to suffer in silence, but she broke that rule by telling Ron she'd leave their marriage if he didn't quit drinking. Now, if Joey gets drafted and sent to Vietnam, she couldn't bear it. Round and round her dark thoughts swirl, dizzying her with waves of terror.

Finally, the music ceases. Her watch indicates it's four in the morning. In the silence, she closes her eyes but keeps listening until the sun comes up.

When Joey appears downstairs around ten, he looks very pale and tired.

Trying for a neutral tone, she informs him, "You've been expelled from school, Joseph."

Shaking his head as if to clear it, he sits abruptly. "What did you say?"

"You've been expelled from Warden. Do you realize what this means?"

"What are you talking about?"

"You could get drafted!" she cries.

"I'll leave the country before I go to Nam."

"It better not come to that."

"Do you think Dad will come chew me out?"

"I called him last night. He can't make it out here right now."

Ducking his head, Joey stares at the table.

ᖉ

Two days later, her father comes by to drive Joey up to a boarding school in Vermont. He found the place and made all the arrangements. The school has a farm on which the students are expected to work every day. Her father thinks it'll do Joey good to get his hands dirty. He tells her that on the drive north, he intends to give Joey a piece of his mind. Harriet cries when she says goodbye to Joey, but she's enormously relieved too.

ᖉ

February 20, 1969

Dear Joey,

I hear that you're at the Green School now, learning something about farming while you finish your high school classes.

You might be interested to know that I had an experience with my father (your grandfather) that is somewhat analogous to yours. After high school I was determined to go to music school rather than Yale. Father forced me to enroll at his alma mater, but I flunked out as quickly as possible, thinking then he'd allow me to go study music. Instead, he sent me to work at a mill in a small town in Minnesota. It was a shock for me, but in some ways it ended up being a good thing because it forced me to start relying on myself, making my own way as I chose.

I hope you can find something to enjoy in your new circumstances, and I know that eventually you will discover how you want to chart your own course going forward. I believe in you.

Love,

Uncle Nat

℘

February 27, 1969

Dear Uncle Nat,

Once I finish my high school credits here, I want to go to the Berklee School of Music. They have real musicians teaching there, and they award bachelor of music degrees. They've even introduced new courses in rock and popular music.

Will you help convince my mother to let me go there? Please!

Love,

Joey

ॐ

In early March Nat calls Harriet and invites her to attend his marriage to Lucy. It's the following weekend at Plymouth Congregational
Church, where they really like the new minister. Nat explains, "We
just want a quiet wedding." She's pleased to have been invited.

Friday afternoon she flies out to Minneapolis with her parents.
Saturday morning they assemble in a small chapel with stunning blue
stained glass windows. Nat's children are there as are Lucy's daughter
and parents, but that's it. Her brother is wearing a navy blue suit. The
bride looks lovely in a pale blue dress that barely reaches her knees.

The minister has light brown hair, and it's surprisingly long. Below
his robe, she spots brown loafers. She pulls her eyes up and gazes
at the stained glass windows while the minister reads a poem about
love by Kahlil Gibran. After explaining that Nat and Lucy have written their own vows, he invites them to make their promises. Then he
blesses them and declares them husband and wife. Harriet glances at
her watch. It's been fifteen minutes since the ceremony started.

The bride and groom look ecstatic. While Lucy dabs her eyes, Nat
pulls out a large white handkerchief and wipes his face. Harriet is
happy that after so many difficult years with Dorie, her brother has
finally found joy.

ॐ

Later that month, Harriet's phone rings at ten in the evening. Nat says,
"Is it too late to call?"

"No, I'm awake."

"Lucy and I were so pleased you came to our wedding, Harriet."

"It was very sweet."

"Thank you."

"I must say, I was a little surprised there wasn't any music—no Bach, no hymns . . ."

"I couldn't begin to choose something that would be sufficient to the occasion," he replies.

"That's interesting."

"Harriet, has Joey broached the idea of going to the Berklee School of Music with you?"

"Does he mean the University of California at Berkeley?"

"No, he's talking about the music school in Boston that *I* wanted to attend all those years ago but Father refused."

"I don't remember that name."

"It was called Schillinger House in those days. You should let him go, Harriet. Joey is passionate about music. Don't make him deny his passion."

"How will he earn a living?"

"That's exactly what Father kept asking me."

Is she really like George?

"I can assure you, Harriet, Joey will figure that out for himself."

"Right now I'm worried whether he'll get into any school. But I'll think about what you said. Thank you for caring about Joey, Nat."

"Of course I care. Joey reminds me of myself at that age."

∾

When her father offered Harriet the job at the Sutton Foundation eight months ago, she couldn't refuse, even though she'd known that working for him again would probably be complicated. She was furious with him over the merger of the two schools and the way he'd handled it, but she wasn't actually surprised. Deep down inside she knows he was trying to be a responsible steward doing what he thought was right. The opportunity he was giving her at the foundation was irresistible; she'd learn a lot and be able to help people in the process, by making the world a better, fairer place through grants that addressed pressing needs.

At the first meeting of the board last September, she just listened, surprised by the board members' informality. Most of their conversation had nothing to do with the requests for financial support, which were presented by her father, as board chairman, toward the end of the meeting. He made all the decisions, agreeing to provide funds for construction of new girls' bathrooms at Warden School and approving requests from Phillips Academy and the Metropolitan Opera Association for annual operating support. The other members of the board simply ratified her father's motions. After all, it was his money.

It didn't take long, though, before she began to think that the foundation needed to get much more professional. After all, they had the fiduciary responsibility for oversight of a $10 million fund, making grants in the neighborhood of $425,000 each year. She'd started taking classes on nonprofit management and grant making at the Foundation Center Library in New York City and worked with the Sutton board and advisory committee to articulate the foundation's funding priorities more clearly. Nat and her parents' friend Dr. Paul Martin from the Plainwood Hospital were helpful in defining the foundation's interest in medicine. Nat's buddy Peter Chase, now a curator at the Museum of Modern Art, weighed in on the arts, and her former boss Janice Braun assisted with their focus on education. A seminar at the Foundation Center Library enabled her to develop detailed grant proposal guidelines for organizations seeking funding from the Sutton Foundation.

Since she's never done this sort of job with a foundation before and has never been responsible for the financial well-being of any entity beyond her own household, she has lots of questions about how things are supposed to work.

Now, as she prepares for their April board meeting, she turns to Gus again. It's Sunday afternoon. She and Gus are sitting at the dining room table in her house, papers spread all over the surface.

"We've got grant requests before us that total $530,000, but I don't see how we can award that much. We're required to give away five percent of our assets, right, Gus? Five percent of $10 million is $500,000."

He tells her, "The five percent includes your operating expenses too."

"Well, then we have less than $500,000 to spend all year. What about proposals that come in for the September deadline? We won't have any money for them."

"Why not have just one deadline a year?"

"I think Father likes board meetings—the members of the board are his friends, and it's his foundation."

"Being admired by his peers is clearly important to George."

"That's right. One of the requests is for $500,000; maybe we could pay it over two years, and we'd still have money for the other requests."

"That could work."

"I really wonder about our executive director, Tuck Foster. Father hired him eighteen months ago. He's responsible for managing the foundation's assets, and I know he has two different brokers he works with, but I rarely see him. I don't know what he's up to. I'm not sure what it is, but he makes me very uneasy, and my gut tells me I should watch him closely."

"I'd be glad to review the brokers' statements if you wish, Harriet."

She leans over to kiss him. "That would be great, Gus. I don't know what I would do without you."

Late in the afternoon the members of the board sit around a table that's been moved into the center of the living room at her parents' home. George, Eleanor, Dr. Martin, Janice Braun, George's banker Ben Goodrich, and his attorney Bill Mairs listen as Tuck opens the meeting and immediately turns it over to Harriet. She'd sent copies f the grant requests in advance to each trustee. Warden School's request is for $15,000 to construct a new space on their campus for field hockey. Phillips Academy asked for $15,000 to renovate the G. W. H. Auditorium, and the Plainwood Hospital is seeking $500,000 for a new wing to house a new research laboratory and expansion of the Rehabilitation Medicine Department.

After she presents each request in detail, she asks for questions.

When none are forthcoming, her father says, "These are worthy projects. Now that the merged schools are housed on the Warden campus, they need to accommodate field hockey for the girls—no question about it. As for the auditorium, it looked threadbare twenty-six years ago when Eddie and Nat performed in Gilbert and Sullivan shows there, so the need is clear. As for the hospital's request, I've discussed it with Nat, and he's interested in the research laboratory because it will enable doctors and residents to experiment and practice using new medical and surgical procedures. Moreover, the Department of Rehab Medicine has outgrown its space elsewhere in the hospital because of the growing need for physical therapy, speech therapy, and cardiac rehabilitation. I say we fund them all."

Dr. Martin says, "If you approve this grant for the hospital, we'd be happy to name it the Sutton Wing."

George replies, "We could name it the Edward Stevens Sutton Wing, in memory of Eddie."

It's apparent this idea appeals to him.

Then she starts to feel angry at her father. Taking a deep breath, she says, "We can't fully fund all the requests right now!" She throws her hands up in the air. "We only have $425,000 to donate this entire year. These requests add up to $530,000. We wouldn't be able to approve any new requests at our fall meeting." She's trying not to lose her temper, but the way her father treats the foundation as his own personal vehicle with which to do whatever he wants infuriates her. This is not his private fiefdom. The Sutton Foundation is an independent nonprofit organization that must abide by IRS rules. She's trying to get it on a schedule with predictable deadlines and established best practices.

Eleanor asks, "What would you suggest, Harriet?"

Calming down, Harriet replies, "What if we make the grant for the hospital payable over two years?"

"Would that work for you, Paul?" says George.

"Of course."

George turns to Tuck. "Do we have enough cash to pay out $280,000 now?"

"I'll sell some stock."

"All right then. I move that we approve all three grants in their full amounts, paying the grant to the hospital this year and next. Is there a second?"

Dr. Martin says, "I should recuse myself from this vote."

Ben Goodrich says, "Second."

Tuck says, "All in favor, say aye."

As employees of the foundation, Harriet and Tuck aren't allowed to vote.

Her father's motion is approved.

Once the meeting concludes, everyone stands. Eleanor sees the departing trustees to the door. Tuck and Harriet wait next to George.

Tuck says, "George, I've learned about a stunning investment opportunity. There's a company in Colorado that has found a way to retort oil from shale—by heating the rock. This is a whole new approach to the industry. It could be really big!"

"Interesting," George replies. "I'd like a lot more information on this. See what you can get."

Tuck says, "Will do, boss." He leaves.

When Harriet sits, George does too. "Father! How can you possibly consider investing foundation assets in an experimental technique for extracting oil? It sounds very unlikely to me."

"I'm intrigued by unusual investment opportunities. Sometimes you have to take a risk."

"Investing in this company strikes me as much too speculative. It's not appropriate for a foundation that's meant to last well into the future."

"Why are you fighting me on this, Harriet?"

"The IRS could come after us. If you don't believe me, ask your tax guy." Why doesn't he see this? Is he starting to lose his critical faculties? She sighs. "Why did you start the foundation, anyway? What did you hope to achieve?"

"It started as a means of avoiding taxation on the sale of the company. When I was going to sell the company in 1964 for $12 million, I would have had to give the government hundreds of thousands of dollars in capital gains taxes. Transferring the stock into a foundation that could sell that stock without being taxed made more sense. Philanthropy has always been important to me. I give away ten percent of my income every year. Creating the foundation is an ideal means by which I can keep giving over the long term."

"I understand that. Let me put this another way. Do you trust Tuck? Do you believe he has sound judgment?"

"Of course I do. He was in the same college at Yale that I was, though he's much younger. He makes me think of Eddie. Tuck fought in Korea, and then he bounced around from one firm to another, looking for the right fit. I think he has a lot of potential."

His reasons for hiring Tuck make Harriet even more nervous.

"What does he do for the foundation, anyway? He's hardly ever in the office."

"He spends his time studying companies and meeting with their principals."

"Hmm."

Eleanor returns. Smiling warmly, she asks, "Can you join us for supper, Harriet? I'd love to know what you hear from Joey. Rosalee is roasting a chicken right now."

"Thank you, Mother, that's very tempting, but Gus and I are going to see *Hair* tonight."

July 1970

The summer of 1969 was very different from previous years, because Harriet and Nat and their families did not go to Sea View. Nat told Harriet that he and Lucy were renting a house on Cape Cod so the members of their newly enlarged family could bond with each other. Joey was spending the summer at the Green School, so Harriet and Gus decided to take their daughters to the Maryland shore for a week.

This summer Harriet and Nat are coming back to Sea View for ten days with their parents. She did not invite Gus to join them. Over the last six months she's been preparing for the tough conversation she needs to have with her father about the situation at the foundation. She's enlisted Nat to help her make her case. Gus assisted her in obtaining concrete details to use with her father, but she doesn't want Gus to witness what she expects will be a nasty family fight. She has to work up her nerve to take on the man she has always admired and loved.

It's a slightly larger group this year, for this is the first year Lucy and her daughter, Olivia, have been to Sea View. Lucy fits in beautifully with everyone except Nat's children, who still seem to be very angry at her. Olivia is a shy girl, usually sitting with a book on her lap. Retta is studying her organic chemistry text whenever she isn't busy making music with her uncle; she hopes to go to medical school after she graduates from Holyoke next year.

Nat and the kids are completely absorbed in practicing old songs and writing new ones about Sea View. Last night Nat told her that Joe, having spent the last nine months at Berklee, has become a remarkably able assistant. She's glad she followed Nat's advice and allowed Joe to attend Berklee, where he has become very serious about his musicianship. He insists on being called Joe, and he smokes cigarettes now.

A few minutes ago Lucy and Olivia left to get groceries for dinner, and George is off playing golf. As Harriet and her mother sit alone on the porch, they catch snatches of lyrics that emerge from the living room, where the musicians are working intently. They hear some of the lines that are sung the loudest. Now it's "Let's climb round the rocks to see/What else the tide's left on the shore." This is her opportunity to prepare her mother for what she intends to do.

"I'm glad we finally have some time to ourselves, Mother. I'm very worried about what's going on at the foundation. I'm convinced that Tuck Foster is taking advantage of us, but Father believes he's doing a fine job. Tuck is so smooth and debonair he seems like an impressive guy."

"He does indeed," Eleanor agrees.

"I'm certain he's cheating us out of a lot of money."

"Oh no." Abruptly putting down her coffee cup, Eleanor leans toward Harriet. "What makes you think that?"

"When I realized that the value of the foundation's portfolio of stocks hasn't been growing the way it should, I asked Gus to take a look. He helped me dig into the numbers, and we discovered that the foundation has been spending $300,000 a year on commissions to the brokers Tuck works with at Paine Webber and Merrill Lynch. That's an awful lot of money. When Gus reviewed the brokers' statements, he noticed a huge number of purchases and sales. For example, one of Tuck's brokers bought Honeywell at 114 in January and sold it three months later at 118, but the commissions chewed up the gain. Every purchase or sale involves a commission fee. Frequent trades generate lots of fees for the brokers."

"That's not cheating," Eleanor replies. "How would that benefit Tuck, anyway?"

Another line emerges from the living room: "We'll take these last treasures home/To keep with us till summer comes once more."

"I'm not exactly sure," Harriet answers her mother. "I do know he has a new Rolex watch, and somehow he got a complete landscaping job done at his house. He travels a lot too. He bragged about going on a trip to play golf at Pinehurst in North Carolina. I don't understand how he can possibly afford those things on the salary we pay him."

"Maybe he has resources you aren't aware of."

"I called the account managers and asked them to look into the matter. They said the fees are accurate, but it just doesn't smell right to me. Somehow Tuck must be getting some sort of kickback from those brokers."

"Sea View/Summers spent at Sea View/Seem the same but still new."

Eleanor asks, "What do you think we board members should do, Harriet?"

"We've got to fire Tuck. The board needs to fire Tuck—I don't have the authority to do it. I've talked to Father about the lack of progress with our portfolio and my concern about all the commissions. He said Tuck is investing conservatively so the foundation will last a long time, but that doesn't make any sense! I think Father just doesn't want to see what Tuck's doing." She shakes her head. Then she leans forward and whispers, "Do you think Father is still as sharp and discerning as he used to be?"

"Oh Harriet, I've been wondering about his judgment myself, and his memory isn't what it was."

Harriet states confidently, "I don't think there's anything really wrong with Father's mind. He's just slipping."

"I like to think he's mellowing with age. Of course that means he's a little easier to live with now." Eleanor smiles ruefully.

"His blindness when it comes to Tuck, though, is terribly serious. I think we've got to get Father to step aside from chairing the board. Then I can make my case for firing Tuck and convince the rest of you to do what's right."

"Oh dear." Eleanor blinks rapidly. "Are you certain this is necessary? Perhaps you're overreacting to the fact that George is simply getting older. He's not the man he was in his prime."

This stops Harriet. "I suppose I am mad at Father for losing his grip on some things—for aging, I guess. But that doesn't change the facts."

"George considers Tuck his protégé, so he may not be able to see him objectively. And he's not going to like being asked to give up chairing the board one bit."

"I know, Mother! I feel terrible even thinking about it. I've spent most of my life trying to please Father. How can I ask him to step back from the foundation he's so proud of creating?" She could cry. "But I have to. It's the ethical thing to do."

"I agree with you, dearie, and I admire you for speaking up. You *are* George's daughter in many ways, aren't you? You'll do what you feel you must, even if it doesn't make you happy."

Her mother's response feels like a vote of confidence.

"Be gentle when you talk to your father, Harriet."

"I'll try."

"We are bound/As if by the parts of a round/Family harmony."

∾

In Harriet's family one doesn't argue in front of an audience, so she needs to find a time she and Nat can be alone with their father. Because she dreads this confrontation, she keeps putting it off. Finally on her last day at Sea View, she corners George when he's alone in the kitchen, pouring himself another cup of coffee.

"I need to talk to you, Father."

"Sounds serious, Harriet. What's on your mind?"

"Let's go to the study. I'll meet you there in a minute."

Her father shuffles down the hall. When did he start moving so slowly?

Quickly refilling her mug, she grabs Nat, and together they head for the tiny room off the dining room.

George is already seated on a rickety club chair, which creaks as he shifts his weight. When he sees them enter together, he says, "Uh oh, I don't like the looks of this."

She and Nat sit. After taking a deep breath, she says it straight out. "Father, you've got to fire Tuck. He's defrauding us."

"That can't be right," George replies. "He reports to me on his activities every single week." His hand shakes as he raises his cup to his mouth.

Harriet insists, "Tuck's brokers should not churn our stock holdings the way they've been doing."

"Churning?"

Nat says, "Buying and selling with great frequency, Father."

"We should make thoughtful investments in solid companies," Harriet says, "and hold on to those stocks for years."

George replies, "We can instruct Tuck accordingly. Perhaps we've given him too much leeway."

"He knows what he's doing. He's cheating us," Harriet states.

Nat says, "Tuck's investing in over-the-counter stocks I've never heard of."

"How do you know where Tuck invests our assets?" George counters.

"Harriet shared her concerns with me, Father, and I have to say, I'm concerned too. Risky investments make no sense for a philanthropic foundation."

George counters, "Tuck says that's where we can get the best returns."

Nat states, "Foundation assets should be invested conservatively, Father."

"Et tu, Brute?" asks George.

"That's what Mother said to me when we asked her to go into treatment," Nat replies.

Her voice trembling, Harriet says, "It just isn't appropriate, Father! Listen to me!" He isn't really listening. He doesn't respect her opinion.

"Harriet's right, Father!" Nat maintains, gripping the arms of his chair. "Listen to her."

She goes on. "You don't think I know what I'm talking about, but I do! Over the years I've tried really hard to earn your respect, but you still don't believe in me. What's it going to take?" All her old feelings of frustration and anger at him surge up so strongly that she wants to scream at him, but then she remembers how fragile he seems these days. She doesn't wish to hurt him too badly.

"I'm listening." His lips are pressed tightly together.

Harriet says, "If Tuck's brokers invested in companies like Eastman Kodak, IBM, and Xerox, the foundation would have been worth $15 million today. Instead, it's hardly grown at all."

"I'll say it again. I think Tuck's doing a good job."

How can she get through to him? "All right, Father, let's look at this from a different angle. Tell me, does Tuck have family money?"

"Not that I know of."

"Then how can he afford a top-of-the-line Rolex? How does he get to play golf at Baltusrol?"

Nat puts his hands in his lap. "We think Tuck must be getting perks from the brokers he uses for foundation business."

George looks a little unsure now. "I'll speak to him."

"He'll deny everything," she asserts. "Just because Tuck went to Yale doesn't guarantee that he's an honest man. This is your responsibility, Father."

His face suddenly looks haggard. "What do you want me to do?"

She reaches over to touch his arm." You should resign as chairman of the board, Father. I hate having to even suggest such a thing, but it would be best if you step aside now." Her eyes fill.

"I agree with Harriet, Father. It's time."

She suggests, "You could be the emeritus chairman." She hopes this would make his resignation easier to swallow.

Shaking her hand off, he shouts, "How dare you! I created this foundation. I gave you this job."

Trying to stay calm, she says, "When you come home, I'll show you all the facts and figures. Then you can decide what you want to do."

"Think about it after you see the numbers, Father," Nat says.

"I'm certain that when the board reviews the outside audit," she says, "it will prove that Tuck has been feathering his own nest at our expense. He and his brokers are eating up a huge percentage of our earnings. This impacts how much money we can give to nonprofits. And isn't grant making what this foundation is supposed to be all about?"

"Of course it is."

Harriet adds, "I think we should bring Nat on the board. Wouldn't that make sense? He's been a great advisor on medical matters."

George thunders, "You're just getting back at me now for the Hartley-Warden merger!"

"No, Father, that's not what this is about—not at all. I wouldn't be saying anything if I didn't have to."

He rises from his chair unsteadily. "I take it we're done here."

She stands quickly. "May I give you a hand?"

With great dignity, he replies, "No thank you, Harriet. I can manage by myself."

Nat hurries back to the living room.

Her heart hurts. This is so hard. Her father is getting old—he's not the capable man he used to be. She detests having to suggest that he retire. If she didn't work for the foundation, she'd happily overlook his errors of judgment. Will he hate her from now on? That would be unbearable.

They don't speak as they move to the porch, where George takes a wicker chair. She sits down next to him. She feels sick. She doesn't speak.

Eleanor emerges from inside the house. She walks over and places her hand on George's shoulder.

The three of them stare silently at the sea.

Inside, the music starts up again.

June 1971

The house at Sea View is buzzing with activity much earlier than usual this year. Nat wants to attend his twenty-fifth reunion at Andover, so the whole family decided to come in June.

Now Nat and his and Harriet's children are busy in the living room preparing to perform their Sea View songs in a concert for the older generation on Saturday night. He invited Aunt Jessica, Uncle Drew, and their children to join them for supper and the show. The kids are rehearsing their parts. He found an instrument for Olivia too—she's playing the handbells. Eleanor and Lucy have gone out to buy groceries.

After three cups of coffee, Nat is practically levitating. He dashes out of the living room and onto the porch, where Harriet and Gus sit with George. They don't interrupt their conversation to attend to him. He stands there vibrating.

Harriet says, "Tell me what you think about this, Father. I believe we should consider refocusing our giving priorities in order to make more of an impact with the grants we do make."

George, who has accepted the role of emeritus chairman of the Sutton Foundation, replies, "Are you suggesting we eliminate some priorities?" His voice is as resonant as ever, but his body seems to have shrunk since last year.

"I thought we might drop our focus on the arts," Harriet says. "If we stop giving to museums and musical groups, we could do more in the areas of medicine and education."

"What are you talking about?" Nat exclaims. "You can't drop the arts! I'll vote against that."

"We could still fund arts *education*," she says.

Leaning back in his chair, George crosses his legs. "Don't ask me. As executive director, Harriet, you must present your thinking to the full board."

Unable to contain his impatience any longer, Nat says, "Harriet, I need someone to go make Xerox copies of the lyrics so the audience is able to follow along. Olivia typed up two sets—would you take one to the copy place and make more? Please?"

Harriet gets to her feet. "Sure. Come with me, Gus?"

"Of course, honey."

She follows Nat back into the living room, where little scraps of paper with words on them litter the floor. When he hands her a stack of pages, he notices the sapphire on her left hand. "Nice ring, Harriet. Have you and Gus set a date yet?"

"We're thinking about getting married in October, but we don't want to make a big fuss."

"That's great, Harriet! He's a good man."

She says, "I think I'm finally learning how to do the dance between independence and intimacy. Sometimes you just have to compromise."

He lifts his glasses to look at her more directly. What is she talking about?

She grins. "Anything else while I'm out and about?"

"I don't think so." He turns his attention back to his musicians. Retta and Abby have their heads together. Since his daughter followed Retta to Mt. Holyoke, the cousins seem to have grown very close.

"All right," says Harriet. "I'm off."

He glances at her. "Thanks for your help." He takes another sip of his coffee, which is cold. He doesn't care. He's having a wonderful time. "Okay guys, let's get back to work."

ᴄᴡ

Friday afternoon Nat sits at one of many round tables under a large white tent on the campus of Phillips Academy drinking martinis with his best friend, Peter. On the table rests the program Peter designed at the behest of their class's reunion committee. It features a large image of Sammy Phillips—a cartoon character wearing a hat tilted back, a wrinkled jacket, a drooping cigarette, a necktie for a belt, and shoes with laces dragging.

"Peter, I love it! Sammy looks even more disheveled than ever."

"I'm glad you like it, Nat, because I have lots more in my briefcase."

Peter is wearing a white suit with a pale blue shirt and a navy silk tie with lots of little red squares printed up the diagonal. His shoes look expensive.

"That's a smashing tie, Peter. As usual."

Peter teases, "Your tie is askew, as usual." He smiles warmly. "You certainly seem better than the last time I saw you."

"I'm very happy. As you know, Lucy and I married as soon as my divorce was final. She's so good for me and my kids."

"That's great news."

After taking a drink from his martini, Nat says, "And you, Peter— how are you and Stephen?"

"We're living together, but I thought bringing him here would be awkward."

"I'm sorry it's like that, but I understand. And your job is going well?"

"Absolutely." He ducks his head a moment, then looks back at Nat. "I'm the curator of drawings at MoMA now," he says proudly. "We're working on an exhibit scheduled to open in September that's terribly exciting. We're assembling four hundred drawings, paintings, sculptures, prints, posters, and photographs from the museum's collection that have to do with social protest movements on subjects such as urban poverty, war, and revolutions."

"That's right up your alley," Nat remarks.

"I'll say! And I finally feel confident enough in my position to participate in anti-war activities. I marched in Washington, DC, last month. It was great—really inspiring—to be part of such a huge crowd. Why don't our leaders listen to the people? What's it going to take to get us out of Vietnam?"

"Good question."

"The Walker Art Center tried to recruit me for a position there, and I was tempted because I'd get to see more of you. I thought about it, but I just can't imagine living anywhere but New York."

"You must be highly regarded in your field. I'm glad—though not surprised—to hear that."

"What about you, Nat?" As Peter lifts his glass, Nat notices the gold ring on his right pinky finger. He's never seen Peter wear any jewelry.

Nat says, "I'm spending more time on research these days so I can be available to my kids. I like doing research. And I've been having a ball putting songs together with my family about our summer place at Sea View."

"I remember some of your songs from our days here at Andover. 'Baggy, tattered rayon hose!'"

"We didn't really fit in very well, did we? We weren't exactly popular with our peers when we were here."

"We were misfits," Peter says. "At least we had our friendship with each other."

"Thank God for that." Nat looks at the men in their jackets and ties, standing in front of the bar. Other guys circulate around the perimeter. No one has come to their table. "I'm only here for the dinner tonight, then I'll go back to Sea View. If things get slow here on campus tomorrow or if you get bored with our classmates, why don't you come out to Sea View tomorrow night? We're mounting a performance of the songs we've been writing. It would be fun to have you in the audience. You could meet Lucy."

"I'll see how it goes here, Nat. Thanks ever so much for the invitation."

"Please come if you're interested. Here, I'll write out the directions on this napkin."

❧

Late Saturday afternoon, Nat directs the young people to move all the furniture off the porch and onto the lawn facing the porch—which is where the audience will sit. His sense of excitement rises as he surveys the "stage."

Joe has become invaluable to Nat. Since last fall they've been exchanging tapes and talking on the phone, tweaking the tunes to fit lyrics Nat wrote. He's proud of how polished their songs have become.

Now the screen door to the living room slams as Joe brings in amplifiers while Ned carries his drums and hi-hat. Abby has her new electric piano in its carrying case and Joe's guitar in hand. Ernie puts down a speaker and returns for more. Nat gets his saxophone case and Ernie's electric bass and places them at the back of the space.

Holding a microphone stand in each hand, Vi asks, "Where should I put these, Dad?" Now that she's a teenager, his youngest no longer calls him Daddy, which makes him a little sad.

"Ask Joe," he replies.

Retta appears with her flute and Olivia with her bells.

He says, "Your instruments can go over on the ledge."

After everything has been brought out, he repositions the microphones and strings cords from each to the amplifiers that sit on top of the speakers, while Joe sets up the recording equipment in the corner.

When Aunt Jessica, Uncle Drew, and cousins Susan and Brooks arrive, he waves them into the house.

Retta brings out the music stands and places them by the mikes.

Then Lucy comes over to him. "Do you think you can tear yourself away? Supper's ready."

"All right, kids, put down your instruments. It's time to eat." He's too keyed up to eat anything, but he makes himself a strong drink and returns to the porch.

Before long, the musicians return. Abby plays scales on her piano, while the others start tuning. Susan and Brooks sit down in front and watch the activity.

After testing the microphones, Joe moves close to Nat and whispers, "I've got a joint if you want to join me after the show."

Mildly, Nat replies, "You don't want to make a habit of smoking that stuff."

"Right." Joe goes back to fiddle with the tape recorder.

Nat is beginning to feel slightly anxious. He turns his back to the audience and asks the kids, "Does everyone have their music? Abby, play a riff on the piano so Joe can adjust the volume on the amplifiers."

Eventually the band is ready, and it sounds like the adults have taken their seats. When he turns to face the audience, he sees his father and mother, Harriet and Gus, Lucy, Aunt Jessica and Uncle Drew, and Susan and Brooks, all watching him expectantly. The women in his family are wearing bright colored summer dresses that make him think of sherbet.

He takes a deep breath. Suddenly he feels very calm. He flashes back to the way he felt when he and Eddie and friends performed *H.M.S. Pinafore* in their living room at home during the war.

Taking another deep breath, he says, "I would like to dedicate this show to my brother Edward Stevens Sutton." His mother clutches his father's hand. Harriet smiles tremulously. Glancing back at his musicians, he sees confusion on a few faces, especially Ned's. He marvels again that he ever got such a handsome son. He realizes now that he needs to tell Ned a lot more about the uncle he was named after.

He looks back at the audience. "Can everyone hear me? Do you all have copies of the words so you can read along if we don't enunci-ate properly? Yes? All right then." He coughs. "Here with me are my daughter Abby on keyboard and vocals; my son Ned on drums and vocals; my son Ernie on bass; my daughter Violet on wooden block and maracas; my niece, Retta, on flute and vocals; my nephew, Joe, on guitar and vocals; and Olivia on hand bells."

Everyone in the audience applauds. Eleanor's mouth is trembling.

He goes on. "The words of these songs are mostly by me, and the tunes were initially by me, but they have been perfected by my nephew, Joe."

He pauses. "This production is not as polished as we'd have liked." Joe coughs.

He turns back to his group. He nods to Abby, who suddenly makes him think of the grandmother she was named for; Abby has the same sense of poise that Abba had. Abby starts playing the introduction while he blows his sax.

Ned sings:

As before,
Now we're here together once more,
Hearts stand still, waiting till

We obtain
A full picture we can sustain,
When apart, in our hearts.

They all sing the chorus:

Sea View!
Summers spent at Sea View
Seem the same but still new;
How do you do, Sea View?

Ned sings:

Memory
Brings back scenes from our history:
Tales of old, some untold
Till we share
Reminiscences and compare
Stories of those we love.

They all sing:

Sea View!
A place, and an idea too,
Touching all that we do
Our whole lives through: Sea View.

Then Ned:

Then we sing
Songs reminding us of the things
That we've shared. Then and there,

We are bound,
As if by the parts of a round:
Family harmony.

Loudly they sing the final chorus:

Sea View!
The place where we grew
Into a family, now, who
Is part of you, Sea View.

When the final instrumental section with piano and drums comes to an end, the audience applauds enthusiastically. Looking over his shoulder, he's struck by Retta's smile, which is so like his mother's, and although her hair's a darker shade, it's red like Eleanor's was when he was a boy. He's very pleased that she's going to medical school at Case Western Reserve University in the fall.

He brings himself back to the present moment, saying, "This next song expresses a sentiment I suspect we all feel at times."

Nat sings:

> *Let's not put the boats away!*
> *Maybe we'll stay for one more day,*
> *Cook out once more and watch the sun*
> *Setting red and gold in Sea View Bay.*

Then Retta sings:

> *Let's not close the house up tight!*
> *Maybe this fall we'll spend a night*
> *And watch the water turning gray*
> *In the Indian summer's fading light.*

Then Abby sings:

> *Let's climb round the rocks to see*
> *What else the tide's left on the shore.*
> *We'll take these last treasures home*
> *To keep with us till summer comes once more.*

Then Nat sings:

See the cove and mica beach!
The tide is out, the raft's in reach!
We just can't wait a moment more,
Oh, let us run down to the beach!

Then they all sing:

Okay, let's not put the boats away!
Maybe we'll stay for one more day,
Cook out once more and watch the sun
Setting red and gold in Sea View Bay;
Setting red and gold in Sea View Bay.

The audience goes wild. Uncle Drew whistles shrilly while someone yells "Yay!" and someone else calls "Whoo-hoo!"

"Crab Rock" comes next. The band members all sing all the verses of that song. Retta and Abby play the melody on piano and flute, Joey takes a solo on his guitar during the instrumental break, and then Ernie has a turn on his bass while Violet, holding a wooden block and drumstick and with a proud grin on her face, provides punctuation. Ned's steady drumming continues throughout. Nat notices that Violet, the spitting image of Dorie, plays to the audience just as her mother used to do. More whistles follow.

Then Nat says, "This next song might be a little sentimental for some. See what you think."

Olivia starts "There Are Times When I Remember" by striking her bells, and then they launch into a jazzy tune. Joe, who looks just like his father Ron now that he's grown, sings the first two verses. All the kids sing the chorus. Then Ernie, all skin and bones and as awkward as Nat was at that age, takes the last verse.

Gus puts his arm around Harriet, and she leans into him.

During "Magic Stories," Nat gets to play a mellow solo on his sax.

They follow with "Get Off That Raft!" which is met with chuckles from the audience.

Nat says, "And finally, a song entitled 'Good Night Sea View.'" Abby sings first, then Ned, then Abby. Toward the end, the music swells, and Olivia plays the bells as Ned sings the last verses.

Happy tears stream down Nat's cheeks. The music is so beautiful, and Abby and Ned have fabulous singing voices, thanks to their mother. He's grateful to Dorie for that.

The audience members all jump up and erupt with sustained applause and cheers. Several of them shout, "Encore! Encore!"

They reprise "Sea View Song." Then Nat says, "That's all, folks. We can't take any more." Turning his back on the audience, he moves over to the case for his saxophone. He pulls off the mouthpiece and blows to clear it out. The kids put their instruments away.

"Wow, Uncle Nat," says Retta. "That was so much fun!"

Abby chimes in. "It was great, Dad, really great. The audience loved us!"

"Absolutely the best high ever," says Joe.

Once Nat manages to pull himself together, he moves toward the edge of the porch. His parents are sitting in their seats holding hands. Everyone else hovers nearby.

"Wow, Nat." Harriet's voice is choked up.

Aunt Jessica says, "Bravo, Nat."

Taking the seat next to his father, he asks, "Well, Father, what did you think?"

George's eyes are wet, which doesn't surprise Nat—he's seen music make his father cry before. His father says, "Congratulations, Nathaniel. You're a fine musician. You make me proud."

His mother leans over to him. "That was marvelous, Nat." Her eyes brim with tears.

Joe says, "I have a feeling we'll be singing these songs forever."

Harriet nods. "I love the lyric 'We are bound, as if by the parts of a round: family harmony." It's such a great image! With these songs, you've created a real glue that will help keep our family singing together for a long time to come."

"I hope so, Harriet," Nat replies. "I don't know what else to say. We loved doing it. Had so much fun."

℺

A little while later George and Eleanor sit with Harriet and Nat gazing out at the water. The sunset has faded from view. It's dark, though stars are twinkling overhead.

George says, "Maybe I should have let you go to music school, Nathaniel. You're very talented."

Nat's heart feels as if it might burst. He's been waiting his entire life to hear his father say something like this—it doesn't matter a bit that it's too late.

"You were right about Dorie, Father," Nat says. "Once I chose her and we started having babies so quickly, that finished off my chances of a professional music career. Not that I was good enough or driven enough to succeed at it. Anyway, I can't regret any of it, because how else would I have gotten these remarkable children?"

"I'm glad to hear you say that," George tells him softly.

Harriet says, "You know, Father, it was wanting to win your love that led me to graduate school and then to work for Sutton Chemical. That's where I learned how different we are. But my job at the foundation has shown me how much like you I actually am. I really *am* your daughter, Father. I learned so much from you about being hard-nosed and realistic. Even if I had to get tough on you about Tuck."

"You were right to do so, Harriet. Tuck Foster sure managed to pull the wool over my eyes. I've always been impressed by how capable and adaptable you are, and I'm happy that you're my successor because I know you'll lead the foundation well into the future. The foundation will probably be my most significant legacy."

They all sit quietly for a few minutes. Then Eleanor clears her throat. "Doesn't it seem like Eddie's right here with us?"

"I know what you mean," his sister answers.

"Indeed," says his father.

Nat sighs. "Yes."

Acknowledgments

Once again I am grateful to my late uncle Benjamin Hazard Stevens, who inspired this novel as well as *Eleanor's Wars*. Most of the song lyrics here came from him.

Many other members of my family have been enormously helpful as well in providing stories and emotional support during the creation of this novel. Thanks especially to Phebe Miner, Anna Phelps, Terry Sheldon, Sallie Sheldon, Jack Sheldon, Phebe Richards, Pete Stevens, Mary Stevens, and Helen Stevens.

Thank you to Marylee Hardenbergh, Louise Miner, Sally Power, Heather Huyck, and Judy Healey, who have accompanied me along this path.

Thanks to Molly Woehrlin, John Brooks, and Brent Dack for providing a tour of the Malt-O-Meal Company mill in Northfield, Minnesota, and thanks to Kate Roberts at the Minnesota Historical Society for providing access to interviews of millers that helped to inform early chapters of this book.

Mike Crandall was an enormous help in figuring out the characteristics of the fungicide Harriet Sutton creates for Sutton Chemical. Alex Cirillo helped on the workings of an industrial chemistry lab. Janice Gepner and Natalie Rasmussen consulted on the teaching of high school chemistry. Ann Hutchins provided invaluable insight into teaching at a private girls' school.

Conversations with Pat Nanoff and Peter Butler, along with sections of Wheelock Whitney's memoir *Keep Moving*, helped inform my understanding of alcoholism and treatment.

Lucia Newell was a great resource for information about performing jazz, while Kay Baker provided background on the St. Joseph's Hospital Auxiliary. Chalmers Hardenbergh assisted with train routes and schedules, Rob Epler helped with Latin, and Hannah Tozer explained tuition remission.

A special thank you to Jan Woolman for her history of Blake School, entitled *Expecting Good Things of All*, especially the chapter on the merger. Stan and Lucy Shepard and Ted and Nancy Weyerhaeuser helped with my understanding of the St. Paul Academy–Summit School merger.

Many thanks to Fred Martin for explaining the unethical practice of churning stocks, Connie Paiement for rules about taxation on the sale of Sutton Chemical, and Allen Bettis for his help on the workings of family foundations.

Quite a few librarians and archivists helped me find information that enabled this story to be grounded in historically accurate facts. Special thanks to David Null at the University of Wisconsin Archives in Madison, Erin George and Rebecca Toov at the University of Minnesota Archives in Minneapolis, Weston Tate at Cornell University Archives, Erika Gordon at Rutgers University Archives, Helen Burke at the Minneapolis Central Library's Business Library, Jamie Stanley at the Northfield (Minnesota) Public Library, Hayes Scriven at the Northfield Historical Society, and the staff in the Minnesota Historical Society Library.

Leonard G. Wilson's *Medical Revolution in Minnesota: A History of the University of Minnesota Medical School* (Midewiwin Press, St. Paul, 1989) was an excellent resource for information about the early days of heart surgery.

A Fierce Radiance by Lauren Belfer (Harper Collins Publishers,

2010) was an engaging tale with lots of historical information about the development of penicillin.

Interchemical Corporation, which no longer exists, was the primary model for Sutton Chemical.

Alice S. Rossi was a source for Dr. Pennington's comments about women scientists in chapter one. See her paper entitled "Women Scientists: Problems and Prospects," Committee on Human Development, University of Chicago, which was delivered to a conference on women in science at the Wisconsin Center, Madison, Wisconsin, on March 19, 1966.

Any errors of fact or interpretation that I have made are solely attributable to me.

I am deeply indebted to the members of the writers' group hosted by Roger Barr, to Roger, Cynthia Kraack, Charlie Locks, Loren Taylor, Terry Newby, Kathy Kerr, and Jim Lundy, for their critical insights as they read the manuscript, their kind support, and their ongoing encouragement.

Thanks to Mary Logue for her most helpful developmental editing and Pat Carlson for her precision in copyediting.

I am very grateful to Brooke Warner and Lauren Wise of She Writes Press and to Crystal Patriarche and Tabitha Bailey of SparkPoint Studio for teaching me a great deal about hybrid publishing and publicity as well as for their excellent professional work on my behalf.

I need to thank my husband Andy for his great suggestions of titles for both of my published novels. Most of all I wish to thank him for his patience, marketing chops, and continuing efforts to make me laugh every day.

About the Author

A mes Sheldon worked as a reporter for two small-town newspapers in Minnesota before becoming lead author and associate editor of *Women's History Sources: A Guide to Archives and Manuscript Collections in the United States*, which ignited her passion for studying and writing about the history of women in America. After that, she worked as a development officer, raising funds for the Sierra Club in San Francisco, the Minnesota Historical Society in St. Paul, the Minneapolis Public Library, and a variety of other nonprofits. She lives with her husband in Eden Prairie, Minnesota.

Her recent novel *Eleanor's Wars* won the Benjamin Franklin Gold Award for Best New Voice: Fiction in 2016.

SELECTED TITLES FROM SHE WRITES PRESS

She Writes Press is an independent publishing company founded to serve women writers everywhere. Visit us at www.shewritespress.com.

The Belief in Angels by J. Dylan Yates $16.95, 978-1-938314-64-3
From the Majdonek death camp to a volatile hippie household on the East Coast, this narrative of tragedy, survival, and hope spans more than fifty years, from the 1920s to the 1970s.

A Cup of Redemption by Carole Bumpus $16.95, 978-1-938314-90-2
Three women, each with their own secrets and shames, seek to make peace with their pasts and carve out new identities for themselves.

Bittersweet Manor by Tory McCagg $16.95, 978-1-938314-56-8
A chronicle of three generations of love, manipulation, entitlement, and disappointed expectations in an upper-middle-class New England family.

Tasa's Song by Linda Kass $16.95, 978-1-63152-064-8
From a peaceful village in eastern Poland to a partitioned post-war Vienna, from a promising childhood to a year living underground, *Tasa's Song* celebrates the bonds of love, the power of memory, the solace of music, and the enduring strength of the human spirit.

Things Unsaid by Diana Y. Paul $16.95, 978-1-63152-812-5
A family saga of three generations fighting over money and obligation—and a tale of survival, resilience, and recovery.

Eden by Jeanne Blasberg $16.95, 978-1-63152-188-1
As her children and grandchildren assemble for Fourth of July weekend at Eden, the Meister family's grand summer cottage on the Rhode Island shore, Becca decides it's time to introduce the daughter she gave up for adoption fifty years ago.